THE SEAL OF SURYA

by

Amritanshu Pandey

The Seal of Surya

Published by PIRATES
Registered Address: 38 Golf Course, Jodhpur 342011
captain@pirates.ind.in

Ordering Information:
Quantity sales: Special discounts are available on quantity purchases by corporations, associations, and others.

Orders by trade bookstores and wholesalers.
Please contact Pirates Distribution: Tel: (+91) 95555 49701; or email: captain@pirates.ind.in

Cover Design by ***Ashish Subhash Boyne***

Typeset in Giovanni 9.5/12
Printed in India by Thomson Press India Ltd.

1 2 3 4 5 6 7 17 16 15 14

Map of Early Aryavarta

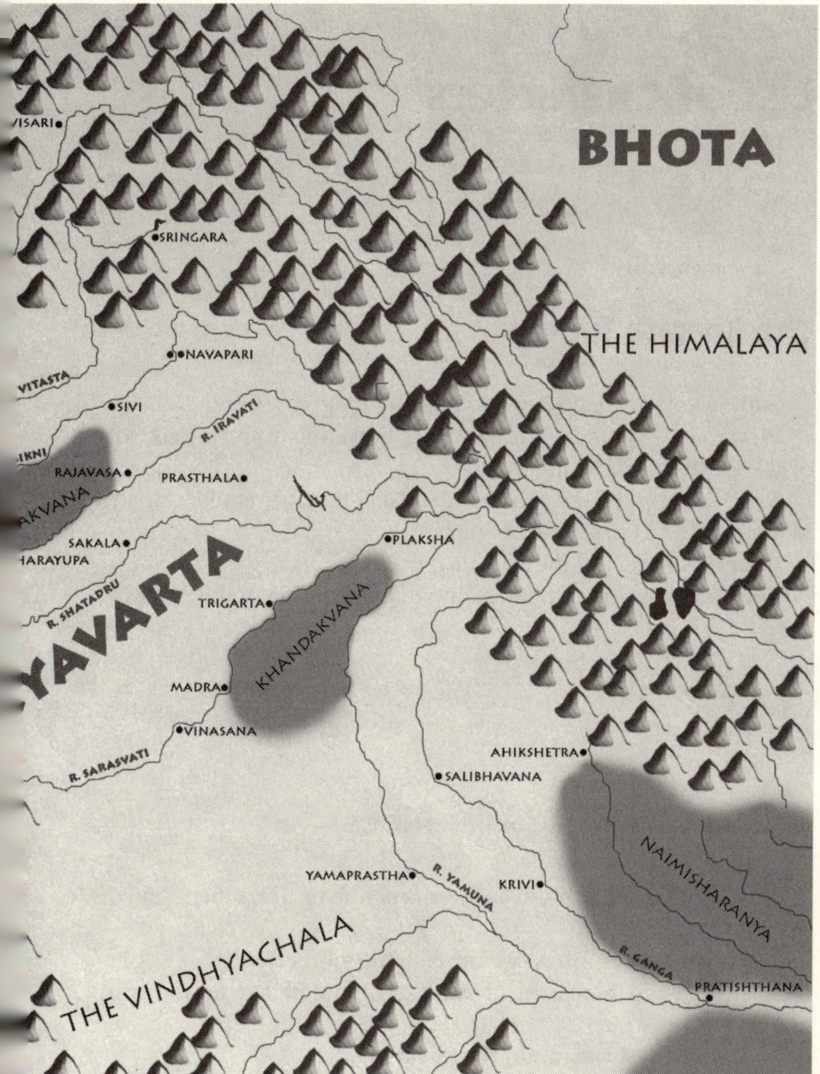
BHOTA
THE HIMALAYA
VISARI
SRINGARA
NAVAPARI
VITASTA
SIVI
R. IRAVATI
RAJAVASA
PRASTHALA
KVANA
SAKALA
HARAYUPA
PLAKSHA
R. SHATADRU
TRIGARTA
YAVARTA
KHANDAKVANA
MADRA
VINASANA
R. SARASVATI
AHIKSHETRA
SALIBHAVANA
NAIMISHARANYA
YAMAPRASTHA
R. YAMUNA
KRIVI
THE VINDHYACHALA
R. GANGA
PRATISHTHANA

List of Characters

The Bharata Tribe

Sudasa-son of High King Pijavana and king-in-waiting.

Pijavana-High King of the Bharata tribe, ruling from Prayaga, son of the Tritsu line of Bharatas.

Rshi Vasishtha-Rajpurohit of the Bharata tribe, student of the Maharshi Vasishtha school of seers.

Bharata-founder of the Bharata dynasty.

Suhotra-elder son of Bharata and first High King of the dynasty.

The Suryavansha (Solar Tribes)

Ikshvaku-founder of the Suryavansha line of Kings, first King of Aryavarta.

Vaivasvat Manu-Ikshvaku's father, settler and explorer.

Kashyapa-first Maharshi of Aryavarta, grandfather to Vaivasvat Manu.

Vivasvana-Kashyapa's son, Vaivasvat's father.

Drishta-cousin to Vaivasvat and first General of Ikshvaku's army.

Maharshi Vasishtha-Kashyapa's pupil and third Maharshi of Aryavarta.

Varman-cousin to Vaivasvat and Ikshvaku's mentor.

Ardra-half-brother to Drishta and first General of Ikshvaku's army.

Haryashva-Ashvak warrior and Ikshvaku's friend and advisor.

Sarmi-Ikshvaku's first wife.

Vikukshi-Ikshvaku's first son, through Sarmi.

Nivritti-Ikshvaku's second wife.

Nimi-Ikshvaku's second son, through Nivritti.

Ila-Vaivasvat Manu's daughter and eldest child, wife to Budha Atreya.

Pramshu, Sharyati, Nabhaga, Karusaka, Narisyanta-the other sons of Vaivasvat Manu.

Revata-second General of Ikshvaku's army and leader of the Aikshvakus.

Marici-Kashyapa's father and last Mahajanapati to the Solar tribes, led them back to Aryavarta.

Havishmana Surya-Marici's grandfather and the last Surya.

Aurvan Surya-shared ancestor of all Solar tribes, victorious Deva of the final Deva-Asura wars.

The Somavansha (Lunar Tribes)

Pururava-founder of the Somavansha line of Kings, son of Ila and Budha.

Budha-father to Pururava.

Atri-second Maharshi of Aryavarta, grandfather to Pururava, founder of Atri school of Rshis.

Devapi-cousin to Pururava.

Ayu-Pururava's son.

Nahusha-Pururava's grandson.

Tapin Soma-shared ancestor of all Lunar tribes, victorious Deva of the final Deva-Asura wars.

Others

Narantaka-Supreme Commander of the Rakshasas of Kamyakvana, later the King of Dasas, also known as Zarath.

Urvashi-Pururava's wife and woman of the Apsara tribe, enemy to Gandharvas.

Devantaka-mythic Asura leader of the ancient Eras, also known as Vritra.

Maghavan Indra-victorious Deva of the final Deva-Asura wars.

Mantradruma Indra-last Indra, left no known descendants.

Older Family Tree

SURYA
PRIYAVRATA RAVI
AURVAN SURYA
VARMAN SURYA
BALVAN SURYA
ASHVAN SURYA
AISHVANA SURYA
AISHMANA SURYA
HAVISHMANA SURYA

SOMA
SOMA II
SOMA III
SAVIN SOMA
SAVIN II
TAPIN SOMA

INDRA
INDRA II
AVASYU INDRA
RISHVANJAS INDRA
SATMANYU INDRA
MAGHAVAN INDRA
TVAJIT INDRA
AVASYU II
MAGHAVAN II
VIRIKVAS INDRA
MANTRADRUMA INDRA AAPYAS

AGNI
VAHNI
HOTRA
VITIHOTRA
JIVALANA
ANGRA AGNI

Later Family Tree

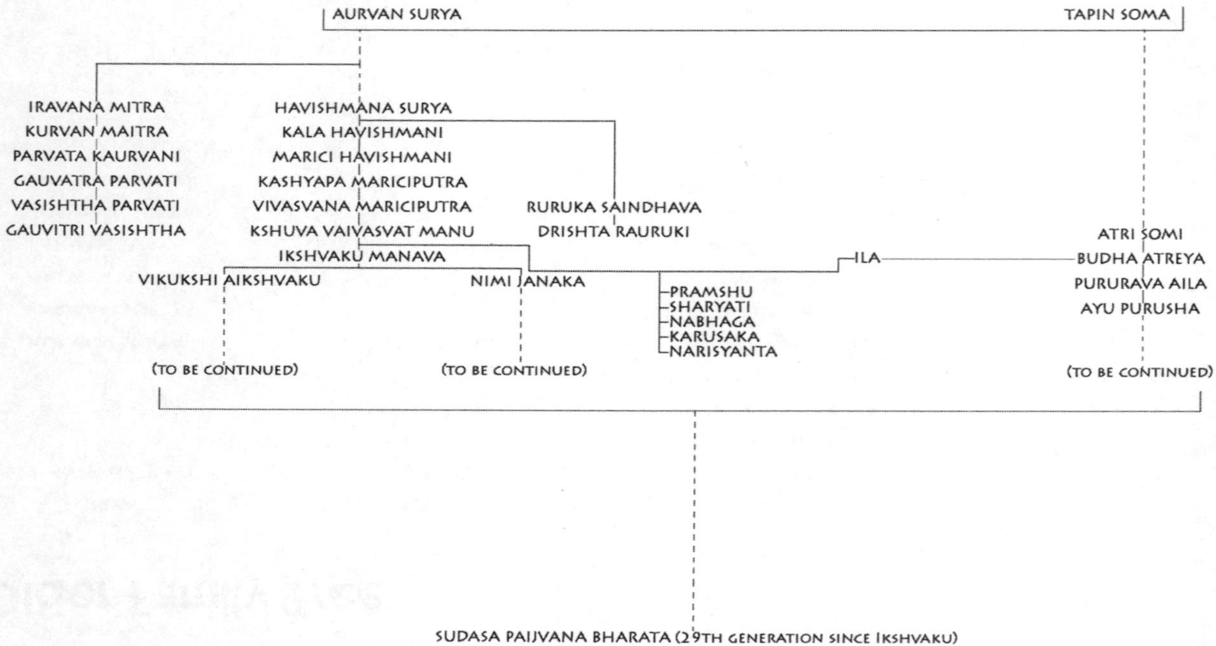

Prologue

Sudasa, Year 920, Seventh era

The King surveyed his visitors with an imperial gaze, his large frame tight with muscle. A dense beard covered most of his face, and bushy eyebrows accented his deep-set eyes. This was Bhagiratha Aikshvaku, King of the Suryavansha and ruler of Ayodhya. His rock-throne was raised on an elevated platform and his visitors prostrated before him. He recognised one face in their midst—Rshi Vasishtha of Prayaga, High Priest to the Bharata tribe. The rshi was old but radiated spiritual authority, much like Bhagiratha's own High Priest.

"King Bhagiratha," said Rshi Vasishtha, his voice deep and bold. "I present to you Sudasa Paijvana Bharata. Son of King Pijavana Bharata and the heir-in-waiting."

Bhagiratha raised his eyebrows in surprise, turning his attention to Vasishtha's young companion. It was a gesture of complete trust from King Pijavana to send his own son to the Suryavanshi capital. The tentative truce between Suryavansha and Bharata tribes was more incidental than planned. They shared the same enemies, and thus seemed to occupy the same side in Aryavarta's great inter-tribal divide.

Young Sudasa bowed before the King again, awed by his hefty, barrel-chested appearance. His own father was a lean, tall man who kept a shaven face at all times. King Bhagiratha admittedly looked more formidable. "My father conveys his respect, King Bhagiratha," Sudasa said with perfect pronunciation. He could not let awe affect his steadied composure.

As King Bhagiratha began his descent down the platform, his ornaments glinted in the sunlight that pierced through the openings in the walls and the ceiling. He touched Rshi Vasishtha's feet with reverence, and lowered himself to his knees to meet Sudasa's eyes. Gold and precious stones layered his bulky frame, far more regal in appearance than King Pijavana's austere trimmings. He studied Sudasa with twinkling interest, and finally spoke in a gravelly, temperate voice. "You resemble your father, young one. How old are you?"

"Twelve," Sudasa replied.

"My son is fifteen," Bhagiratha remarked. "Yet, you are already taller. No doubt Pijavana awaits the day you outgrow him with pride."

Sudasa smiled at the Suryavanshi King, liking his amiable personality instantly. Despite his appearance, Bhagiratha was not stern and grim like the Kings Sudasa was familiar with. There were four Kings in the Bharata tribe. In power and authority they were equal, but in lineage Pijavana was of direct descent from their great founder. He was the High King, and he ruled from the Bharatas' dynastic capital of Prayaga. Sudasa's memory of his uncles was of gaunt, tall men who constantly talked of war and ritual. But King Bhagiratha seemed different.

"King Pijavana has directed me to remind you of an ancient tradition, King Bhagiratha," said Rshi Vasishtha. "A tradition of Suryavanshi Kings training princes of allied tribes, turning them into warriors of great ability. He suggests you consider starting the tradition anew with his son and heir."

Bhagiratha looked from Vasishtha to Sudasa. "Do you know of this tradition, young one?"

Sudasa nodded. "Rshi Vasishtha has explained it to me."

"And are you willing to leave your home for five years? To live among men and women of a different tribe?"

Bhagiratha's easy nature gave Sudasa the confidence to reply. "Both our tribes are guided by the Vasishtha Rshi School. A Vasishtha is your High Priest as well, thus our ways cannot be too dissimilar."

Bhagiratha smiled. "Well said! I expected no less from the student of a Vasishtha." Then the King turned to the rshi and said, "I accept Pijavana's offer, but not out of sentiment for a bygone tradition. The last allied prince to enter Suryavanshi tutelage lived more than six centuries ago. This is a new Aryavarta, and we must shape a new destiny for ourselves. I will take Sudasa under my wing out of hope for a grander, better future for our respective tribes."

Rshi Vasishtha bowed in acknowledgment. "Your sagacity and judgement are unrivalled, King Bhagiratha. I would respect any decision you take without question."

Sudasa stared at Bhagiratha in open curiosity. It was not common for a rshi to defer to the wisdom of a King. What was Bhagiratha's story? His attention went to the medallion hanging around Bhagiratha's neck. Thick metal nuggets had been fused together to form the chain, and at the bottom hung a chunky, circular disc embossed with gold. The Sun was drawn at its centre, its golden rays extending to the disc's edges before disappearing. The medallion shone brighter than any other ornament on Bhagiratha, yet it also looked extremely ancient. There were countless cuts and scratches on its surface, and the chain bore signs of being frequently repaired. It was the most fascinating object Sudasa had ever laid his eyes on.

King Bhagiratha spotted his interest and said, "This is the seal of Aurvan Surya, my great ancestor. It is more than 1,500 years old. Would you like to know its history?"

Sudasa hesitated and looked to Rshi Vasishtha, who nodded in encouragement. "Yes!" he exclaimed.

"It was created by Aurvan Surya, in an age long before ours. But its history in Aryavarta begins with Ikshvaku. Do you know who that is, young one?"

Sudasa tried to remember his lessons. The name was familiar, but he could not place it. Aryavarta's history was vast, and it began nearly 1,000 years before his time. Then it clicked into place. "He was the first King of Aryavarta!" he shouted, unable to keep the triumph out of his boyish voice. "And founder of the Suryavansha—your great dynasty, King Bhagiratha."

Bhagiratha looked pleased at that, complimenting Vasishtha, "With you as tutor, I have no doubt that the boy's education has no gaps."

"Except for the very critical skills of war and combat," Vasishtha replied modestly. "But five years in your kingdom will bridge that."

Bhagiratha nodded and turned to Sudasa, taking the medallion off and placing it in his eager hands. It was as heavy as Sudasa expected, evidence of the purity of its components. "Aurvan forged it to emphasise his claim to the title of Surya," Bhagiratha narrated. "A title that few men have ever held. Some believe that the gold that went in its making was of an even earlier era—the time of an original and divine Surya."

Bhagiratha's tone made it clear that he held no such beliefs. "It has been lost by our tribe many times, but it always finds its way back," he continued. "And the first man in Aryavarta to find and wear it was Ikshvaku. I will tell you his tale now, and when you return to your father you can tell him that I will train you to be an Aikshvaku—a figurative son of Ikshvaku himself. Five years hence, you will emerge with the skills and ability that propelled Ikshvaku to become the first King of our now-fractured nation."

Raja

"Once, there was life and culture in the Great Deccan—but ages have passed since then. Now, our land begins from north of the Vindhyachala and culminates at the Himalaya. To the east, Ganga shows us the limits of our country, and Sindhu binds it from the west. This is the great land of Aryavarta."

Vaivasvat Manu to his son Ikshvaku

Ikshvaku, Year 32, Seventh era

Ikshvaku stepped back and evaded the attack, his movements calm and measured. Varman, his opponent, was older and far more experienced. But Ikshvaku could not afford to lose this duel. He allowed his opponent to attack hard and fast, forcing him to drain his stamina. Their swords were wooden, but Ikshvaku pretended they were made of metal, sharp and lethal. That kept his concentration alive, the danger real. From the corner of his eyes he saw his father observing impassively. Vaivasvat Manu was no longer the formidable warrior he once was, but he had passed on every crucial skill to his fourteen-year-old son.

Varman feigned left and brought his sword swiftly across to the right, slashing at Ikshvaku's exposed plexus. He quickly hid the look of pain upon his face, not wishing to give that satisfaction to his attacker. Taking a deep breath and moving his attention away from the bruise, he executed a rapid sequence of attacks that took Varman by surprise. This particular sequence was a modification of Manu's own style, designed for pace and fluidity than brute strength.

The final two lashes of his attack hit hard against Varman's torso, and if the sword were metal it would have sliced across his waist with deadly effect. Ikshvaku's face lit up with a sly smile, his eyes triumphant. Only father was known to beat Varman in a duel, and now he was the second to earn that honour. But Varman was too stern a tutor to be anything short of critical. "You still move slowly," he said. "In the heat of battle, enemies are upon you from all sides. Speed could make the difference between life and death."

Taking note of Varman's comments, Ikshvaku silently followed him back to the armoury and threw his sword into the pile of practice weapons. Varman was Ikshvaku's tutor and Vaivasvat Manu's childhood friend. They had learned and perfected swordplay together, and now they were passing on their knowledge to young Ikshvaku. Father and son began their walk back to the hut, winding through muddy alleys and narrow passages between the markets and residential settlements that formed the village of Sakala. As far as Suryavanshi villages went, it was a modest one, populated by only a few hundred Solar tribesmen and women. Most were cowherds or farmers, some were from the elite warrior lines. To the north lay great cities like Prasthala and Avisari, while Harayupa and Vitabhya lay to the south. Powerful bastions of Solar power, they were nevertheless isolated fortresses with a small perimeter of protection for the surrounding villages. The once mighty and united Solar clan was now a loose confederation, and it troubled Ikshvaku.

"Why are we not a united people anymore, father?" he asked.

As he was known to do, Vaivasvat Manu replied with a question of his own. "Who says we are not? And who are 'we' anyway?"

It was a test, and Ikshvaku replied confidently. "We are the Solar clans, or the Suryavansha. A confederation of people descended from the great patriarchs—Havishmana Surya, Aurvan Surya and others of that title before them. We are united by ties of blood and family, more binding than any of our ancestors ever held dear. We should be one force, one people. Instead, we exist as fragmented cities and clans."

"Who would unite them?" Manu asked, not missing a beat. It was a daily habit for father and son to debate such matters, as had been a tradition in the family for many generations. "Each city is ruled by a regent, a representative of the main Solar clan that inhabits it. And our law dictates that no regent holds more power than another."

"And what was Marici?" Ikshvaku challenged.

Marici was their forefather, a pivotal figure in the early decades of Aryavarta. His strong, undaunted leadership united the scattered, nomadic Solar clans and brought them east of the Sindhu river. Marici was who Varman often referred to as the last Mahajanapati, Supreme Clan Head, of the Suryavansha.

"A great leader certainly," Manu conceded. "But his son and my grandfather, Kashyapa, abdicated rule when it descended to him. The Solar tribes have been a confederation ever since." He eyed his son shrewdly, deducing what was on his mind. "Kashyapa's abdication means that our line can never claim the title of Janapati again. Our fate depends on the regents now, and none among them can claim supremacy over another."

"But what of a King, a Raja?" Ikshvaku asked. "He would hold supreme power, would he not?"

Manu studied his son. "Where have you heard of a Raja?"

"From Ila," Ikshvaku replied, speaking of his elder sister. Ila was Vaivasvat Manu's first child, born fourteen years before Ikshvaku. "She says that a King is sovereign, his authority undisputable."

"And has she also told you that we have never had a King in Aryavarta?"

"What of the earlier eras? Surely we had kings back then?" Ikshvaku countered, referring to the previous six eras of Man. They were a broad division of ancient history that Manu taught him long ago, and there was no better teacher on this subject.

"On that we can only speculate," replied Manu. He caught the dissatisfied look on Ikshvaku's face and continued."Our forefathers before Marici were Suryas, claiming descent from the first and original Deva of that name. But we do not know whether a Surya ever called himself King." He did not tell his son the whole tale–the title of Raja was offered to him once, by a council of regents from Avisari, Harayupa and Vitabhya. But Manu was as disinclined towards rule as his grandfather, Kashyapa. He was content with his favoured vocation: transmitting knowledge from village to village, bringing agriculture and stable settlement to the scattered Solar clans.

Ikshvaku fell silent, withdrawing into deep thought. He was a boy of fourteen, but Manu could tell that he was mature beyond his years. But Sakala was too mundane a settlement for lofty ambitions to find fruition, and Manu knew that the day had come when he would have to part with his son. Villages such as Sakala were humble enough for him, but they were no breeding grounds for aspiring kings.

"There can always be a first time," Ikshvaku speculated aloud. "Just like there was a first Surya, there can be a first King." And the clans needed one, he thought. The Solar tribes were growing more distant than ever before, their cities suffering frequent raids from Rakshasas and Gandharvas, hostile tribes that did not follow the Arya ways.

"I agree," said Manu. "Your desire is neither misplaced nor over-ambitious. But to see it come true requires exposure and resilience. You are a formidable warrior, Varman and I agree on that. But you will not become King by the sword alone. You need to inspire people. You need to win over the traders, farmers, potters and fishermen as much as the warriors. It is time you leave Sakala behind, my son."

"Where must I go first, father?" Ikshvaku asked immediately without hesitation. Manu marvelled at the look in his son's eyes. Where did the boy get his resolve from? And how had it remained hidden for so long? Then Vaivasvat realised that Ikshvaku's ambitions were at least in part those of Ila. His daughter had voiced similar thoughts in her childhood, but he ended those dreams when he married her off to secure a lasting alliance with the Lunar tribes of Plaksha.

"To Avisari," Manu replied. "The old warrior families still prefer mountains to our river-lands. You must rally them together under the banner of Marici, for that is the last name they ever swore loyalty to."

"I can do it," Ikshvaku said confidently. "The blood of Surya is scattered across this land, waiting for the line of Marici to stake its claim. Will you not come with me, father?"

Vaivasvat Manu shook his head, his expression turning grim. "I cannot join you on this path, my son. Aryavarta has never seen a King, and even tribal chiefs rarely come as young as you. You are undertaking a venture fraught with risk, but my duty is to peace and stability." Lest that dishearten his son, he added, "It is good to imagine great things. Once imagined, you only need to act to make them real." It was in line with the optimistic philosophy he had imparted to his son all his life.

Ikshvaku nodded determinedly. "Very well then, father. I will take mother's blessings and make way for Avisari in the morning. I will enlist the help of uncle Drishta along the way." Drishta was Manu's cousin, born from the line of one of Havishmana Surya's younger sons. His was the clan that settled the city of Prasthala and nurtured it to the growing town it was today. Unlike other Solar settlements, Prasthala was not established along a river. It lay boldly halfway on the vast tract of land that separated the two tributaries of the mighty Sindhu river. And it was a waypoint for all travel, north or south of the many rivers that eventually merged at Vitabhya. It was a city of farmers and merchants, the only one to be ruled not by a regent but a council of clan elders.

Manu frowned. "Drishta might not be happy at the thought of travelling to Avisari. There is a past to him that you do not know about, my son. But there is another who will be more difficult to persuade. He was friend to my father and pupil to my grandfather, now a Maharshi in his own right."

There were three Maharshis in Aryavarta. One was Atri, who was of the Lunar tribes and lived in Plaksha. Then there was Maharshi Kashyapa, Ikshvaku's notoriously hermetic forefather. That meant that father referred to… "Maharshi Vasishtha!" Ikshvaku whispered in awe, surprised that the Maharshi was so connected to his family. "He was a friend to grandfather?"

"Indeed. Vasishtha and my father were childhood friends, and Vasishtha studied under Maharshi Kashyapa before gaining that title himself. He resides at Sringara now, running a school of pupils who will take his name one day."

Maharshi Vasishtha was a figure of legend in Ikshvaku's mind, and the mere thought of coming face-to-face with him was far more terrifying than thoughts of battle or kingship. "What would I say to him?" he wondered aloud.

"Tell him who you are, tell him of your lineage and then fall at his feet. But be ready for the most important question he will ask you—*why*."

Ikshvaku frowned and repeated, "Why?"

"Yes. The Maharshi will want to know your purpose, the reason for your mission. If you waver in that response, you will not gain his faith."

Ikshvaku nodded, resolving to stand up to Maharshi Vasishtha's expectations. Manu continued, "You will have to win over many more people. The regents, especially Ardra of Avisari, are proud men who will not simply stand aside for you. I wish you well, my son." Then he added mysteriously, "And when we meet again, I hope to have with me something that will establish your right to rule over the Solar tribes beyond all doubt or dispute."

Drishta

"Young Ikshvaku was fortunate to have many mentors, and nearly all of them were elders of the Solar tribes. One of them was Drishta Rauruki. He never married and had no known progeny, and perhaps looked upon Ikshvaku as the son he never had."

King Bhagiratha to Sudasa

More than six decades had passed since the Suryavansha migrated into Aryavarta under Marici Havishmani's ambitious leadership. Most of his own descendants settled at Sakala, which was modest enough to afford the sort of anonymity they desired. Others made Prasthala their home, not able to shed their ancestral suspicion of all water bodies, a characteristic their horses readily shared. Another band settled at Harayupa, which was now Aryavarta's most bustling city. It was home to countless people that Ikshvaku could count as aunts, uncles and nephews even. The vast confederation of people that claimed descent from the Suryas of previous eras was scattered across these and other settlements. And born four generations after Marici, Ikshvaku was determined to become their King.

"A King!" exclaimed Drishta. "Why not! Marici was more or less a King to us once, as were the Suryas before him. But I guess your father was not too keen on the idea, was he?" Drishta was in equal parts amiable and boisterous, and an easy smile perennially rested on his lips. Father was not the first to hint that in his past lay war and bloodshed, but Ikshvaku found that hard to imagine. Beloved uncle Drishta was a simple, bumbling farmer, though this did not mean that Drishta had never held a sword. As an eight-year old, Ikshvaku had seen his uncle fight hard and defend Sakala during a Rakshasa raid. He assumed it to be born of necessity, and Drishta certainly never spoke of any warrior past.

"Father is more supportive than I can ask for," Ikshvaku said humbly. "And the concerns he has raised are quite valid. For one, I *am* far too young."

Drishta scoffed. "I have seen you wield the sword. Even at fourteen you can better most men."

"Prowess with the sword is not the only skill a King needs," Ikshvaku replied, feeling pleased nevertheless. "There are several complications to uniting a tribe-hood as scattered as we are. Marici managed it only after legendary endeavours."

"And everyone remembers those legends!" Drishta countered heartily. "It took supreme effort to unite the many Solar tribes. But once it was done, it took us to a state from which we could never return. You have not been to Avisari before, or Harayupa and Vitabhya. You do not know that the people wait for Marici's prime line to take hold of Solar leadership once again. Your throne awaits you," he added wryly.

"Avisari is where I am headed now," Ikshvaku said. "And I will be greatly aided in my endeavour if you join me, uncle."

Drishta turned grim at that, which was an odd expression on him. "It has been years since I went beyond Sringara," he said, "And more than a decade since I stepped into Avisari." There was darkness in his eyes, a look that Ikshvaku had never seen before. Suddenly, it made him look unfamiliar.

"But you would welcome a trip to the Himalaya, would you not?" Ikshvaku asked tentatively. For all his ability and resolve, he was but a boy. And his uncle now looked increasingly like the man people warned him about. This was not the man who used to shelter Ikshvaku from his parents' fury after every mischievous prank.

Drishta sighed and said, "I come from a warrior line, son, just like your father. Battle and death is in our blood, and we have seen enough of both in our lives. But at Prasthala I have put that behind me. It has been years since I even held a sword, let alone fight Rakshasas."

Right then Ikshvaku realised what would bring him Drishta's submission. If he wanted to be King, he had to behave like one. Supreme authority was not a violable concept, his sister had once taught him. "When I am King, will you not submit to my sword?"

he asked. "Will you not bend your knee and accept the son of Surya incarnate in front of you?"

This appeared to throw Drishta off. This was not his young nephew anymore, but someone more mature and poised. "I will," he said uncertainly. "You are heir to Marici's prime line. And a King is exactly what our people need, with savage tribes growing in strength all around us."

"A King will need strong, reliable men to lead his armies. And ours will be no small force," Ikshvaku said, speaking of the enormous horde of warriors that could be summoned if all Solar cities united their numbers. "Your duty to our tribe is no less than mine, and when I claim authority in the name of Marici, will you not accept? When I ask you to take up the sword again and lead our armies, will you not return to your old life?"

Drishta's lips curved into a wry smile as he realised that his nephew had outwitted him. There was a hint of pride in his eyes as he bowed his head and said, "I will."

"Then I am your King already, uncle Drishta! I am King of the Suryavansha, and as a fellow son of Surya, you must obey my every command." Ikshvaku felt a rush of adrenaline as he said that, realising that he would remember this as the moment he first asserted himself as King.

Drishta exhaled deeply, marvelling at the maturity set upon Ikshvaku's face. The boy had a lithe, chiselled body, and muscle flexed beneath his skin. Drishta knew that he was right. The young nephew was already his ruler, and he was thus bound to loyal obedience. "Very well then," Drishta said. "To Avisari we go, my King."

Ikshvaku nodded. "To Sringara first, to seek the blessings of Maharshi Vasishtha. And there is another thing. I think father has set himself upon a search. He said he would have something for me the next time we meet. Something that could seal my claim to Suryavanshi kingship. Do you know what it is, uncle?"

Drishta scoffed. "Do I know anything about what Manu is ever up to? Not in the slightest."

The Maharshi

"Along with Kashyapa and Atri, but surpassing their legends, Vasishtha was among Aryavarta's first great Maharshis. Your family retains many prayers of his composition, and it was a Vasishtha who first legitimised the Kingship of your forebear."

King Bhagiratha to Sudasa

Born and raised in Sakala, Ikshvaku had no experience of the Himalaya. Everything he knew about them was learnt vicariously, and nothing could prepare his senses for the first view of their majestic glory. They became visible only when Drishta and Ikshvaku crossed north of the Iravati river, their peaks rising high into the clouds in the north-east. Beyond it they rose higher and higher till one was already amid the foothills. The Asikni river marked a final crossing point, for north of it the Himalayas rose without hesitation–each mountain taller than the one before it. Even though it got colder as they ascended, Ikshvaku found that his body barely seemed to mind. He said as much to Drishta, who remarked, "Your blood comes from people who once called the mountains their home. Winds of the lower Himalayas should scarcely affect you. But let us see how you fare after we cross Sringara." Despite his initial reluctance, Drishta looked at ease once they set off. Quite a few times he let his horse work up a gallop and felt the wind rush onto his face. There was so much to him that Ikshvaku was yet to learn, but the same applied in reverse as well. For all the confidence Drishta had in Ikshvaku's skills with the sword, he had seen only a fraction of it on display. Yet that could remain true for only so long, as Manu had once said, good warriors hold many secrets, a great warrior holds a great secret.

Sringara was situated deep in the lower Himalayas, overlooking the vast Dalasarovara lake. This was the spot where Marici and his tribes had realised that they were finally in Aryavarta, establishing their first village and commencing their transformation from nomadic to pastoral and agrarian. Ikshvaku had never imagined that such beauty could exist on earth. Sringara was a valley of flowers blooming in all possible colours, lines of deciduous trees adding a dash of green to the visual tapestry. "Back when our forefathers were nomadic," Drishta narrated, "Sringara was the farthest they ventured into Aryavarta. You are not the first to be amazed by its beauty, and it is not for nothing that they named it Sringara–a jewel. The name is obviously ancient, for even the Rakshasas know it as *Srinagara*."

"What family lines reside here?" asked Ikshvaku. He imagined the people of Sringara to be fair and gentle folk, more craftsmen and artisans than warriors.

But the truth was quite different. "Sringara is home to Solar lines descended from the brothers of Havishmana Surya. Their forefathers were the fierce warrior-nomads that populated his elite contingents. They are a harsh and grim people, son. And they have to be so, to make a home in a place so cold and remote. Only Avisari offers conditions more hostile than those in Sringara."

Their passage from Prasthala to Sringara took close to five weeks, at the end of which Drishta's conversion from uncle to loyal subject was complete. He looked upon himself as Ikshvaku's guardian, though he knew from the way the boy moved in practise that he needed no protection. Vaivasvat Manu had trained Ikshvaku well, raising him to be an expert swordsman and archer. Varman's maverick but highly disciplined rigour endowed Ikshvaku with a flexible technique. It was on their second night in Sringara that they managed to meet Maharshi Vasishtha. His ashrama was located on the banks of the Dalasarovara lake. Here was Aryavarta's first rshi school–a place of learning for students who wished to take the path of a seer. The venerable Maharshi Vasishtha guided them and the worthy got his name. But for now, there was only one Vasishtha, and when Ikshvaku finally found him face-to-face the young boy was tongue-tied. He had imagined this moment for weeks, visualising the meeting and memorising the words he would utter. But all speech failed him, and it was Drishta who mercifully stepped in to save his King.

"Maharshi Vasishtha," he said, "I present to you the boy Ikshvaku, son to Vaivasvat Manu and great-grandson to Maharshi Kashyapa. Born in the line of Aurvan, Havishmana and Marici, he is heir to the prime Solar line."

The seer turned his attention to Ikshvaku, who now remembered what his father had taught him. His introduction already made, he fell at Vasishtha's feet. "Pranama, Maharshi."

Maharshi Vasishtha bent down and raised the young boy up by his shoulders. His gaze pierced through the son of Manu, scrutinising him, as though to assess his core. Ikshvaku returned the stare, perceiving in those luminous eyes the wisdom of ages coalesced into a single personality. "You have your mother's face," the Maharshi finally said. "But your flaming orange eyes are uncannily like those of Marici."

Ikshvaku raised his eyebrows in surprise. "You knew Marici?" Marici was his forefather by four generations, more a figure from legends than someone real and tangible.

"I barely knew him," Vasishtha admitted. "I knew his son somewhat better, and knew his grandson best. To Marici we were but boys, aloof to his grand visions, and I doubt he even knew my name." Maharshi Vasishtha was more than sixty years old, and though much of his hair was still black he simply *looked* old. It was hard to imagine him as a boy, and harder still to imagine the boy being around Marici. Yet Ikshvaku could perceive the history around him, the memory of a tribe's migration ingrained in his personality. It was not unlike father's aura, and Ikshvaku realised that Maharshi Vasishtha's support was vital in reuniting the Solar confederation. But what family line did he descend from?

The seer seemed to sense his mind and said, "Havishmana Surya had six brothers, and I was seeded in the line descended from the fourth. My father was Parvata Kaurvani, general and counsellor to Marici."

Ikshvaku bowed with as much humility as he could, knowing that it was a special privilege to hear of Maharshi Vasishtha's lineage in his own words. But now came the difficult part. Explaining his intentions to his father or uncle was a different matter. They knew and understood him even if he could not articulate himself very well. But with Vasishtha there were no filial benefits to be gained, and Ikshvaku had to convince the Maharshi of two things. One, that the Solar tribes needed a King and two, that he was suitable for that role. "I come to take your blessings, Maharshi," he said. "And to tell you a tale of history and ambition."

Behind him, Drishta's lips curved in a grin. It took a special boy to make the Maharshi's eyes grow wide. "A tale of history and ambition!" the seer repeated with interest. "I have tutored many teenage boys, but none have ever offered so intriguing a proposal. What is your tale then, son of Manu?"

"There were once Devas and Asuras in Aryavarta, though this was not yet the land's name," Ikshvaku began, and the Maharshi leaned imperceptibly closer. "Great wars were waged between these two ancient tribes, and in the final war the Devas won. Asuras were driven out from what was *not-yet*-Aryavarta, and many found shelter in the forests and mountains."

Drishta exhaled deeply at Ikshvaku's pause, evidently taken in by his oratory. "Continue," said the Maharshi.

"And then for reasons unknown to us, the Devas decided to leave this land. Some went into the mountains, like Tapin Soma and Angra Agni. Others went west, like Maghavan Indra and Aurvan Surya. Centuries passed, and the line of Surya grew vast. For generations they wandered as nomads in lands that no man of Aryavarta is familiar with. And then a fundamental change happened."

Ikshvaku paused again, his gaze locked deeply with that of the Maharshi. "Where have you received this history from?" the seer asked.

"From my father and grandfather," Ikshvaku replied. "And from the many Solar tribesmen and women that inhabit Sakala, for I have not ventured out of the village before this."

"You received it in parts, did you not? And you welded the narrative yourself, combining all you learnt or overheard?"

Ikshvaku nodded.

"How old are you, young Ikshvaku?"

"Fourteen."

The Maharshi chuckled, his dense beard bobbing up and down. "I was there at Vaivasvat's naming ceremony," he said, eyes twinkling in reminiscence. "It was I who gave him the name of Kshuva Vaivasvat Manu–which lends itself to your patronymic–Kshauva Manava. How did you acquire the name of Ikshvaku?"

Drishta stepped in once again. "The boy has a notorious fondness for sugarcanes," he said. Sugarcane was called *ikshu* in the prime Solar dialect. "As a boy of four years, he was responsible for theft in seven out of the eight sugarcane growing households in Sakala." Drishta did not add that Ikshvaku's mother would have thrashed him all night had he not intervened and volunteered to counsel the boy. Such counselling sessions usually meant a few days of active farming and bantering between uncle and nephew.

The Maharshi chuckled again, louder this time. "Continue then, *Ikshu-vaku*. What was this fundamental change you speak of?"

"The Devas lost the labels that held them together," Ikshvaku replied. "The title of Deva fell out of vogue in a few generations after Aurvan Surya, and with Havishmana the title of Surya ended as well. That was the final step in losing our unity. Without the ancient labels of kinship to bind us, our eventual disarray was inevitable. Marici's attempt was valiant, even successful, for a while. But this unity was lost with his son's abdication and we became a divergent confederation. Where once there was one ruler, one voice of decision, there became many."

The Maharshi looked at Ikshvaku again, and appeared to assess him in a new light. "Marici was grandson to Havishmana," he said. "Do you not wonder why his father did not take the title of Surya?"

"The boy has been asking this question ever since he learnt of his ancestry," Drishta offered. He did not need to add that Ikshvaku had never received a satisfactory response. It was one of the greatest Solar mysteries-why did the name of Surya die with Havishmana?

"It was not given to him by the people," Vasishtha said simply. "They implicitly and unanimously decided that there could be no Surya after Havishmana, and that their era had come to a close. There was nothing Marici's father could do, which is not to say that he did not try. And so, Marici took a more dignified route. He never claimed the title for himself, choosing to lead by example and merit. His unification of the Solar tribes was achieved piece-by-piece, taking decades to fructify. And it was not without its fair share of blood and war. Are you ready for the same struggle, young one?"

Ikshvaku did not ask how the Maharshi had guessed his motives. "I am," he replied. "This uneasy confederation between Solar cities will not last long. Soon the regent of Avisari will look over the valleys to Sringara, and the regent at Vitabhya will grow wary of his counterpart in Harayupa. All that Marici achieved in his lifetime will be undone in a matter of years. And this does not even include the threat we face from Rakshasas, Gandharvas and other tribes descended from the Asuras."

"I agree with you," the Maharshi said, having leaned closer to Ikshvaku by now. "But what is the solution?"

This was the moment Ikshvaku was waiting for. He delivered his response like a well-rehearsed speech. "The scattered Suryavanshi strength needs to be yoked together. The old labels may not work anymore, but the ties of kinship are still present and tangible. The time has come for a Solar raja to take his place. And Surya's prime line is well-placed to honour this duty."

Maharshi Vasishtha eyed the boy for a long time, feeling in his words the passion that people had always desired from Vaivasvat, and even Vivasvana and Kashyapa before that. Suryavanshi history remembered a glorious past, a time of great men like Aurvan Surya who brought lasting victory against the Asuras. The consequent tribal aspiration to regain that past was natural, and born in Aurvan's own line, Ikshvaku was its logical culmination. Vasishtha said nothing, but his eyes seemed to shine in agreement.

"Will you come with me to Avisari?" Ikshvaku asked, pressing his victory. "Will you support me when I claim kingship over the old mountain families? Over Harayupa, Vitabhya and all the land that lies between them?"

"I will come with you to Avisari and beyond," the Maharshi replied. "If the dynasty of Surya rises to stake its claim, then I will be its humble priest. And yet the seal is missing."

Ikshvaku frowned. "The seal?" he repeated.

"The seal of Aurvan Surya, an ancient piece of our history. But it is not my place to tell you this. The seal of Surya is something you must learn from Vaivasvat Manu, when he decides the time is right."

Avisari

"Founded in an age before ours, Avisari is a place of history and legend. Some hold that it was the birth place of Aurvan Surya, though I have reasons to doubt that claim. But that does not diminish its important and almost sacred status in Suryavanshi lore."

King Bhagiratha to Sudasa

Avisari—the Opportune Place. Home to more than 7,000 people, it was still far from being one of Aryavarta's most populous cities. For it was the harshest and most remote. Situated on the Sindhu river's western bank, it looked across to the grand Himalaya peaks that the early Suryavanshi crossed before settling along the river's many tributaries. This was de-facto capital to the Solar people, and all clans could trace their ancestry to men and women who once crossed east of the Sindhu from here.

Ardra, the Bear, regent of Avisari in the name of Surya, stood tall over Ikshvaku. He was easily the biggest man Ikshvaku had ever seen; tall and barrel-chested with a fierce grimace to match. It was an intimidating sight and few men could stand under Ardra's shadow and not quail. "I am a regent to Surya," said Ardra, his voice bold. "If you are born in the line of Havishmana and Marici, then you *are* a Surya. I will gladly step aside and give you the rule of Avisari. But I will not call you King, boy."

Ikshvaku was aware that all eyes had turned to him. And he had the distinct feeling that Maharshi Vasishtha was watching with interest. How would the young king-to-be react now? It did not bother him that the Maharshi did not speak up in his support, or uncle

Drishta. This was a battle he had to fight for himself, for he could not truly call himself King until he acquired the resolute loyalty of all Solar regents combined. It would not have daunted Marici, Ikshvaku imagined. And it would not daunt him. "I am indeed a boy to you, great Bear," he said, bowing his head slightly. "A boy from Sakala, on his first journey to the outside world. And you are the regent of Avisari, a man as fine as Solar blood has ever bred."

Ikshvaku paused and Drishta knew that he already held his audience captive. He inched a step closer to his nephew, feeling a profound sense of solidarity towards the boy who was now his King. Ikshvaku continued, "It is a mark of your honour that you willingly step aside for me, but your greatness lies in your refusal to call me King." Ardra raised an eyebrow. The boy was a fine orator, and he spoke with the confidence of an older man. He glanced around and knew that each of his counsellors was listening spellbound. This was truly the son of Vaivasvat Manu, and the ability to hold people captivated came naturally to him.

"I am only fourteen," Ikshvaku said. "With a slender body that is nowhere near the strength of a grown man. There is no hair on my face, and my voice shows hints of having only recently cracked. I am clearly not a worthy King of the Solar tribes. And being a loyal Solar son yourself, it would be irresponsible of you to accept me as your King. Is this not how you perceive me, great Bear?"

The Bear grunted, clearly unsettled by Ikshvaku's demeanour. "You are right," he said. "A King is a tiger among men, better than any other warrior in his clan. You might be that man many years from now, but you are not him yet. And before you call me vain, let me confess that I am not that man either."

"You are far too humble," Ikshvaku said. "My uncle Drishta tells me that you are the fiercest Solar warrior alive. No man has ever bested you in combat."

Ardra turned to Drishta, and as their eyes met, Ikshvaku realised that the two had faced each other before. He became painfully aware of his youth. He was not even born when most of these men lived their best years. "Your uncle is humblest among us here," Ardra said, his gaze still locked with Drishta. "I have been bested in combat once, by none other than him. If you seek the fiercest Solar warrior alive, then you need not look further."

"I did not know that," Ikshvaku said, loud enough only for Drishta to hear.

"It was fortune on my side," Drishta said to the Bear. "Your foot slipped, and I was able to pin you down. Again, something passed between them that told Ikshvaku that these men shared a relationship he knew nothing about. He silently resolved to learn it one day, and allowed himself to imagine the ferocity of an army led by men such as Drishta and Ardra. Who would dare make an enemy of the Suryavansha then?

"An excuse no honourable warrior would allow himself," Ardra said after a while. "But let us not digress. I believe the boy has not yet completed his point."

Ikshvaku nodded. "I sought to challenge you to combat, great Bear. Only by beating the best among us can I convince you of my kingship, that is the nature of Avisari's warriors. But if, as you reveal, the best among us is uncle Drishta, then my duel will have to be with him."

Drishta's eyes widened, and even Maharshi Vasishtha looked surprised. "Combat with me?" Drishta repeated. "It would serve no purpose, Ikshvaku." He had seen the boy move with the sword in his hands. He would make a finer warrior than most men Drishta had known. But he also knew his own past. He was a retired but undiminished warrior; Ikshvaku was only a boy in training.

"On the contrary," said Ardra to his old rival. "The son of Manu is right. We are all warriors here. Swords, arrows and horses are the things that matter in our lives. And so there must be three tests for the aspiring King of Avisari. By sword, you will test him. By arrow, I will. And by horse, let the gathered council set a worthy test. If he succeeds, then every man and woman of Avisari will kneel to their first King."

The key to every victory is finding a calm place for your mind, Manu had once said to Ikshvaku. If you can be dispassionate, if you can see the warrior and not just the man, you will be invincible. But for this, your mind needs to be silent. The stillness inside you must mirror the chaos outside, and then I assure you, son, with the right methods you can beat any man. But to perfect the art of invincibility requires great and infinite practise.

Ikshvaku took confidence from the words, observing Drishta stretch his limbs and prepare for the duel. Ardra entrusted them with real swords, and the rules of engagement dictated that he who drew blood first would be declared the victor. Ikshvaku had held true swords before, but this one was heavier and somewhat unwieldy. Its handle was long, obviously made to be held with two hands in the usual Solar way. It was odd that tribes that favoured horses fought with both hands, a rider with one hand on the reins could scarcely swing with a double-grip. Ikshvaku had expressed it to Manu once, who explained: *Our forefathers discovered horses only a few centuries ago. There were no horses in the time of Aurvan Surya, for horses are not native to Aryavarta. Our weapons and fighting styles have remained more or less unchanged since those times.* But Varman rarely followed the usual techniques, and often fought with a single-handed grip that Ikshvaku had naturally picked up. He had not hitherto revealed it to Drishta, but now he held the blade in his right hand and stared at his uncle for a reaction. It was not the only secret ability he possessed, but he hoped he would not have to reveal the other so early in his journey to kingship.

Drishta frowned when he saw Ikshvaku hold the sword with a single hand. How could he balance so much weight in one arm, at his age? He circled around Ikshvaku with intent, noticing with discomfort that his nephew stood utterly still and calm.

Every warrior needs a personalised strategy to be beaten, Manu had said. Give the enemy time to move and lunge, slash and withdraw. Watch his motions, watch which limbs he favours. Does he use power; or does he rely on motion? Does he strike from above or the side? Your eyes must conduct a deep inquiry for you in the initial moments. Then use the knowledge gained to formulate a perfect sequence of motions to make your kill. Ikshvaku had last put this to practise against Varman and come out victorious. He had no doubt that it would yield him success again, although this time, the stakes were infinitely larger. If he lost here, his journey to kingship would end even before it started. And yet, this only added to his composure, and the boy stood ready, fully confident of himself.

But Drishta was losing patience. Ikshvaku stood still as a rock, and he did not want to strike at the boy first. So he swiped his sword, its tip cutting inches away from Ikshvaku's face. The boy smiled and shifted his stance from right side to left side forward. Drishta swiped again, this time aiming for the body. But instead of parrying or blocking, Ikshvaku simply moved away at the last instant. He looked up and down at Drishta, glancing briefly at his uncle's left knee. Drishta's eyes narrowed. His left knee was victim to an old wound, causing him to limp so barely that none had ever spotted it. Till now.

Does he sustain any old injuries? Does he lose breath quickly? Does he cover a wide arc when he swings or does he prefer fighting within a small perimeter?

Ikshvaku lunged and slashed at Drishta's knee with the blunt of his blade, smacking it at the exact spot where an arrow had pierced in decades ago. Drishta roared in frustration and fell to one knee, but not before swinging his sword mightily through the air. Ikshvaku anticipated the angry strike and moved away with an ease that surprised his uncle. Drishta picked himself up and grunted in annoyance, he was going easy on his nephew. He clasped the sword tightly and adopted his favourite stance, satisfied to see Ikshvaku frown.

The enemy will assess you in a new light when you reveal your perceptive skill. He will seek to throw you off by showing you something new, something he thinks you are not familiar with. But the same skills will hold you in good stead through this ruse.

Drishta executed eight perfect motions of attack, his sword flashing up, down and sideways faster than observing eyes could follow. Each swing was deadly, its intent so real that there was no time to stop it mid-flow. When the motion was complete, all attention turned to the young boy standing unnerved at the tip of Drishta's outstretched sword. Ikshvaku had evaded every move with fluid, exact motions of his own. Even mighty Drishta could not hide his amazement, and Ardra the Bear got up from his seat and moved closer.

"You are still going soft on me. But I can handle more, I assure you," Ikshvaku said before jogging some steps away and circling his uncle. From the look on his face, there was no doubt that he had perceived every injury Drishta nursed, every niggle in bone and muscle acquired through years of hard combat. Drishta frowned, both angry and relieved that Ikshvaku had avoided each lethal blow.

There will always be an opening, and timing is essential. Your enemy is frustrated and thinking of ways to foil you. This is when you must make your move. When the enemy is at his weakest and slowest.

With a speed faster than Drishta could ever muster, Ikshvaku executed a thirty-two step attack of his father's invention. Drishta could evade less than half of them, and for the rest, Ikshvaku's sword rained hard on his body, always making contact with the blunt side. On the last swipe he let the blade cut through his uncle's skin, only enough to let a sliver of blood trickle out. Both were sweating profusely, and Drishta knew then that his young nephew was already a better warrior than any he had known. He marvelled at his cousin, Vaivasvat Manu. It was one thing to be a great fighter, but it was another to train a student that excelled the master.

"Do you yield, uncle?" asked the boy.

"I do," said Drishta, adding-"My king." Ikshvaku had won the test by sword. And there was no doubt in Drishta's mind that he would pass the tests by arrow and horse as well. The warriors of Avisari had found themselves a King.

Haryashva

"Of all the scattered Solar clans, none drifted so far as the Ashvaks, who were at the fringes of Suryavanshi society, even by Ikshvaku's time. In the earlier ages, however, they provided a constant supply of both heroes and horses. They remain one of the most elite, war-hardened Solar sub-clans."

King Bhagiratha to Sudasa

The regents of Harayupa, Vitabhya and other settlements found little reason to dispute Ikshvaku's claim to kingship, endorsed as it was by the powerful trinity of Maharshi Vasishtha, Vaivasvat Manu and Ardra the Bear. He rode through their towns swiftly, halting long enough only for the formal exchange of horses, cattle and metal that evidenced their submission to the first Raja of Aryavarta. Just as Ikshvaku had suspected and hoped for, the Solar clans were happy to welcome Marici's prime line back to leadership. But he took care to remember that this imposed on him an obligation, not mere privilege. The realisation was crucial to his growing ideas of duty—both to the tribe and to his purpose. He would have to wait to discuss these concepts with father though, for as it was turning out, a King had many duties to attend to.

When his convoy returned to Avisari, people were out in the streets, decorating their city in celebration. Streams of dyed fabric ran between rooftops of multi-storied huts and domes. Thin, coiled strings in various hues fell to the ground in vivid curls. Horses stood in pairs, facing each other along Avisari's main, intersecting streets, their faces painted with the Solar insignia. Town criers ran through alleys and connecting pathways, singing of the royal coronation and adding to the din of ceramic trumpets and wooden drums. Ornate, processional boats floated along canals dug from the Sindhu river. They carried choirs and criers of their own, zealously proclaiming the glory of the first Raja.

Haryashva could hear the noise from a distance as his horse trundled towards Avisari. Six weeks ago he had set out from Kapisa, mountain settlement of the Ashvaks, a clan of horse-warriors that occupied the periphery of the Solar tribes. Word of a Solar King had come to them only the night before, and his clan head had immediately declared that the Ashvaks needed to voice their allegiance. Haryashva imagined the King as a huge, fiery man, taller and stronger than any that stood before him. After all, true Solar blood could produce nothing less. But it wasn't just allegiance that the Ashvaks needed to voice. The ancient wars had only seen the Asuras defeated, not wiped out. And now their descendants roamed the lands as tribes, just like those of the Devas. Of them all, the Yakshas were particularly wretched–subsisting on frequent raids on Ashvak and other nomad tribes. Only a united Suryavanshi could deal with them for good. And with the rise of a King, this finally seemed possible.

After a long, arduous journey through rough mountainous terrain, both the mare and rider were relieved to see the city within reach. From where they stood, Sindhu's waters sloped gently towards the right and disappeared into the mountains. Himalayan peaks formed the entire skyline across the river, and Haryashva counted at least five that were hidden among clouds. Two horsemen approached him when he approached Avisari's main entrance. Their horses were smaller, but appeared fit and muscular. With vivid orange, yellow and red paint on them, they looked far more fierce than his ageing mare. When the men reached closer he noticed bright, gleaming swords hanging by their sides—forged recently and yet to draw blood. Then his gaze went to the turrets mounted next to the main gate, where he saw archers standing ready with their aim pointed at him. That the main Solar tribes had militarised heavily since the days of Marici was not unknown, but until now Haryashva had never witnessed the extent of it. Avisari looked more like a closed fortress than the ancient tribal town it was.

"Halt, rider," one of the approaching men called out. Haryashva's horse was already progressing at a casual, slow trot. He frowned and brought the beast to a complete stop. His left hand instinctively went to the dagger tucked beneath his robe, though he mused at what good it might do in case the archers decided to fire.

The riders reached and flanked him on either side. "Introduce yourself," one of them commanded.

Haryashva looked at one and then the other, trying to perceive their skills with the sword. He could take them on, if need be. But what about the archers in the distance? "I am Haryashva of the Ashvaks, from Kapisa" he replied. "I come to submit my clan to the King."

"Foreigners cannot enter Avisari today," one of the riders replied indifferently.

"And who is a foreigner to you?" Haryashva shot back. "Are we all not the people of Aryavarta, or does the King discriminate among the various Solar tribes?"

"Anything west of Sindhu falls outside Aryavarta, does it not?" one of the riders asked the other, ignoring that Avisari too, was on the western bank.

The other shrugged. "On this day, you are either a resident of Avisari or you are not," he replied. "You simply cannot enter."

"But I must," Haryashva said stubbornly. He tightened his grip around the dagger and nudged his horse in front of a rider, hiding himself from the archers' aim.

The first rider smiled arrogantly. "Kapisa is a noble city," he conceded, "And Ashvaks are famed horse-warriors. But you cannot hope to stand the might of Avisari combined. There is a small village near the river bank. Take rest there tonight and visit Avisari at the break of dawn tomorrow."

Haryashva raised an eyebrow and appraised the riders. "I cannot do that, my friends. I have travelled long and far for a single purpose. I must meet the King today, at the earliest."

The two riders chortled. "Meet the King?" one asked incredulously. "And who are you anyway, Ashvak? You think the King has time to meet the likes of you?"

"I will gain passage to your city today, and I will meet the King whether you like it or not. I bring a message he needs to hear."

"Then you will give it to his Generals, Drishta and the Bear, and you will do so tomorrow."

"Again, you fight a lost cause. Move aside now, riders. I *will* gain passage to your town." His own intractability surprised him, for it was not like his usual self. Perhaps it was the insularity of this new

King. No ruler could refuse meeting with a visitor in so remote and impersonal a manner. Especially if the King were Solar and the visitor an Ashvak.

He made a move past them, and both riders pulled out their swords with surprising swiftness. He leaped off his horse in a flash and yanked hard at one of the rider's reins. In the distance, the archers waved their bows about helplessly, unable to find aim. The rider fell to the ground with a loud thud and lost his grip on his sword. Haryashva drove his left foot into the rider's plexus and kicked the sword away. Then he felt the back of his skull explode in crucifying pain, and lost consciousness in an instant.

He dreamt of Kapisa, his place of birth and only home. He saw the joy of that semi-nomadic settlement, felt its ruddy-brown colours and smelled the distinct stench of horses. Then the vision erupted in blood, and he saw demons descend upon his people. It hit him like a hammer to the head, and he found the pain again just as he found wakefulness. By the time he opened his eyes, his skull was throbbing. His vision was still blurry, and he smelled the metallic tang of dry blood on his face. He was firmly tied to a wooden post, his arms behind his back. When he came to, he saw he was surrounded by a group of men and a young boy of not more than fifteen or so. They were all attired regally, golden sashes running diagonally from their left shoulder, to the waist. Under that they sported strong, copper armour and long, menacing swords. All were tall and muscular, including the boy. His young age was belied only by the smooth, hairless glow of his skin and the curious look in his eyes—in direct contrast with the others' dark expressions.

Ikshvaku observed the Ashvak, trying to hide his admiration at the dense, rounded beard he sported. Ashvaks occupied a unique position in the tribal structure of Aryavarta, made all the more strange when one considered that they inhabited lands that were entirely outside its borders. But descended from Aurvan Surya much like the Suryavanshi, theirs was a kindred tribe. Ikshvaku nodded at a soldier, who walked up to Haryashva and brought a pot of water to his lips. He gulped it down greedily, realising all of a sudden that his throat was painfully parched. He emptied the pot, and the soldier moved away. Pain swelled up in different parts of his body, from his jaw to left knee.

"You gave my city-guard quite a scare, Ashvak," Ikshvaku said. "They were in half a mind to chop your head right off."

Haryashva found no reply to that, and his throat still hurt.

"But when I heard of it," Ikshvaku continued, "I decided that there must be good reason for an Ashvak to travel all the way from Kapisa just to visit me."

With a start, Haryashva realised that this boy was in fact the King. His eyes widened in surprise. Who knew that the King was so young?

"So tell me, stranger," Ikshvaku said, his voice cutting through the many questions running in Haryashva's head, "Why did you want to meet me?" He gestured again, and another soldier walked up to Haryashva with a moist cotton swab and cleaned the blood on his face with warm water. Drishta and Ardra stood behind Ikshvaku, who eyed Haryashva curiously, never having met an Ashvak before. But their expertise with horses was famed, and there were many stories of Ashvak stallion contingents making decisive runs in the Deva-Asura wars. Would they accept him as their King, and did they even consider themselves Suryavanshi anymore?

"If this is how the King treats his guests," Haryashva replied in a hoarse, broken voice, "Then he is not a King I wish to meet." To his surprise, he saw Ikshvaku look almost contrite.

"I realise that," Ikshvaku conceded. "The city-guard was too zealous, but I cannot blame them much. Avisari has faced raids from Gandharvas and Rakshasas recently, and their numbers are growing larger. Today is my coronation, and the city-guard was particularly jumpy. I would have them untie you now, but even I choose to exercise caution where I can. Tell me of your intent, and I will have you rested and refreshed as an honoured guest. I'm told your name is Haryashva, is that right?" The name was not new to Ikshvaku, for it meant bay horse in Solar dialect. Horses permeated every aspect of Ashvak culture, and he was yet to hear of an Ashvak name that did not have ashva for a suffix or prefix.

"As I told your soldiers, I came here to offer my tribe's allegiance," Haryashva said. "While you are troubled by Gandharvas and Rakshasas, Kapisa faces attacks from Yaksha raiding parties every quarter. We heard that the prime Solar line rises in the near east, and I followed the trail that led to you."

"Gandharvas, Rakshasas, and now Yakshas," grumbled Ardra with clear distaste. "These Anarya tribes are swarming around like ants!"

"Gandharvas are not so bad," Ikshvaku said, repeating an opinion held by his father. "They can be negotiated with."

"But Rakshasas are exclusively hostile," countered Ardra with emotion. "And now it seems that Yakshas are turning belligerent as well. We are going to have our hands full, young King."

Ikshvaku nodded in agreement and signalled to a sentry. Haryashva found his hands and feet being untied. "There," Ikshvaku said, "Now tell me all, Haryashva. What message do you bear for the Solar King?"

"I would like my robe and dagger back," Haryashva said, flexing his wrists gingerly. "And I hope my horse is being taken care of." He still could not get over the sight of this young boy as King—who would have thought?

"Your horse is well-fed and rested," Ikshvaku assured him. "I recognise a fine beast when I see one. You cannot, however, have your dagger back just yet. My generals will be scandalised if I was so careless. Let us talk more and get to know each other. You will notice that I carry no armament myself."

"The men around you do," Haryashva countered.

Ikshvaku sighed. "Yes, they do," he conceded. He turned to the men around him and nodded for them to leave. Drishta protested only with his eyes, but Ardra grunted in objection. "I will be alright, Bear," Ikshvaku said to him. "Surely you know that by now." The Bear relented, and they reluctantly filed out. Haryashva was amazed at the sight. How could a mere boy command formidable men with such ease?

When they were alone, the young royal smiled warmly and gestured to the seating slabs on one side of the room. Haryashva sat down warily, Ikshvaku followed. "These Yakshas you speak of," he began, "How many do they number?"

"Our scouts have spotted six Yaksha settlements among the valleys. Each settlement has hundreds of Yakshas, give or take a few hundred. And every year more arrive from the far-east."

Ikshvaku nodded thoughtfully. "We've noticed increased migrations from that side too. Numbers are on the rise everywhere, ours as well as theirs. But that does not explain what brought you here, Haryashva. How can we help you?"

Haryashva looked at him blankly. "You are a King," he replied, "A leader of men. You have thousands of soldiers in your army. And Yaksha encroachments threaten the borders of Aryavarta itself, surely that is a threat to your nascent kingdom?"

Again Ikshvaku nodded carefully, his pensive gaze telling Haryashva that he was wiser than he looked. "I appreciate your logic," he said. "But we have troubles of our own here. Even if I ignore Rakshasas for now, how can I defend Aryavarta when I have no Aryavarta to rule over? I must first look downstream along the Sindhu and consolidate the kingdom. And I have not even started, my official coronation is today!"

"But you have much to gain from helping us," Haryashva insisted. "Even half your army would be enough to eradicate Yaksha settlements once and for all. And in return, we offer our own horsemen. Ashvak steeds are the finest war-bred horses in the world, and Ashvaks are experts in the art of equine warfare. Our numbers will strengthen yours."

"Ashvak cavalry would indeed make my army quite formidable," Ikshvaku admitted. "And it would be easier to patrol the banks of Sindhu with your faster, stronger horses. But I will not decide on this before consulting with my advisors. And for that, we must wait till we are done with the coronation."

"Time is of the essence," Haryashva warned. "We must strike before more Yakshas arrive from the far-east and fortify their existing settlements."

"I understand," Ikshvaku replied. "But my generals will not allow me to commit soldiers to an Ashvak cause while we are yet to consolidate our own kingdom."

There was an awkward silence before Haryashva confessed, "I expected you to be older."

Ikshvaku chuckled. "I am fifteen, and most people seem to agree that it is a fine age for a King." He found himself drawn to Haryashva's candid, blunt nature. And the Ashvak did not look older than twenty-two, which was a welcome departure from a world inhabited by veterans, elders and Maharshis.

"Is it true that you claim descent from Surya Deva himself?"

"It is not a matter of claim," Ikshvaku replied. "Havishmana Surya was grandfather to Marici Havishmani, who is my forefather through a direct line. We have held the duties of a Solar leader for countless generations."

"Then are you related to Vaivasvat Manu?"

"He is my father."

Haryashva's eyes widened. "Why would he not declare himself King?" Manu was a familiar name in Kapisa, looked upon as one of Aryavarta's wisest figures. Haryashva remembered his father and uncles taking Manu's name with deep reverence, and even the Clan Head often jested himself to be only a regent to Vaivasvat.

"Vaivasvat Manu has larger roles to play," Ikshvaku answered, referring to his father's remarkable prolificacy in setting up towns and villages. "The banks of Sindhu and Shatadru are replete with villages set up under his care and guidance."

"And such growing numbers need protection," Haryashva said, finally seeing how father and son played two different, but vital roles.

"Yes, and they need men willing to die for that protection. They need weapon and metal, horse and authority. A mere chieftain cannot wield such power, he cannot rally an army around him. But a King can."

"Certainly one descended from Surya himself," Haryashva added.

"*Only* one descended from Surya himself," the boy King corrected. Haryashva was beginning to like this young, forthright son of Vaivasvat Manu. He was fifteen not too long ago. He did not think his eyes shone with such maturity and ambition at that age, or that they did so even now.

Boy King

"Listen closely to the tales of Ikshvaku's early years, when he was but a boy like you. His devotion for duty and obligation sowed the seeds of what we today call Dharma. Indeed, the unsaid standard that every Suryavanshi King, including I, strives for is Ikshvaku."

King Bhagiratha to Sudasa

Year 33, Seventh era

Ikshvaku was young, but he was no longer a boy. Haryashva realised this gradually, over the six months since he first arrived at Avisari. There were very little rules around a kingship, no legal precedents to define Ikshvaku's powers. He was the First King—*Adiraja*—an unprecedented event among the tribes of land, horse and river. But he inspired fierce loyalty in the men around him, carrying himself with maturity and authority. Haryashva travelled the length and breadth of the Suryavanshi kingdom, visiting famed cities like Harayupa and Vitabhya to witness the extent of Solar prosperity with his own eyes. At Vitabhya, he saw the boy fishing and farming with the citizens as if the vocations were a part of his daily routine. At Harayupa, he talked of currency and writing with the traders, poring over hundreds of clay tablets with strange inscriptions and suggesting trade routes to the guilds. Haryashva initially wondered where the boy had learnt it all from. But wherever they went, he found people who said one thing to Ikshvaku over and over again—*You are a true son of Manu.*

And in that aspect Ikshvaku was finally delivered with rivals. News arrived from Prasthala that Vaivasvat Manu's wives had blessed him with three more sons—Pramshu, Sharyati and Nabhaga. Manu had a large family, and one of his wives was Gandharvi. Haryashva suggested that Ikshvaku send assassins to kill these competitors. It was a common practice among Ashvaks, and he felt no reluctance in proposing it. But the very idea was absurd to the young King. These were his brothers, he solemnly told Haryashva, bonded to him by blood. It took Haryashva many weeks before he realised that this was not a sign of Ikshvaku's naiveté but of his sense of principle.

Besides, Haryashva soon found, Ikshvaku and the Suryavansha had enough threats from the outside world. Rakshasas were the scourge of Solar villages and towns, though they rarely approached the larger cities. The most recent raids were at Navapari, a river-crossing town situated on either side of the Asikni river. Haryashva learnt through hushed murmurs that Sakala was raided as well, and that the King had taken the attack on his village personally. In the decades past, the Solar people had tried to negotiate with Rakshasas, seeking barter over war. But their attempts became unsuccessful by the end of Marici's reign, and under the confederation that followed, each city fended for itself and the villages under its protection. A King changed all that. Now the Suryavansha was one—from Avisari to Vitabhya. A vast army under the command of one voice patrolled the kingdom in search of Rakshasas. But after the attack at Sakala, Ikshvaku finally decided it was time to take the battle to the enemy. And that meant venturing headlong into the Rakshasa den, Kamyakvana.

Kamyakvana was the largest forest Haryashva had ever seen. The mountains to the north were peppered with firs, spruces and hemlock trees, but nothing was as dense and suffocating as Kamyakvana. This was a lush, verdant Aryavarta unknown to any nomadic tribes. A few steps into the forest and one was immediately engulfed in darkness. Teeming branches intertwined with each other and created an almost endless cover of black. Even in the day they entered with lamps and torch lights, for the forest was perpetually dark. Haryashva was warned that Rakshasas were natives to the forest, used to living in dark conditions after generations of inhabitation. He was to expect an ambush anytime, from any quarter. A chill went up his spine when they walked into the forest, and the brave horseman found comfort from the boy King beside him, who declared with the confidence of a far older, experienced warrior, "Fear not, my Ashvak friend. Stay within my sword's arc and you will leave this forest unscathed." Haryashva realised two things that moment—Ikshvaku had faced Rakshasas before, and he did not fear them.

The King lived up to his promise that night. Haryashva certainly pulled his own weight, but Ikshvaku managed to save his life on three different occasions. No matter what the King did or how many Rakshasas he took on at once, his one eye remained on Haryashva. When an arrow came at Haryashva, Ikshvaku was by his side to slice it away. When a Rakshasa came from behind, Ikshvaku jumped in between and sawed him in half. He slew dozens more than Haryashva, moving at speeds no Ashvak could. When the fires died out and the battle was over, the son of Manu was radiant even in the dark. Blood appeared black on his armour and face, his eyes glinting like metal. That was when Haryashva finally understood why the Suryavanshi had accepted this boy as their King—he was like Surya descended on earth once again.

More than eight months and several battles later, Ikshvaku finally promised Haryashva a meeting to discuss plans for the north. Winter was to set in soon, and once the snow started falling the passes to Kapisa would be closed. Fields would be barren of both plant and animal life-hardly the conditions for an army to march. The time to cleanse the northern mountains of Yakshas was now.

Avisari was the declared capital, the official seat of the nascent Suryavansha kingdom. Settlements sprung up outside the city walls, complete with markets and hutments. At the centre of the town lay what was now called the Nripalaya–the King's Quarters. Larger than any man-made structure Haryashva had ever seen, it was an elaborate complex of halls, yards, gardens and private chambers built over generations by General Ardra's predecessors. Baked bricks were the only building material available, and the complex survived the decades thanks to the diligent upkeep of its inhabitants. Ikshvaku's chambers were towards the west wing of the Nripalaya, overlooking the Sindhu's powerful currents flowing downstream. Once there was a rope bridge there, a means for the rulers of Avisari to escape the city and cross the river swiftly, should that need arise. But Ikshvaku had the bridge dismantled. *If I cannot defend my city, he explained to Haryashva, then I deserve to die with it. What King would flee while his subjects are being put to death?* That was Ikshvaku as Haryashva had come to understand and respect—moral, just and propelled by a sincere sense of duty. It was close to evening when Haryashva walked into Ikshvaku's chambers, a gentle river breeze carrying through the Nripalaya, cooling its sun-baked rooms.

"Ah, Haryashva, come. I've been making plans since last night." The King looked less and less a boy as the months wore on, the first wave of hair appearing densely on his face and giving him a scruffy look.

"Some say that the descendants of Surya need no sleep," Haryashva jested as he sat down.

Ikshvaku chuckled. "They say many things about the descendants of Surya. But fight me without my armour and you will find I'm not as invincible as they say."

"You're invincible enough," Haryashva replied, and he meant it. No man was as powerful on the battlefield as Ikshvaku, even at his young age.

Ikshvaku nodded, looking uncomfortable when praised. "It is time to help your people," he said. "We've lost some good men in Kamyakvana. But many more have joined us since. Have you visited the barracks of late?"

"No," Haryashva replied, "But I have heard as much from Drishta and the Bear." More and more Solar families were willing to set their sons on the warrior path since Ikshvaku's rise as the King. Veterans who had turned to other vocations, mostly farming and herding, now proudly enlisted their grandsons and granddaughters into the burgeoning Suryavanshi army.

"And our training program has improved. The Bear has devised certain military formations that are tailored to the tactics we use."

Haryashva nodded. "Just the other day I saw a unit practise something called the Snake formation."

Ikshvaku beamed. "You saw it? What did you think?"

Haryashva shrugged. "It might be efficient against an organised military, but it is unsuited for the Rakshasas and Yakshas' unconventional methods."

Ikshvaku did not take offence at that, which was one of his traits that Haryashva was coming to admire increasingly. The Solar King exerted his authority when it came to making final decisions, but till then he allowed for debate and even dissent. "I agree," Ikshvaku said. "But there are other formations in the making as well. I am working on one that we can call, for the lack of better words, a Sugarcane formation."

Haryashva's lips curved in a suppressed grin. "Are you really that fond of them?"

"Sugarcanes? Of course! Have you ever tried one?"

"Unfortunately not," Haryashva replied. "Sugarcanes do not grow around Kapisa."

"Well, that will have to be corrected. But first, I have a promise to keep. My army in Avisari is more than 4,000 strong now, enough that I can leave a sufficient number behind when we march against the Yakshas."

"I'm happy to hear that, young King. I fear that if we do not drive the Yakshas out this winter, we will lose the opportunity forever. One more season and they will build permanent settlements there."

Ikshvaku nodded. "My thoughts exactly. In any case, my scouts report that the Rakshasas that fled Kamyakvana have made their way across the Sindhu. There's nowhere for them to go from there but north or west. Another month or so and they could join the Yakshas, making things even more difficult for us."

"So what do you plan to do?"

"Mobilise immediately. I've already instructed General Drishta and the Bear, and they will prepare our forces the moment I give command. We need to chart our routes now. You say that there are at least six settlements. Assuming that at least another two could have sprung up in the months since you joined us, I'm splitting the army into two contingents of 1,000 each. Drishta will lead one and I will take the other. It is up to you to organise the Ashvaks, Haryashva. I understand that yours is a proud, independent clan. But for this campaign they will have to submit to the Suryavansha banner."

"You may keep in mind that I came to your town to submit to the King, and ask for his help. Ashvaks welcome the son of Manu as their ruler. We trace our descent from early Solar lines as well, and as such we are kinsmen." It was true enough—when Aurvan Surya migrated west after the Great Wars, some of his clansmen stayed behind around the Sindhu. While Solar tribes roamed nomadic in the central plains of the vast continent, these clansmen remained on the periphery of the Aryavarta kingdom. And when the Solar tribes returned, the clansmen were too attached to their lands and horses to follow them back into Aryavarta.

Ikshvaku smiled. "And how many Ashvak kinsmen can I expect on this campaign?"

"All of them. More than 1,000 riders."

Ikshvaku's eyes widened. "1,000? Kapisa cannot be more than a few hundred strong. Are you telling me that hundreds of Ashvaks roam the mountains?"

"I am," Haryashva confirmed. "And Kapisa is not a town in the way you consider it. It has no permanent residents save a single family of priests. To Ashvaks it is simply a place to stop by from time to time-gather news, deliver babies, conduct important rituals and trade goods. We are of the older ways, semi-nomadic in true sense."

"Well, that changes plans considerably. I expected no more than a few hundred Ashvaks. But with the 1,000 riders we can support three contingents and cover a larger amount of territory. This is heartening, Haryashva. Your riders and my Suryavanshi warriors will be more than a match for Yakshas."

"I never doubted that, young King."

"Drink," Haryashva insisted as he passed the bag of water to Ikshvaku. "A parched throat allows the cold in."

Ikshvaku obliged, though Haryashva suspected that it was more out of politeness. The young King seemed, for the most part, as impervious to the cold as he was to heat and the sun. He did not even don his armour, claiming it would be unjust to pile that weight on his horse during the harsh journey. Clad in a simple goat-skin robe, he looked more at home in the cold mountains than Haryashva. Even the steed accepted Ikshvaku with grace and readiness, and Ashvak horses were known to be wary of outsider blood. *He is not just the Suryavanshi King,* Haryashva thought, *he is my King, and the horse knows this.*

"When this campaign is over," Ikshvaku said, "Remind me to assign a bard to Kapisa."

"And what do these bards do?"

"Think of them as record keepers. They memorise genealogies, town proceedings, birth and coronation dates and the like."

Haryashva snorted. "You Suryavanshi place far too much importance on genealogies and progeny. A man's skill with the sword does not depend on that of his fathers."

"True," Ikshvaku agreed, "But if one's father is a skilled warrior, and knows how to pass on his ability, then does one not stand a better chance? We do not speak of the strength of an individual, we speak of the strength of a family, a tribe. This is how we ensure our survival through the ages. And that comes from producing strong and capable lines. Think of the way Ashvaks breed horses. Do you not look for the best stock, and separate it from the weak?"

"You are comparing men with horses," Haryashva said, but he marvelled at Ikshvaku's mind. How much of this boy was his own ambition and originality, and how much was but the echo of Vaivasvat Manu? And then Ikshvaku often mentioned the influence of his sister, Ila.

"The purpose is the same," Ikshvaku countered. "To produce a lineage that is supreme."

Two scouts returned from the front, and Ikshvaku signalled for the line to stop behind him. Haryashva heard a few horses neigh in protest. It was in the beasts' instinct to gallop across the landscape, and a night ago they had picked up the inviting musk of a wild herd nearby. The riders came up to Ikshvaku and stopped smartly, clearly familiar with their stallions.

"A minor stream diverts off the Sindhu a yojana ahead," one of the scouts reported. "The foothills beyond it are scattered with Yakshas. One of the hills holds their settlement, King Ikshvaku."

Ikshvaku nodded, his jaw tightening. "Well done," he commended his scouts. "Join your contingents and prepare for battle." He signalled to his guardsman, and the rider set off along the line, delivering his message.

Haryashva felt a familiar wave of adrenaline rise, one that preceded every battle. "Full formation ahead?"

"No," Ikshvaku said. "We can be sure that these mountain Yakshas are familiar with the art of guerrilla warfare. Pushing all our formations forward make us vulnerable to a surprise attack."

As if on cue, they heard the crunching sound of rock upon rock and looked up to see a boulder rushing down the mountain. It took only a second for Ikshvaku to calculate that the boulder was well outside the path of their line. Then his gaze went further up, and he saw dozens of black Yaksha figures descending rapidly in the boulder's wake.

"Well," he said grimly. "Looks like they've brought the battle to us."

The Yakshas were a ferocious and formidable enemy. They were tall and hefty, their arms long and their swings wild. Most had axes, but many charged with simple clubs and spears. Ikshvaku found himself admiring their tenacity. Slice and hack at one as much as you'd like, but he would not back off till he bled to death. The best way to end the fight was to simply cut the Yaksha in two, but even that, Ikshvaku learnt, was not as easy as expected. The brutes were both strong and cunning, unlike the dumb, hostile Rakshasas of Kamyakvana. When they charged, they came with the power of stone and rock, enough to knock a man off his feet and fling him some distance away. They snarled and snapped, cursed and spat, their battle cries were loud. Their surprise attack denied him the use of his archers, some of whom were fatally injured. He knew that the Ashvaks would hold their own, but many of his warriors had been caught off guard and disoriented.

Two Yakshas came at him together, sensing that he was the leader. They circled around him, eager to strike. He felt no fear, for this was the life he expected when he claimed kingship for himself, and now Ikshvaku revelled in the pleasure of warring for his tribe. The Yakshas came in ones and twos, not wanting to risk being slashed by each other's weapons by charging all at once. Undaunted, Ikshvaku whirled his sword all around, easily following the stances and thrusts his father taught him many years ago. Since then he had modified the style, but the basic angles of swing and the pattern of breathing between attack and defensive stances remained the same. Out of the corner of his eye, Ikshvaku saw Haryashva hacking his way through the circle of Yakshas that had gathered around. He ducked under a swinging club and sliced his sword straight through the legs of another Yaksha. As he rose, he pressed his shield against the onslaught of a third Yaksha and knocked the second one off his legs. Blood spattered across Ikshvaku's face, but he was getting used to this by now. The Yaksha's scream of agony drowned out the charging yell of a fourth, who came at Ikshvaku from behind and knocked the helmet off his head. Ears ringing, he turned around just as the third Yaksha came crashing at him again. He heard his shield break and felt his wrist shatter as he flew in the air and landed painfully some distance away. Agony shot up his spine and exploded all over his body, before he gave in to the pain and lost consciousness.

When he came to, the first thing that hit Ikshvaku was the chill in his bones. He was shivering, and a blurry figure draped another blanket over him. Almost instantly, the pain resurged and he remembered every injury. His right wrist was broken. He knew that as much from the memory of the Yaksha crashing into him as from the pain of it. His spine had sustained severe damage, and he could vividly picture the fall that had caused it. His face felt swollen and his ears throbbed with a faint ringing sound even now. For the first time in his life, Ikshvaku spared a thought for the dangers that lay in his path as King. But the moment passed and he reminded himself that everyone from his father to Maharshi Vasishtha had warned him that the path would not be easy.

"The moment I take my eyes off you," a voice broke into his thoughts, "You get into trouble."

He opened his mouth to speak, but it was parched and he coughed. With each cough his abdomen tightened and hurt, and the pain had now spread to his feet. He tried to lift his head, to find the source of the voice. A figure moved into his vision and placed a soft hand under his head to guide it back down. He looked up and the worried, bearded face of Haryashva swam into view.

"Rest, my friend," Haryashva said, running his hand across Ikshvaku's forehead and through his hair. Then he lifted his head gently and brought a pot of water to his lips. Ikshvaku sipped, feeling some relief as the warm, soothing water washed down his throat.

"Haryashva," Ikshvaku asked after drinking water. "Where are we?"

"Not far from where you were injured," Haryashva replied. "In your condition, you could not be moved too much."

"How long has it been?"

"Two weeks. You have floated in and out of consciousness since then."

There were many questions Ikshvaku wanted to ask, but the pain made him foggy and irritable. He asked the one that seemed the most important. "What of the battle?"

Haryashva gave him a broad smile, showing as many teeth as possible. "Worry not, my King. The Suryavansha was victorious, and the Ashvaks aided them valiantly. You can hear all about it when you recover. And you must do so quickly, for the Yaksha threat may be finished, but we still have Rakshasas to deal with." And with that, Haryashva also delivered his implicit promise—that he would remain at Ikshvaku's side even after relieving the Ashvaks of the Yaksha threat. The decision had come to him gradually, partly out of a renewed sense of adventure that could only be satiated in the company of the Suryavanshi King. But there was also a growing loyalty, and an admiration for the sense of duty and responsibility that Ikshvaku so sincerely embodied. Haryashva smiled as Ikshvaku drifted back to sleep.

The Generals, Drishta and Ardra invited him to dinner that night, a sign that the other Suryavanshi were warming up to him as well. The Suryavanshi warrior dinner was much like the feasting ceremonies followed by ancient Deva tribes. Warrior men and women gathered around the fire as equals, and even the Generals held no higher status at the dinner circle. Hunted deer and rabbit were roasted to choruses of tribal ballads and prayers, most of them in praise of Surya and his allies. There was much banter and boastful reference to powerful forebears, but beneath it Haryashva also sensed an abiding sense of kinship. Every member of the dinner circle was related to the other by some measure and was aware of this blood bond. This was something Haryashva could relate with, for there was nothing stronger than the blood bond among Ashvaks.

"Drishta tells me that you have decided to stay back among us," the Bear grunted to him when the celebrations subsided. Haryashva always found it difficult to read Ardra. The formidable regent of Avisari had many legends about him, and Haryashva had fought at close quarters to him to know that none of them were untrue. But Ardra was distant, guarded even.

"I have," Haryashva replied. Then, feeling that his response might appear too curt, he added, "And hundreds more Ashvaks will return with your forces to Avisari."

The Bear nodded in terse approval, passing a cup of cloudy, silvery drink to Haryashva. "What is it?" he asked as he took the cup.

The hint of a smile passed across the Bear's face before his grim bearing recovered. "Soma," he said, his tone suggesting there was something sacred about this drink. "A brew passed on to us by Maharshi Kashyapa, who in turn received it from his tutor, Bhrigu." Catching the lost look on Haryashva's face, he continued, "It is a drink unique to Aryavarta, young Ashvak. And its distillation is an art known only to a select few."

Haryashva took a sip, liking its bitter and thick palate. "I did not know that you drink, General Ardra," he said before gulping the rest in one go.

Ardra ignored the comment. "Be careful," he warned. "Soma is not like other liquors you may know. Its full course through your body will be a unique and overwhelming experience. Do not indulge in it as freely as you would in a common brew. King Ikshvaku has denied himself the experience so far, and at his age that is advisable. You are not much older."

Before Haryashva could reply, Drishta walked up to them boisterously. Putting an affectionate arm around Haryashva's shoulders, he shouted into his ears. "Haryashva my boy! You did your ancestors proud in this campaign." The General was clearly drunk, and the Bear eyed him with wary distaste. Oblivious, Drishta continued, "And I'm happy that you've decided to stay. Ikshvaku will be better served with a friend around him."

"You drink far too much, Drishta," said the Bear, his voice gravelly with disapproval. "It sets a bad example."

"And you remain far too grim, Ardra," Drishta countered amiably. "I am simply following the traditions of our forefathers, back up to Aurvan Surya and beyond!"

Ardra grunted, disinclined to debate with an inebriated Drishta. Ikshvaku had mentioned that Drishta and Ardra shared a tense history. It was made all the more strange by how deeply familiar it looked, and yet Haryashva could not place the familiarity. It was the Soma beginning to take effect, though he did not yet realise it.

"Come Ardra," Drishta said, oblivious even to Ardra's distant demeanour. "Let us at least partake Soma together."

Haryashva could have sworn that he had heard those very words before, and yet that could just not be true. A barrage of connections suddenly whirled in his mind before it provided him with a moment of clarity. "You are brothers!" he blurted, looking from Drishta to Ardra. And in that clarity he also understood why he knew this. Drishta and Ardra were born of the same father, but their mothers were different. Haryashva too, had a half-brother, and the tension between them was remarkably similar to what existed between Ikshvaku's two generals. He knew now that it was the Soma that allowed him to make this almost implausible connection.

Ardra looked angry at Haryashva's declaration, but Drishta smiled knowingly. "The Soma has begun working on you, young Ashvak," he said happily. Then he turned to Ardra. "Come now, Ardra. Do not deny me your company at the tribal feast. And let us escape before the Soma makes this one blurt any further accusations!"

They left Haryashva without another word, though Drishta winked mischievously as he pulled a reluctant Ardra away. They neither confirmed nor denied what he said, but he did not need them to. Soma was running strong inside Haryashva now. A world of colours and fractals consumed him, laid out on a landscape of lucidity with its own peaks and valleys. He came to several epiphanies, resolved countless moral dilemmas. But no uninitiated mind could withstand the eventual onslaught of Soma-induced hallucinations, and Haryashva was no rshi. Come morning, as the last embers of the tribal feast turned to ashes, Haryashva would remember only some of the profundity.

Rakshasa

"Rakshasas are the Suryavansha's oldest, most reviled enemies. The seeds lie, of course, in the older Deva-Asura rivalries. But ever since Ikshvaku's time, we Solar tribes have been fighting a brutal and unrelenting war with the Rakshasas. They surround my capital, Ayodhya, even today."

King Bhagiratha to Sudasa

Year 35, Seventh era

"Here, this is Avisari," said Ikshvaku, pointing to a spot on the wide slab of clay.

Haryashva nodded. The slab was etched and contoured at various places, several lines weaving up and down its length and breadth. It was a map of Aryavarta, as Ikshvaku had explained to him, created through the research and travels of Vaivasvat Manu. And given that Manu rarely stayed at one place for too long, this particular map was already outdated.

A thick line ran along Avisari, starting way south at the Mansarovara lake before taking a sweeping route that finally landed into the ocean's mouth. "Is this the Sindhu river?" Haryashva asked, pointing to where it ran past Avisari.

"Yes, and then the tributaries, Vitasta, Asikni, Iravati, and Shatadru. Between them, the other settlements of the Suryavanshi kingdom." Ikshvaku looked at the map with pride. Not even Marici or the Suryas before him had been able to visualise their lands like this. Baked clay was a relatively recent technology, acquired only in the closing stages of the last era. Its earliest applications were in brick-building, fuelled by the early settlers' need to build better, stronger constructions than what their nomadic roots had taught them. But soon the crafty artisans of Harayupa found other uses, clay tablets being one of them. Variations of this invention were being used by traders, artisans, and rshis across the kingdom.

"Do we know how far Kamyakvana spreads?" Haryashva asked. He knew that the forest bounded between the Sindhu's various tributaries, but he wanted to see its extent on the map.

"More or less," Ikshvaku replied. "Maharshi Kashyapa established his first ashrama at the forest's southern periphery, which is now the town of Kashyapura." He pointed to another spot. "To the north the trees range wider and wider till they reach the Iravati. Beyond it the forest takes over completely, running all across the land between Iravati and Asikni, and often crossing over on either side."

"That is a lot of land," Haryashva remarked, looking at the map.

"Enough to accommodate 4,000 Rakshasas or more," Ikshvaku added grimly. "And you have seen battle in the forest—a most dangerous and fatal venture. I cannot win this through sheer force."

Haryashva nodded in agreement. "As long as we continue these skirmishes, we only fight the unknown." Despite their frequent forays into Kamyakvana, the Suryavanshi had not made any significant dent in Rakshasa activities. Ikshvaku's armies had managed to protect the villages from their raids however, and the last damaging attack had been more than ten months ago.

"I need to understand their hierarchy," Ikshvaku said, frustration creeping into his voice. "Do they have contingents, or sub-clans? Who is their chief, one or many?"

"In any tribe so confined, there has to be a supreme head," Haryashva reasoned. "Rakshasas fight with the same weapons and tactics, whether you enter Kamyakvana from the north or south. Their raiders bear similar armour and use similar tactics, whether around Prasthala or Vitabhya. This shows organisation, which in turn needs leadership."

"And until we can get to that leader, we are but fighting in the dark," Ikshvaku summed up. He was pleased with Haryashva, happy to find in him a man of agreeable opinions. But Generals Drishta and the Bear were not of similar thought. To them the Rakshasas were a savage tribe, incapable of any consistent, organised endeavours.

"I've heard you tell General Ardra that the Rakshasas cannot truly be called Anarya," Haryashva said. "Do you really believe this?"

"We cannot really speak of these matters before defining Arya first, my friend," Ikshvaku replied. "What does Arya really mean? To the farmers of Harayupa it only means a simple man, one who tills the land and tends the cattle. To the ancient families in Avisari and Vitabhya, an Arya is noble in thought, speech and deed. To the warrior lines in our tribe, only one who can hold a sword and ride a horse deserves the title. To my father, every man or woman is born Arya unless they prove otherwise through unworthy conduct."

"Then Rakshasas are Anarya to the farmers, to the warriors and to Vaivasvat Manu as well," Haryashva pointed out.

Ikshvaku smiled, admitting silently that Haryashva had a fair point. Aloud, he said-"To me, an Arya is one who follows his or her duty. Their basic responsibility in the order of nature and tribe."

"And what is that?"

"It is different for everyone, is it not?" Ikshvaku asked. "The cowherd's duty is different to that of the warrior, but neither's is any less compelling. If either of them abdicate from their role, the tribe is in trouble. How can I judge the Rakshasas as Anarya when I do not know what compels them? What drives them to belligerence? Is the Rakshasa warrior's duty to his tribe not as great as a Suryavanshi's?"

The questions were rhetorical, and Haryashva saw their point. Then his Ashvak pragmatism made him say, "Arya or *un-Arya*, Rakshasas are our enemies. They raid our villages, steal our cattle and destroy our livelihoods."

Ikshvaku's face lit up in approval. "I completely agree," he said. "And it is our duty to defend against this threat to our people. Even if that means taking the attack to the enemy."

That seemed to settle the matter for now, but as a sly smile crept up Haryashva's face, he said, "Perhaps you should let Generals Drishta and the Bear handle things for a while. A King has other duties as well, you know."

Ikshvaku caught the hint and blushed. "I wish I could say that I'm too young for such things. But if I can be King at this age, I can scarcely use the excuse for anything. Even father insists that I must get married at the earliest."

Haryashva scoffed in good humour. "Some of your customs are quite strange, my King. Marriage is an alien concept to the Ashvaks. I would have you ride to Kapisa now and charm a fair Ashvak maiden.

Spend some time with her—as much as you like in fact. And then, when you are both satiated, you move on. Man is not meant to be permanently tied to a single partner. And I mean this for both genders!"

Ikshvaku smiled wryly at his horse-warrior. "Our traditions are somewhat similar, but with a distinct male inclination. We seem to have no problem with men having multiple partners. My father has fathered children with four different women, for instance. But a woman may have only one partner her entire life."

"Yet our forefathers were the same," Haryashva said. "How have these differences come about?"

"Maharshi Vasishtha has a few theories. And I have some of my own as well. It has a lot to do with the ideas of ownership and succession. But come, my Ashvak friend, there is much time for us to share our tales. For now, if I am to keep my advisors happy I must find myself a wife. And before long we must join Generals Ardra and Drishta in Kamyakvana. As much as I acknowledge the Rakshasas' claim to the forest, I must eliminate their threat if our renewed Solar unity is to survive."

The last time Ikshvaku's vast family had gathered in such numbers was at the wedding of Ila to Budha Atreya, a son of the Lunar tribes that centred around Plaksha. As Ikshvaku grew older, people often commented that his wedding would be a grand affair. That was no idle promise, as he was finding out. Past lessons on his genealogy notwithstanding, he had no idea that his family numbered in hundreds of living relatives. Aunts, uncles, grandfathers and grandmothers, nephews, nieces and cousins of all degrees had descended upon Vitabhya for the marriage of Aryavarta's first King to Sarmi, daughter of Tauranga Medhi, Vitabhya's regent. It was a wild, raucous affair, the guest-list running into 1,000s. Food and liquor were consumed in copious quantities, numerous ballads and prayers sung loudly and often incoherently. Lewd jokes about the virgin's first night were shared with abandon, women participating with equal gusto. But the wedding rituals themselves were an exhausting set of ceremonies, running for a fortnight. Bride and groom had to be present through every ritual, always breaking at sunset and recommencing just before sunrise. Tradition disallowed them from viewing each other's faces before the rituals were over, and Ikshvaku went through it all with growing anticipation.

On the first day of wedding, Vaivasvat Manu had taken his son aside, looking guilty and apologetic. Ikshvaku knew what bothered his father. "The last time we met," Manu had said, "I promised you that I would find something that legitimises your rule beyond all doubt. It would have been most propitious had I succeeded before your wedding."

"It's the seal of Surya, isn't it?" asked Ikshvaku.

Manu nodded, not asking how Ikshvaku had known about it. "Forged in the time of Aurvan Surya from the purest metals he could acquire, it is an unmistakable, overpowering symbol of Surya descent. To garland the seal around your neck is the greatest act I can perform as your father."

"How did we lose it?"

"The seal was lost many times as it passed along the six generations between Aurvan and Havishmana," Manu explained, "But it always found its way back to our family, or maybe it was the other way round. From Havishmana it descended to his son, Kala, and then to Kala's son, Marici. He wore it proudly as a medallion around his neck when he led our people back to Aryavarta. After him, it should have descended to his son, Kashyapa. But as you know, Kashyapa declined to rule over Solar tribes as his father had. In the chaos that ensued after Marici's funeral, the seal was lost."

Ikshvaku had listened with concern, but then relaxed a little. "It is still in the possession of a Suryavanshi then," he said. It was a safe conclusion to make, for only someone of the Solar tribes could have been present at the funeral.

Manu nodded in agreement. "But *which* Suryavanshi?" he said. "When I was younger, perhaps a few years older than you are now, finding the seal was the only goal in my life. I followed every thread, annoyed the living descendants of those that had attended the funeral, and wasted years in the search. I gave up later, when I realised that it was nothing more than a childhood whim for me, not the crucial symbol it can become for you."

Ikshvaku had no words in response, feeling overwhelmed at the rare glimpse into his father's past. "But you returned to the search," Ikshvaku said, "Or perhaps found a new clue. That's why you hoped to find it, the last time we met."

"Yes, but I was wrong. The trail led me to Plaksha, Prasthala and Sringara. But it was in vain."

"We will find it yet, father," said Ikshvaku, feeling confident. Manu was but one man, Ikshvaku had armies of men at his disposal. He would scour the length and breadth of Aryavarta for it, and even beyond if need be. The seal of Aurvan Surya, which later became Marici's prized medallion, was Ikshvaku's by birthright.

Father and son had then set thoughts of Aurvan's seal aside, for the wedding ceremonies faced them all. The rshis had chosen the spot well, nestled on a flat cliff that overlooked a sheer dive to the Sindhu river. Vitabhya was built on a vast plateau, one of the only three distinct physical contours that existed for yojanas around. Two sharp, rocky hillocks and the plateau gave shadow to the Sindhu river as it passed by, having just been met by the Shatadru and Iravati. By the fourteenth evening, much of the ceremonial energy had dissipated. Now the head rshi invited Vaivasvat Manu to bring a formal closure to the ceremony. It required an accurate oration of the bride and groom's ancestry, and there was none better informed on this than Vaivasvat. In invoking their forefathers, he would bind them to a lasting tie, one blessed by generations of Solar elders across the past eras.

"Both these children share a common ancestor," Manu began, "As do we all. We do not know his real name, but we do know that he was first to take the title of Surya in the Sixth era. He fathered Priyavrata Ravi, and through his line came each one of us. These two—Ikshvaku and Sarmi—share this line right up to Havishmana Surya, from where it splits. I shall narrate the bride's ancestry first. From the third son of Havishmana came the clan of Medhi, founded by Medha Paravara. His eldest son was Kumara Medhi, whose eldest son is Tauranga Medhi. Tauranga Medhi has fathered four children, and of these the youngest is his daughter, Sarmi Taurangi."

Tauranga Medhi bowed to Vaivasvat Manu in humility. "I could not have narrated this better myself," he confessed with gratitude.

Manu bowed in return before continuing. "And now we come to the groom, where I must admit a certain partiality, for the boy is my own son. I hope this will excuse me for proclaiming the groom's ancestry with greater zeal!" The line was delivered in humour, and it had the desired effect on Manu's audience. Seated at the centre of the ritual structure, Ikshvaku's vision was covered by the ornate headgear mounted around his forehead. But he smiled at his father's natural appetite for wooing the crowd. Manu's voice boomed loudly. "From Havishmana's eldest son came Marici Havishmani, the great leader who led our nomadic forefathers back to Aryavarta. To Marici came Kashyapa, who abdicated rule and achieved the title of Maharshi. From Kashyapa was born Vivasvana, who in turn gave life to me-Vaivasvat. Of my six children, the groom is my eldest son, Ikshvaku Manava."

With that the wedding was over, though a further two ceremonies remained before it would be truly consummated. The first of these was the Ceremony of Gifts, and Ikshvaku had last experienced it as the bride's brother. That meant watching a steady stream of cattle, metal and other commodities flow towards the groom's side, meant as gifts from the bride's parents. Now he could enjoy it as the groom, watching the elaborate parade of presents Tauranga Medhi had prepared for Vaivasvat Manu—2000 cows, 500 young horses, 500 sheets of copper and countless uncut pieces of lapis lazuli, agate and other precious stones. It was a fine dowry, one that befitted a Suryavanshi King. And knowing Manu, it would later be distributed among the villages around Vitabhya.

The second ceremony, of course, was the Union of Mates. Bride and groom were taken to separate quarters, where tribal elders stripped and bathed them in scented waters. Then they were dressed in fresh, flimsy robes translucent to the light. After a lot of singing, dancing, teasing and taunting, Ikshvaku was pushed into the private chambers where his bride awaited him. Sarmi was only a year younger, and her slender frame was in stark contrast to his muscular, hard body. Even from afar, Ikshvaku could sense the tension in her. He could not deny a certain nervousness in himself as well. Wading into battle seemed a simpler task than what he must do here, now. He was trained for combat and war, but nothing had trained him for this, save a few lessons from Haryashva that could not be entirely true. He walked closer to his wife, feeling desire awaken within him as he got nearer. Sarmi's robes stuck tight to her wet body, accentuating her soft curves.

Ikshvaku sat beside her, for the moment content to admire her form and allure. He had spent too many years in the drive for kingship, occupied solely by the vision of himself as the supreme Suryavanshi leader. Living by the sword and horse, he had scarcely paid attention to women in the manner young men of his age did. Now with the knowledge of what the "union of mates" was all about, combined with Sarmi's young, fair presence next to him, Ikshvaku felt alive like never before. He raised an arm to bring her closer, and she responded by shifting closer. She looked up, and for the first time they finally gazed upon each other's faces. She was the most beautiful woman he had ever laid eyes upon, and her look confirmed that she too liked what she saw. No words needed to be spoken as they ripped apart their flimsy robes. Her body was pliable to his inexperienced but certain hands, moving into the exact position he wanted. She moaned softly at his first attempt and he desisted, but she pulled him closer and whispered, "Don't stop."

They made love twice that night, exhausting themselves in each other's young, eager bodies. It was love in a form Ikshvaku had never experienced before, vaguely aware as he was of its very existence. But he was disciplined enough not to spend himself quickly, taking care to pleasure her as much she needed him to. It was late when sleep overcame them, the fatigue of a fortnight of intense ritual and eventual culmination finally washing over their weary, spent bodies. Come morning, they were awoken by a loud and abrupt banging at the door.

"King Ikshvaku! A rider brings an urgent message," a deep voice shouted out.

Ikshvaku frowned and replied, "I'll be right outside." He experienced a moment of reluctance, but then the King inside him stood firm. "I must go," he said to his bride somewhat brusquely. She did not see his pain as he left, but how could a seventeen-year-old boy describe the concerns of a newly-wed King whose forces were at war with the Rakshasas? He had surrendered himself to a higher duty, and his personal desires could not come in the way of it.

The rider's message was brief but pertinent, adding to young Ikshvaku's growing troubles—General Ardra's force of 1,000 men had splintered, and the General and his elite 200 were surrounded by Rakshasa forces. The Bear was in need of immediate assistance.

Fear was an emotion Ardra Aditya had never experienced. His fearlessness had been passed on to him by his forefathers, who carried the same blood that coursed through his King. He thought of the boy King now, finding comfort from the fact that the Solar tribes finally had a ruler to unite them. He could die in battle here, today, and Avisari would live on. What else could a regent hope for?

The Rakshasas snarled at him malevolently, reeking of brew and ash. Their indiscipline always amazed him. They could be a far more efficient force if they fought sober and with co-ordination. But abandon and chaos was in their very nature, and Ardra had fought enough battles to be familiar with it. He studied the lead Rakshasa, perceiving his power and authority. The others gathered behind, waiting for the leader to make the first move.

"Do you know who I am, Suryavanshi?" the Rakshasa asked, his voice grating like a saw on wood.

200 Solar warriors lay dead around Ardra, and even now he could hear the wounded ones being finished off systematically. He marvelled at how viciously each man had fought, taking countless Rakshasa heads before being slain himself. Their stand against 1,000 Rakshasas was valiant, yet they were routed. But the Bear only towered higher, giving the Rakshasa his best condescending look. "Do you know who I am, Rakshasa? I am General Ardra of the Suryavanshi. My people have always called me the Bear. It is a title I proudly earned when I once mauled one of your kind to death with my bare hands."

The Rakshasa chuckled dryly, not intimidated by Ardra's large appearance. He was a tall, muscular man himself, his skin dark and his eyes blood red. "And I am Narantaka, General Ardra," he declared calmly. "Supreme Commander of the Rakshasa force of Kamyakvana. This is *our* home, and we are far too skilled at hunting bears than you might assume."

"You can save your life yet," another Rakshasa added. "Surrender to the Supreme Commander, and carry his message to your King."

Ardra raised an eyebrow. "What message might that be?" he asked. There was no way he would surrender, but he did allow himself some curiosity.

"Ikshvaku is just a boy, is he not?" Narantaka asked. He bore the aura of unmistakable power, and added to it with a disdainful confidence. "How old is he? Fifteen? Sixteen? How does a beast such as yourself come to call a wimpling his King?"

"Face the King in a duel, Rakshasa. All your questions shall be answered by his blade."

Narantaka shrugged, looking unfazed. "Carry the tale of your defeat to him, General," he said. "Tell him to accept Rakshasa sovereignty over this forest and the waters that pass through it. Or decimation shall visit your cities as sure as it has visited your men here."

The Bear smiled. "I will carry no such message."

"I did not think you would. You Suryavanshi do overvalue this thing called pride, after all. Will you join your men in death then?"

"I will take dozens of your men along with me," Ardra said, priming his sword for attack.

"I do not doubt it. But I can spare the lives of these men. You have only the one life. Let us see how hard you fight for it."

"Steady," Ikshvaku commanded to his line of soldiers. "Do not fear what comes now. Glory awaits us, and a meeting with Surya Deva himself-our magnificent ancestor. Come now, warriors! Let us shine Solar light on this Rakshasa darkness!"

An army of 2,000 men roared with Ikshvaku's chant, and even Haryashva beside him felt reassured. His King and friend was with him, ready to protect him with his own life. And he was determined to do the same in return. He bared his teeth as the approaching sound got louder in the darkness. The Suryavansha had learnt not to use lamps inside Kamyakvana. Their light only illuminated a small distance around them, at the fatal cost of throwing the distances beyond into a deeper pall of black. The torches also made them visible to any observant eye hidden in the forest, and one had enough reasons to make do without.

The sound came closer and stopped just at the periphery of their tentative, hazy vision. "Are you there, Ikshvaku? Solar King, Son of Vaivasvat and Marici?" a loud, grisly voice broke out from the black. Malevolence was unmistakable in its tone.

Haryashva pressed a hand on Ikshvaku's shoulder to stop him from shouting out in reply. *Wait,* he gestured before moving some distance away from his King.

"I am here," Haryashva shouted, and then changed his position in a flash. A spear shot out from the darkness and sliced through where he stood moments ago. There was silence for a while before he shouted, "Now that the silly trick is done, what do you want, Rakshasa?"

The Rakshasa laughed confidently. "I did not really expect you to fall for it, King Ikshvaku of the Solar. But one must always try the most straightforward tactic first."

"The time for petty tactics is over," Ikshvaku said. No spear flew out this time, but he did move away just in case. Haryashva nodded approvingly.

"I agree with you, boy King," said the Rakshasa. "And to commemorate the war games soon to commence, I have a gift for you. Here, I think you will quite like it."

Something landed near Haryashva's feet in a damp thud. He bent down and peered, taking some time to recognise the battered, semi-pulped head of General Ardra. Rage seered through him like ice, and then the smell hit him. It hit Ikshvaku the moment he came closer, just before he too bent down and recognised the head of his General lying there defiled. The stench was unmistakable, the Rakshasas had obviously relieved themselves on it. Ikshvaku could only hope that the deed was done after the beheading. "Rakshasa!" he roared in fury. "Who are you? Reveal yourself to me!"

The Rakshasa laughed from the darkness, without mirth. "I am Narantaka, boy King! I lead the Rakshasas, who did that to your General. A fine Arya, I will admit. It took three of my largest men to bring him down, and the finest sword we possessed to severe that neck. The rest was easy, but I was not involved in it. I am saving myself for you after all!"

Ikshvaku needed to hear no more, and neither did the men around him. Solar fury coursed through their ranks as word passed around of what had happened to their beloved General. The King issued no command, cried no rally of attack. He ran into the darkness with sword in hand, ready for death as much as the men behind him. They hit a forward line of Rakshasas almost immediately, cold blades clashing with wood and stone. Ikshvaku waved his sword with relentless will, killing all that strayed near with brutal, wild swings quite unlike his usual precise style. Haryashva fought behind him, almost staying back to back. In the forest's pitch black darkness they were unsure of whether their blades cut through enemy men or their own, but the King allowed himself no hesitation. Cries of both Rakshasa and Arya rang through the air, creating a chaotic din that did not really befit a forest otherwise so quiet.

But Ikshvaku was not the only one driven to traumatised fury. General Drishta rampaged through the Rakshasas like an immortal on a merciless killing-spree, such was his rage at the Bear's fate. He sliced and hacked ruthlessly, countless Rakshasa heads falling lifelessly to the ground in his sword's wake. Yet, the anger was but targeted at random, slaying the more dispensable Rakshasas while Narantaka remained elusive. Ikshvaku knew that he could not hope to find him in these conditions, especially since Rakshasa leaders bore no differentiating marks or attire. Each was like the other—ash smeared and stinking of blood, flesh and brew. He maintained one eye on General Drishta, feeling a sense of responsibility towards his uncle's safety. Yet even the valorous boy King found enough to admire in his veteran warrior. Drishta was death personified, rampaging through the Rakshasas and notching up an admirable kill-count.

Ikshvaku remembered Varman's lessons, playing out attack sequences and defensive parries in his mind moments before executing them live on the Rakshasas around him. He did not stop to observe his kills, nor to wipe blood off his face. I am a King, he reminded himself. *I must be the best among my men, the most fearsome warrior that Solar blood can produce*. The motion and violence threw him into a trance, Rakshasa blood splashing off his sword in thick streams as he swung it around almost mechanically. He was Surya, a rapidly flowing blur of death, cutting across Rakshasa lines with alarming ease. When some of the chaos dissipated, he stood surrounded with the largest pile of Rakshasa corpses, surpassing even Drishta's kills. Haryashva had witnessed such a scene before, two years ago. But the King looked different now, bigger and stronger. Blood trickled down his sword and torso freely, though none of it was his. Ikshvaku looked around and saw many of his own men slain among the trees, their blood being soaked by the soft earth. When he turned, for a moment it was as if he did not recognise Haryashva. Then the rage in his eyes blinked away and Ikshvaku returned.

"Narantaka," Ikshvaku said, repeating the Rakshasa's name almost as if it were a curse. "I will avenge the death of Ardra the Bear, and I will not find rest before I do." The Bear's body was not found, but Drishta insisted on cremating the head just the same. At the funeral he confessed what Haryashva had suggested long ago. "Ardra was my half-brother, born to my father's third wife. There was no particular love between us all our lives, but there was always a grudging respect. We will avenge him together, you and I."

Pururava

"After the final Deva-Asura wars, Tapin Soma was among the victorious Devas. He left his clans behind in the plains and foothills that stretched in the shadow of the Himalaya. They became the Lunar tribes of Plaksha, the Somavansha. You will learn later why the name of Suryavansha still survives while none declare the banner of Somavansha anymore."

King Bhagiratha to Sudasa

Year 36, Seventh era

Situated on the eastern bank of the Sarasvati river, Plaksha was home to the Lunar tribes of Aryavarta. Descendants to the legendary Deva, Tapin Soma, they were nevertheless a simple people. There were no warrior lines among them, no elite dynasties with a history of rule and authority. The venerable Maharshi Atri, born in the line of Tapin Soma, led them as guide and counsel, his years of administration extended by the abrupt death of his son, Budha Atreya. Atri was aided in his governance by Budha's widow, Ila Manava, the wise daughter and first child of Vaivasvat Manu. Her marriage to Budha had secured an alliance that would sustain itself for decades to come. Hundreds of years later, fragmented tribes could look back in their genealogy and find a blood-relation among themselves solely through the link that Ila established between the Solar and Lunar people.

Her bulging convoy of caravans and horse-guards wheeled into Avisari, led in by an elite set of escorts sent by the King himself.

For Ila was his beloved sister, a mentor to him almost as much as Vaivasvat Manu himself. And this was a fine occasion—King Ikshvaku's wife Sarmi had delivered a son. The Solar dynasty now had an heir, and Ikshvaku's messengers had insisted that Ila must visit. She was accompanied by a set of attendants, a single priest and her son, Pururava, the son of Budha. While her features were distinctly Solar, Pururava had taken after his father. His fair skin, light hair and greyish eyes were reminiscent of Maharshi Atri.

Inside, the convoy turned onto Avisari's main street, from where young Pururava had a panoramic view of the city. Colours invaded his vision from every corner, new smells wafted in and out, and all sorts of noises floated in from the busy alleys. Large, tall complexes lined Avisari in organised patterns, and the Nripalaya was the biggest of them all. There were no such structures in Plaksha, only humble brick and mud constructions that paled in front of the Nripalaya's daunting walls. He followed his mother through its imposing doorway, where his eyes went to the tall, straight men that stood by the sides, dressed in copper and wood armour.

Sarmi was waiting when they entered, and she walked up to them with a broad smile on her face. "Ila, how great that you could make this journey!" There was genuine delight upon her face, and a captivating fragrance surrounded her presence. Her jewellery was stark and profuse, unlike the dull ornamentations favoured by women in Plaksha. Pururava had heard of Solar prosperity, but his Lunar austerity had left him with no means of imagining it. Now he could see it all around him, testifying to the glory of the Suryavansha.

"How could we not come?" Ila replied, sharing a tight embrace with Sarmi. "And Pururava has been dying to meet my brother!"

That was unwarranted, Pururava thought. Sure, he was eager to meet his uncle, but did mother have to embarrass him like that? He was thirteen now, only a year short of the age at which his uncle ascended the throne. And mother always said that to be a King, he would have to grow into a man as soon as possible.

Sarmi turned her attention to Pururava and her smile widened. "How handsome you look!" she exclaimed. "Come. Ikshvaku will be pleased to see you." She led Ila and Pururava through another doorway where the boy found two men seated on mats of grass and laughing over a joke. At their entry the younger man's eyes widened and he stood up in a flash.

"Ila! Finally you arrive! My scouts reported sighting your convoy more than a day ago." He pulled Ila into a tight embrace, but not before he bent down to touch her feet. Then he turned his attention to his nephew.

Ikshvaku was taller than anyone Pururava had ever seen, and he stooped low to bring his head to Pururava's level. "This must be my little nephew," he said. That was when Pururava realised that this was Ikshvaku, the First King of Aryavarta. His appearance was nothing like he had expected. He looked much older than his seventeen years. His hair was long and wavy, and a strong stubble layered his face. His hands were thick and muscular, while his chest and shoulders jutted out wide and firm. When he held his hands out to hold Pururava, the boy noticed numerous cuts and scars on them.

"Pururava," Ila said. "Pay your respects to the King."

Pururava folded his hands in the traditional greeting, but Ikshvaku clasped them with a wide grin on his face. "He looks so much like our father," he said to Ila, "The same nose and jaw line."

Ila beamed. "Father has said as much himself. But Pururava has taken the hair and grey eyes from his own father."

"That is good," Ikshvaku commented, "Maharshi Atri must be proud." He turned to the man next to him and said, "This is Haryashva, my dear friend and an Ashvak from Kapisa."

Pururava had heard much about this Ashvak, who was well known as the King's right hand man. *When you grow to be a ruler of men yourself*, Ila always said, *you must find loyal and capable men like Haryashva*.

Haryashva bowed and brought his palms together in a namaskara. "It is an honour to meet you, Ila devi. The King often talks of you."

Ila nodded with a smile, giving her brother a fond look. "I hope he remembers some of the things I taught him! And I have heard much about you, brave Haryashva. I have you to thank for saving his life."

"Only after he saved my life a dozen times," Haryashva replied humbly.

Ikshvaku chuckled pleasantly. "Haryashva is stubbornly humble, Ila. Except when it comes to his abilities as a rider. He calls me his King, but he refuses to accept that I handle a horse better."

"Because you don't," Haryashva replied firmly. Both men exchanged a chuckle, and Ila smiled at their mirth. "Can I see the boy now?" she asked.

Ikshvaku turned to Sarmi. "The new-born is sleeping," she said. "But I will bring him out shortly. We have decided to name him Vikukshi."

"Vikukshi?" Ila asked. "I thought you named your firstborn Kshuva, after our father."

"We would have," Ikshvaku replied. "But Maharshi Vasishtha suggested that a name beginning with *Va* was more auspicious, and Sarmi favoured Vikukshi. His official title is Vikukshi Kshuva Aikshvaku. That way our father is honoured as well."

"Enough chatter," Sarmi interrupted. "Come, let us seat ourselves. Ila and Pururava must be famished after their long journey."

Pururava was famished indeed. The journey from Plaksha to Avisari took two long months, and only because Ikshvaku sent the best horses from Kapisa to carry them. They subsisted on wild berries and baked flour all along the route, and Pururava was eager to have a real meal. He followed the elders as they sat on grass mats, and waited hungrily while food was placed in front of him. The rice here was slender and longer, more appetising to both eye and palate. The spices were milder, with a sweet aftertaste that went well with the smoked rice. Pururava knew that the Solar tribes also had a heavy dose of flesh in their diet, but meat was missing here, perhaps in deference to the Lunar tribes' vegetarian ways. The elders made more small talk as they ate, and Ikshvaku and Haryashva made several quips and japes at each other that Pururava did not understand. On a few occasions his gaze met Ikshvaku's, and the King looked at him with friendly, twinkling eyes.

After the meal, Pururava was introduced to another famed figure among the Suryavanshi, Maharshi Vasishtha. A rshi in Plaksha once assured Pururava that Vasishtha was more than 100 years old, but Ila had rubbished it for him right away. Vasishtha was younger than Kashyapa and Atri after all, and the streaks of black in his beard were evidence of his relative youth. They were joined by another man, fierce and barrel-chested. Pururava soon learnt that he was General Drishta, formidable commander of the Suryavanshi army. Sarmi disappeared and returned a little later cradling infant Vikukshi, depositing him in the eager arms of Ila.

"Maharshi Vasishtha," said General Drishta. "Please share with the King what we discussed earlier. He refuses to heed my counsel on this." A lot had changed since Ikshvaku and Drishta had first arrived at Sringara three years ago, seeking the Maharshi's aid and approval. The young boy was a confident King now, his authority reinforced by his ever-growing popularity amongst Solar warriors and civilians alike.

Ikshvaku's demeanour changed visibly. He looked more like a King now, than the teenage cousin that greeted Ila some moments ago. There was a grim and regal bearing upon his face. "Are you talking about the proposal to shift our capital, uncle?" he asked.

"I am, my King, and Maharshi Vasishtha agrees that the proposal is wise."

Ikshvaku turned to Vasishtha, who said, "Avisari is no place to build a capital, Ikshvaku. You are inaccessible here, your armies surrounded by mountainous terrain. Now that Kamyakvana has become the focus of our campaigns, it makes sense for you to shift south near the Iravati."

Ikshvaku bowed his head, indicating that he respected the Maharshi's words. "I hear your counsel, guruji. But I see it differently. Avisari's remoteness makes it an impenetrable capital. On the plains of Iravati we could be surrounded from all sides, vulnerable to siege."

Ikshvaku turned to Haryashva for his opinion, who shrugged and said, "You are building a military outpost at Kapisa. It can protect these lands should the need arise. If the eventual aim, as you often state, is to colonise Sindhu and Sarasvati down to where they meet the ocean, then at some point you must shift south."

"I need not do the shifting myself," Ikshvaku countered. "I have a son now, who can be my regent when he comes of age. And what of my brothers, Pramshu, Sharyati, Nabhaga, Karusaka and Narisyanta? They need lands to colonise as well. What of my sister's son? If I send my forces down to the Yamuna, Lunar tribes will hold no claim over those lands. Pururava would have nothing to rule over. Are we ready for that?"

No one replied, then General Drishta spoke up. "At least take my counsel on the other matter. Your brothers and son will come of coronation age around the same time. There is no law stating that your son should be Suryavanshi King before your brother, and so Pramshu or Sharyati could stake a claim to the throne as much as Vikukshi could."

"Your counsel being?" Ikshvaku asked. He knew what Drishta was going to say. This was a discussion that Ikshvaku was growing weary of.

General Drishta turned to Vasishtha again, who said, "Primogeniture. The right of the firstborn to inherit the wealth and powers of his father. Institute this practise before your brothers are of age to protest it. Make it law that the firstborn becomes King after his father. That way your son will be protected."

Ikshvaku chuckled. "And what will become of any future sons, those who haven't even been born yet?"

"As the King it will always be in your discretion to split the kingdom among your sons," Vasishtha suggested. "But no other Manava could stake a claim to kingship."

"I have no right to deny them of any such privilege," Ikshvaku argued. "Why does my son have greater claim to Havishmana and Marici's legacy than my brothers?"

"Primogeniture has always been an unsaid law for our people," Drishta insisted. "Even the title of Surya passed down only to the eldest son."

"A practise I do not find much prudence in, uncle," Ikshvaku challenged. "There is no assurance that Vikukshi will be more capable a ruler than my brothers. And I cannot pass a law that may rob our people of a better King." He said that in a tone of finality, no further discussion could happen on the matter. Pururava stared in admiration. How could Ikshvaku command so much power at such a young age?

"Let us turn to our search," Ikshvaku said, shifting the topic with ease. "What has the group from Harayupa found?"

Pururava frowned reflexively, not knowing what Ikshvaku meant. "Nothing yet," Drishta replied with a frown of his own. "Finding the seal will take time, my King. Whoever possesses, it now knows of its import. They will either wish to retain it, or fear your fury if they come forward."

"There is no assurance that it remains in Aryavarta," added Maharshi Vasishtha, his voice grave. "It could have been traded away long ago. Its metal could have been melted and re-forged into something else. I do not mean to dishearten you, young King. But you must be prepared for any possibility. If the seal remains lost, how many years will you spend searching for it?"

"All the years I have," Ikshvaku replied, undaunted. "If not for me, then for my successors." Then he turned his full attention to Pururava. "Come now," he said, "Let me spend some time with my nephew. Can you ride a horse, Pururava?"

"I can," Pururava said confidently.

"Then let us take a ride," the King said. Haryashva stood up to follow them, but Ikshvaku placed a hand on his shoulder and said gently, "No, my friend. I wish to have this ride with my nephew alone." Haryashva made no protest, and Pururava followed his uncle in anticipation.

"Your lineage is as glorious as mine, if not more," Ikshvaku commented once they were trotting their horses out of Avisari. "Quite a lot of expectations rest on your young shoulders."

Pururava simply said, "There were a lot of expectations on your shoulders too."

"Did you learn that from your mother?" Ikshvaku asked shrewdly.

It occurred to Pururava now that Ila had a life before he was born. How many years would she and Ikshvaku have spent together? He turned to his uncle with this query in his eyes, but Ikshvaku was in a pensive mood now.

Ikshvaku ignored the silence and asked, "How fares your grandfather, Maharshi Atri?"

"He is getting old," Pururava replied, happy to have something normal to converse about. "He rarely steps out of his hut now, and prefers to meditate in isolation."

"The first generation seers are all getting old," Ikshvaku commented. "My own great-grandfather, Maharshi Kashyapa, has seen more than eighty years." Ikshvaku said it casually enough, but his expression turned perceptibly taut. Pururava could guess the reason. Maharshi Kashyapa was notoriously ascetic and withdrawn. As a young man he had rejected the leadership over Solar tribes that passed to him from Marici, and as an accomplished seer he rarely made contact with any of his tribe. In all likelihood, Ikshvaku had never even met Kashyapa.

"This seal you are searching for," Pururava ventured. "What is it?"

"A thick, heavy chunk of metal, with the sun embossed on it in gold—at least from the way it has been described to me," Ikshvaku replied. "It was created by Aurvan Surya, my ancient ancestor and a contemporary to your own, Tapin Soma. But it was lost after Marici's death. I wish to find it again."

They passed out of the town walls and made way through the crowded market streets outside Avisari proper. The people recognised Ikshvaku, many rushing to fold their hands in namaskara around his horse and shout words of praise and gratitude. Quite a few young women placed themselves around his path, hastily brushing their hair or adjusting their dresses strategically. Ikshvaku had not opted for a second marriage yet, but for a son of the famously polygamous Vaivasvat Manu it was only a matter of time. Once beyond the market, the land stretched flat before climbing steeply up to the high mountains. Here Ikshvaku set his horse at a gallop. Pururava followed, his pace matching Ikshvaku's. They raced till they reached the rising climb and worked up a healthy sweat. Pururava felt sore and tired but Ikshvaku looked positively rejuvenated.

"This is why I cannot leave Avisari," Ikshvaku said as he sipped some water from a pouch and tossed it to Pururava. "I belong with the horses and mountains, neither of which are found in the river-lands. Were I not the King it wouldn't matter, I could be an inconspicuous rider in the far north, battling Yakshas by day and sleeping huddled in blankets by night. But such anonymity is not available to boys like us, is it?"

Pururava noted that Ikshvaku used the term boys, not men. For the first time since he met him, he realised that his uncle was a boy too. He was only seventeen after all, and the bulk of his experience and wisdom lay ahead of him.

"There is something I want to discuss with you, Pururava," Ikshvaku continued. "I need your mother's permission for this, but I want to know if you are ready. Your mother is preparing you for reign, I know that, but there are many areas where her preparation will fall short. She is well protected by the men our father has served her, and by extension so are you. But no man can be King till he can protect himself and those around him. And you have had no training yet. You do not know the ways of sword and shield, of blood and grime."

"Mother says that I am too young for that," Pururava said. Then he hastened to add, "But I disagree."

Ikshvaku nodded approvingly. "Good," he said. "Then come join me here in Avisari. You will train under Varman and Haryashva. You will learn archery, sword fighting, horse riding and much more. You will join raids against Rakshasas, learning by doing. I began training at the age of nine, had my first battle at the age of thirteen, and was crowned King by fifteen. Since then, I have battled more than ruled. If you are to be a ruler as your mother desires, then you must be trained for it. In Avisari I can provide you with that training. Will you join?"

Pururava's face lit up in excitement, and Ikshvaku smiled at his nephew's enthusiasm. "We will need your mother's permission, of course," Ikshvaku added. "But I think I can convince her. It will be good for my young boy to have an elder brother around him. And Varman and Haryashva will appreciate having a ward to train. Their skills are ones I would like to see passed on."

Narantaka

"Narantaka, founder-figure to both Rakshasas and Dasas. His name literally means 'Ender of Men', and enough Solar men and women gave their lives to prove that title true. He was Ikshvaku's greatest enemy, a hero to Rakshasas much like Devantaka was to Asuras in the previous era."

King Bhagiratha to Sudasa

Year 36, Seventh era

"I will cut you to pieces," Narantaka threatened, keeping his distance nevertheless. He had seen enough of Ikshvaku's combat prowess to know that he fought no simple boy.

"An empty boast," Ikshvaku said calmly, casting his shield away and facing Narantaka like the Rakshasa faced him—a single weapon in one hand. His eyes had the hungry look of vengeance, and he stepped closer to Narantaka, speaking in a low, sinister tone. "But I have three cuts to make on your body, Rakshasa. First is for the Bear, for that is a debt you have owed us far too long. Second for the countless raids your people have made through our lands. As their leader you shall bear the crime. Third, for all the men that have died to bring us here today."

But a Rakshasa was not a man to be cowed, and Narantaka was their commander after all. He charged angrily, and Ikshvaku noticed within moments that this was not a crazed, unrestrained run. Narantaka's steps were measured, his head still even as he built up pace and closed the gap between them. Soldiers from either side backed away to watch the duel unfold. Ikshvaku braced himself at Narantaka's leap, and sharpened his eyes at the gleaming sword in the Rakshasa's hand. It came down in a smooth arc as Narantaka descended, and rather than moving away Ikshvaku brought his sword up to block it. Metal met metal in a resounding clash, and Ikshvaku moved a few steps back to absorb Narantaka's sheer momentum. Their eyes met for an idle moment when time itself seemed to stop. Then the blur of their swords began. Within a few blows Ikshvaku perceived fatal flaws in Narantaka's technique. The hirsute Rakshasa left his back open when he swung hard, his follow-through long and hefty. When he slashed downwards, the recoil was not swift enough to defend a counter to the throat. But King Ikshvaku took his time. This was his final enemy, a man he had pursued since the day he became King. And a few technical errors apart, he was a worthy adversary. Blood crept up in Ikshvaku's Solar eyes, and General Drishta and Haryashva allowed themselves to stand back. They recognised the look on their King's face. He was playing with his enemy, putting up a show that soldiers on both sides would not forget too soon.

The first promised scar cut across Narantaka's chest, spurting blood out of him in a carmine display. The Rakshasa reeled in pain but stood his ground, transferring his sword to the other hand to display an ambidexterity that Ikshvaku knew to be common among Rakshasas. But Manu had trained him for this, and Ikshvaku was satisfied to spot the swiftly revealed look of surprise on Narantaka's face when he transferred his sword from right to left as well. And this was Ikshvaku's greatest secret—he was *naturally* left-handed. He gripped his sword with a familiar wave of comfort, made all the more warm for its rarity. Narantaka charged again, indiscipline evident in his movement this time. With the cold look of a practised killer, Ikshvaku moved aside at the last moment to evade Narantaka's swipe. The Rakshasa's back was open once again, and in a quick flash Ikshvaku ripped open the second promised cut. This was turning easy for him, and it was evident to Narantaka's warriors as well. But then Narantaka turned around with a jeering grin on his face. Slowly and deliberately, he licked his bloody fingers one by one, seemingly impervious to the pain he ought to be in.

Ikshvaku frowned, thrown off more by Narantaka's tolerance for pain than anything else. For a split second he looked like a boy, confused and vulnerable. Then he grunted and braced for another charge. Just then a horn shouted in the distance, its blare erupting muted through the dense foliage. It was not Solar, and a strange sensation crept up in Ikshvaku's gut. He did not know it, never having felt it before. It was fear.

"Ah," said Narantaka. "That's a few of my friends, I think. Probably a few more than you calculated for, King Ikshvaku."

Ikshvaku did not let his surprise show, walking towards Narantaka now with the intent to kill. General Drishta flanked away with his contingent, seeking the horn's source. Haryashva ordered his Ashvaks into a tighter circle around their King, pushing the rejuvenated Rakshasa force into a wider arc. Narantaka moved to attack just as Ikshvaku came close, but then the horn blew a second time, from *further* away. Distracted, Narantaka failed to notice Ikshvaku manoeuvring himself behind him. The Solar King's sword was at his throat in a flash, and the son of Vaivasvat Manu whispered into his ear. "The third and final cut-as promised, Rakshasa. But I will not deliver it here. You shall receive it in the full view of my people."

General Drishta returned less than a day later, explaining the mystery of the two horns. "Narantaka had another contingent of 500 Rakshasas hidden in the forest. They were supposed to rise to his aid at the last moment, catching us unawares. But there was some sort of falling out, and their leader elected not to help him on this day." Drishta did not need to add that his men slaughtered them all. The blood on his face and armour was testament enough.

The Supreme Rakshasa Commander was bound and tied to a horse, fated to journey back to Avisari with his captors. The remaining Rakshasas surrendered, accepting Ikshvaku's terms—cross west of Sindhu and never return. It was time to leave Kamyakvana. The war was finally won, Narantaka captured and Rakshasas ousted from Aryavarta. But relief did not wash over Ikshvaku yet, and as he scoured the battle site one last time he came upon a band of Rakshasas. They were from Narantaka's surrendered bunch, but had not come true on their promise to leave Aryavarta yet. Ikshvaku's men had disarmed them before letting them go, but one managed to retain his petty dagger, which he now held to the throat of a fair-skinned Rakshasi. An infant lay abandoned by her side, its cries drowned by the other Rakshasas egging the first one on.

There was no fear in the Rakshasi's eyes, even for her child. She stared back defiantly. "Do what you want!"

The Rakshasas shouted out several suggestions, each as imaginative as the other. Ikshvaku discerned one comment: "Rip her leather off, let us see what Narantaka fancied so much!" This was Narantaka's wife then, or at least one of them. Ikshvaku felt a sudden wave of responsibility towards her and the infant.

Another one shouted. "Be done with the infant first. The screeching is turning me off."

And yet the Rakshasi spared no look of anxiety for her child. Ikshvaku had fought Rakshasis before, and he was no stranger to their courage. But what sort of mother did not fear even for her hapless infant? Needing no further cue, Ikshvaku charged with a loud battle cry. These men were familiar with his voice, and without their weapons it was all they needed to flee into the forest's darkness. One fool rushed at him valiantly, seeming to realise at the last moment that he held no axe. Ikshvaku's sword sliced through him even before he completed the thought. The last Rakshasa stood his ground, slashing his dagger in the air in warning. "Back off!" he said. "I will slice her throat before you move."

"You think I care for the life of one more Rakshasi, when I have slayed countless in this forest?" Ikshvaku bluffed. Deciding that it was not worth the risk, the Rakshasa threw his dagger to the ground and fled. Ikshvaku approached the Rakshasi cautiously, wary of any concealed weapons in her possession. "You are Narantaka's wife?" he asked.

The Rakshasi nodded curtly, picking her infant up and quelling its wail to a sob. "And this is his son. Your effort is a waste, Suryavanshi. Another group will surely find me and finish the job."

"Narantaka has enemies within your tribe?"

"He does now," the Rakshasi replied. "A Supreme Commander that loses is not worthy of that title. As punishment for his failure, his family and name must be wiped out. It is the Rakshasa way."

"Then come with me," Ikshvaku said immediately, knowing that he could not leave this woman and her baby to their deadly fate. He felt a surge of guilt, finally realising something he had never thought of before. How many Rakshasa families had his campaign destroyed? And how many women and infants were slain internecine as a result?

The Rakshasi gave him a condescending look, one that King Ikshvaku was not used to. She did not know his identity, and probably thought him to be just another Solar warrior. "Your King will never allow the blood of Narantaka in his city," she said to him, faintly patronising in her tone.

"You do not know the King," Ikshvaku replied. "So you cannot presume to tell me what he will or will not do. Come with me to Avisari, I will give you and your son the protection you need." He did not stop to consider the consequences, seeing in Narantaka's infant son the possibility to repair Suryavanshi and Rakshasa relations. If he could be raised among the Solar, if he could be taught the Arya ways, would that not reconcile the two tribes?

The Rakshasi frowned, assessing his armour and insignia anew. "You speak with the confidence of a leader, one who is used to having his commands fulfilled. Who are you, Suryavanshi?"

"I am Ikshvaku, King of the Suryavansha. And I offer you and your son refuge in my kingdom."

"You would kill the husband and lay with his wife?" the Rakshasi asked, not caring to keep disdain out of her voice.

Ikshvaku was not offended. Years of war had taught him many things about the Rakshasa way, and sexual candour was a part of it. "That is not my intent," he said honestly. "As the man who defeated Narantaka, his family is now my responsibility. Especially since his defeat places you in such direct danger. I hold no desire towards you, Rakshasi, though I do not mean that as a diminishing comment on your beauty. But if I take you to Avisari, it must be as my wife. Solar ways will allow no other relationship between you and me. Your son will be my son, I assure you. But let me take you away from this threat to your lives."

The Rakshasi sighed, looking to the infant in her arms. "I care for his life, not mine. Were he not here, I would have ended my life the moment Narantaka lost to you. But I will come with you on one condition, Solar King, knowing well that I am in no position to negotiate."

"What is your wish, Rakshasi?"

"Spare Narantaka's life," she said. "I do not ask for his freedom, or that you forgive him for whatever crimes he has committed. But do not take his life, do not orphan this young boy. A father who is alive, even if enslaved, is better than no father at all."

"He has a father," Ikshvaku said. "Me. He will never feel the need for another. And for my people to find closure against the Rakshasas, Narantaka must die. His crimes are too severe for mercy."

But the Rakshasi fell at his feet, her haughty demeanour finally breaking. "I beg you, King Ikshvaku. Make Narantaka your slave, make him a stable-cleaner, imprison him for life even. But do not take my lover's life."

Ikshvaku picked her up, taking care not to let the blood on his hands smear on the boy. "Do not beg me for what you know I cannot give," he pleaded gently.

The Rakshasi nodded, then suddenly changed her line of attack. "You search for something," she said, surprising him with her knowledge. "It was common talk among Narantaka's generals. Your soldiers have been hunting for it across Aryavarta."

"What do you know of it?" asked Ikshvaku, his voice cold and tight.

"Nothing," the Rakshasi said. "But Narantaka does. A distinct-looking Suryavanshi artefact had once come into his possession, and I know that he had sent it somewhere for safekeeping. It may be what you are looking for. But even if it is not, if Narantaka knows of one important Suryavanshi relic he may know of another."

Ikshvaku moved closer to her, looking into her eyes and trying to determine whether she was lying. Was it just a ploy to buy her husband some time? "I could torture Narantaka to pry this knowledge out of him," he said. "Would you not prefer that he receive a quick death?"

The Rakshasi's confidence was growing, and she gave Ikshvaku a wry smile. "Has any Suryavanshi ever tortured a Rakshasa, in all the years of war between us? Your Arya principle disallows it, and it will prevent you from torturing Narantaka."

Ikshvaku returned her smile, drawn to her shrewd mind. "For all you know, what I search for could simply be that important," he said. "But let us accept that torture is beyond the Suryavanshi way, and I will believe you for now. What is your name, Rakshasi?"

"Nivritti," she lied, wishing to put her Rakshasi past behind her. "And my son's name is Nimi." With those names they would enter Avisari as King Ikshvaku's second wife and recently-born son.

Making Peace

"The events after Narantaka's capture affected Ikshvaku's innocence. His transformation from an ambitious, sincere Solar scion to a driven, single-minded King began with the secrets he had to keep. They weighed him down, teaching him what he did not naturally possess-wile and dishonesty."

King Bhagiratha to Sudasa

"Back straight!" barked Varman. "And point those toes forward! Remember the golden rule, your toes should point in the same direction as the tip of your sword."

Pururava failed to understand how one could remember so many rules in the heat of battle. But Varman assured him that with adequate practise they would become a part of his instinct. The last few months had been spent learning tactics, sequences, military divisions and formations, but no perceivable battle-instinct had developed yet. But it was in no way a commentary on his tutor, the stern and demanding veteran Varman. He was a beefy, intimidating man, his barrel-chest surpassing even General Drishta's famed hulk. He was also Avisari's deputy regent, acting as its ruler whenever Suryavanshi armies marched to war. Pururava learnt that Varman was Vaivasvat Manu's childhood friend, and the two had battled Rakshasas together in their younger days. He was also ex-duelling partner and master to Ikshvaku, which made Varman the perfect man to tutor Pururava.

Pururava tucked his toe inwards and straightened his back. "Good," Varman said approvingly. "Moving from stance to stance should be as fluid as breathing itself."

Pururava whirled his sword around and pivoted, minding to keep his toes pointed in the right direction as he moved. "Good," Varman said again, though he did thrust his stick at Pururava's spine to make it even straighter. "Stand tall in front of your enemy," he said. "So you may strike at him from above."

The lesson continued till Pururava's feet were chafed and his arm hurt from swinging the sword around. He was learning Ikshvaku's single-handed grip, not the Suryavanshi warriors' traditional two-handed hold. The regiment barely left him enough time to take another bath before lunch and enjoy a content nap after. On days he was lucky, Ikshvaku would be around and he could spend time with his uncle. The latter happened rarely though, for Ikshvaku was often away on campaigns against Rakshasas. In Avisari, Varman issued orders and made decisions in the King's absence. Pururava longed to accompany Ikshvaku on these campaigns, but Ila had commanded her brother not to put her son in any real danger. Under no circumstances was the boy to experience real battle till Ila felt he was of adequate age. But what that age was, she never specified. So Pururava was left to train in empty barracks each time Ikshvaku took on Rakshasas.

The military training was alternated with spiritual tutelage under Maharshi Vasishtha, at Ikshvaku's special request. Mornings started before the break of sun, and Vasishtha would march a drowsy Pururava to the Sindhu for the morning ritual prayer, Suryanamaskara. The first time Pururava saw Vasishtha do it, he couldn't figure out what the big deal was. It was just a few sequences of stretching and bending, nothing more. But a full circle of just ten Suryanamaskaras left him breathless, and Vasishtha insisted on increasing the number by one every consequent day. The Suryanamaskara was followed by another set of asanas, and he dreaded the Shavasana, which was really nothing more than lying down with one's eyes closed. After the gruelling Suryanamaskara, Shavasana was all Pururava needed to fall into a deep sleep, something that Maharshi Vasishtha looked upon as a sign of extreme weakness.

Pururava had never seen anyone in his family conduct such exercises. Maharshi Atri simply took a dip in the river in the mornings, and Ila rarely showed any spiritual inclination. Why did *he* have to do all this then? He never even spotted Ikshvaku doing the Suryanamaskara, and the Sun was supposed to be his banner! One day he found the courage to point all this out to Vasishtha, who replied, "Ikshvaku is the King, he may do as he pleases. You are my ward, you may do only as I please." Pururava was unable to counter that.

But the truth was that he was having the time of his life in Avisari, and it was only with guilt that he thought of his mother, for he did not miss her as much as a loving son should. Avisari was more alive and populated than anywhere he had ever been. There were markets here selling all sorts of things-beads, pots, pouches, figurines and more. He even found some tablets with strange figures carved onto them, and learnt from Vasishtha that it was a crude writing system, in vogue among trading guilds of the southern Sindhu. Capital of the Suryavansha kingdom, Avisari attracted a wide mix of people. There were tall and gaunt Ashvaks; bronze-haired and fair Sringaras; dark, burnt-skinned boatmen from the southern Sindhu and even the odd few marsh-dwellers from Yamuna. This multi-ethnic and dynamic populace engaged in various sports and rituals that were completely alien to him. Life here was lived to the fullest, unlike the sparsely populated lands around Plaksha.

The next morning Pururava returned from the day's rituals with Maharshi Vasishtha to find commotion in the Nripalaya. Soldiers were afoot everywhere, looking nervous and busy. Then a few senior warriors entered through the Nripalaya's gateway; bloody, scratched and looking fresh out of battle. Finally, they were followed by Ikshvaku, looking weary but kingly nevertheless. Behind him came Haryashva, and as Pururava was pushed to the side by the crowd, he saw a bound and tied figure walking in behind Haryashva.

Pururava jostled, trying to push his way back to the front. But by the time he got there the convoy had passed through the doorway. He sprinted towards the main hall, where a crowd had already gathered. Pururava recognised many prominent citizens of Avisari. They whispered to each other, and he heard one say excitedly, "They've captured the Rakshasa leader!"

The murmurs and mutterings grew louder till the curtain behind the throne parted and out stepped Ikshvaku. The throne was carved out of a single piece of stone and engraved with figurines made of purified gold, bought from the independent city of Trigarta in return for 800 cows. Plush cushions layered the seat, hand-rests and the back. As Ikshvaku took his throne, Varman and Vasishtha sat down beside him. General Drishta stepped in after the prisoner, who was the most hirsute man Pururava had ever seen. His arms and face were entirely black with a dense covering of hair. He sported furry bearskin, and a chain of random bone fragments hung proudly around his neck. He walked with a limp, and a violent slash across his chest had been hastily wrapped up. But his eyes were defiantly belligerent, and he showed no sign of fear. Seeing him, Pururava finally realised why his mother had protected him from battle so far. There was no way a boy like him could stand against a beast like that, training or no training. Then guilt at this cowardice washed over him, and he glanced abashedly towards Ikshvaku. The King was staring back at him, and at eye contact he gave him a faint, reassuring smile. Haryashva led the Rakshasa up to a short distance away from the throne, and stood by his right while General Drishta took the left. Behind them, dozens of soldiers walked in and stood some distance away, hands on their swords. This was clearly no ordinary prisoner.

"Rakshasa," Ikshvaku said in a voice that boomed loud and clear across the hall. "You are leader to the Kamyakvana Rakshasas. Do you accept this?" The Rakshasa only growled and stared malevolently.

"No matter," Ikshvaku said, looking beyond the Rakshasa to the growing gathering of men and women. Duty demanded that he give these Suryavanshi what they deserved—justice heaped upon Narantaka for the crimes of his people. But if the Rakshasa had any clue to the whereabouts of Aurvan's seal, then Ikshvaku could not afford to lose him. Was it not also his duty to find that important tribal relic, as a proud son of Havishmana, Marici and Manu? "This is Narantaka, leader of the Kamyakvana Rakshasas. You may also know him as the man who beheaded Ardra the Bear," Ikshvaku declared decisively. A loud ripple of chatter and curses passed through the hall at his announcement. He waited for it to subside before turning back to Narantaka. "You were captured under the rules of battle. By right you are my prisoner, and I can have you executed. But that is not my intent. War is damaging to both our sides, Rakshasa, and a ceasefire is beneficial to both. I have brought you here to negotiate a treaty between us."

Pururava frowned, noticing a similar expression on other faces as well. What was Ikshvaku doing? Rakshasas were vile and corrupt men, without any honour. What sort of treaty could be negotiated with them? Had Marici not tried once and failed? Even General Drishta and Haryashva looked surprised.

Nevertheless, Haryashva nudged Narantaka, urging him to respond. "There can be no treaty between us," Narantaka replied in a hoarse, guttural voice. His pronunciation was off, he enunciated where there was supposed to be none and ate up the vowels that needed stressing. Pururava realised that Sanskrit was not the man's native tongue.

"An answer your predecessors once gave to mine," Ikshvaku said, referring to Marici's attempts to broker truce between the Solar settlers and Rakshasas. "But look where that has brought us. The war between us must end at some point, to be replaced by a lasting friendship."

The Rakshasa snorted in derision. "I need not your friendship, Suryavanshi." He pronounced the title as if it was a curse. "You killed my kind, drew us out of our homes, and had me bound and tied by your men. There is no way we can meet as equals now. I am a captive. Treat me accordingly."

"Damage has been done to both our sides," Ikshvaku reminded him, not missing a beat. "For decades your people have raided and looted as you pleased, preventing our boats from passing through the forest. You have stolen our cattle, metals and our women. And we have not forgotten what you did to Ardra the Bear. Do you deny this?"

Narantaka did not reply, and Pururava realised that the man's defeat was more psychological than physical. The burly, big Rakshasa had lost to a young Solar boy. His ego would take some time to repair from that. "I'll take your silence as acceptance, Narantaka," Ikshvaku continued. "So we can agree that both our sides are hurting, exactly the scenario that calls for a truce." As long as there was a possibility that Narantaka knew something about the seal of Surya, Ikshvaku could not kill him. He would keep Narantaka in Avisari, working on him slowly to see if he could glean clues. But till then, he could also enlist the Rakshasa's aid in making peace between their people.

"Don't make truce with this creature, Ikshvaku!" a voice shouted from the gathering. "Kill him and be done with it!"

Ikshvaku's eyes found the source in a flash and glared at the offender. The man quailed under his King's gaze. "I see only a man standing before me," Ikshvaku said in a deeper baritone than his usual. "A man as proud and stubborn as a Suryavanshi, it seems."

Narantaka stared at Ikshvaku, suspicious of the unexpected compliment. For the first time since he was brought in he stared around the hall, gathering its architecture and the people that stood in it. His eyes lingered at Haryashva before moving to Vasishtha, where they lingered longer still. "A glorious capital, Ashvak guards, and a Maharshi guru," he said finally. "You surround yourself well, boy King." This time there was no malevolent inflection when he pronounced the title.

"I must," Ikshvaku replied. "For I am charged with protecting my people."

"As was I," Narantaka said proudly. "But as my presence here indicates, I have failed in that responsibility. You ask me to meet you as a leader, but I am a leader no more. Already, another of what's left of my people would have assumed that title. If I return to them now, they will kill me themselves." He did not add that they would have already done so with his family.

"Then stay here," Ikshvaku said. "And give your strength to the Suryavanshi. There is much we can learn from you."

The Rakshasa's eyes widened, and to everyone's surprise he laughed—a hoarse, broken laugh that was cut short as Haryashva stubbed him with the back of his sword. He coughed and spat out blood that fell deep red on the painted white floor. "And what exactly is it," he said between coughs, "That I can teach you, King? Why would I do so when you will only use it against my own people?"

"Bringing us back to my first proposal," Ikshvaku replied, ready with his response. "Let us have a truce between us. Your people may not allow you to join them again, disgraced as you are. But surely you can act as an intermediary, and there may yet be peace."

Narantaka did not reply, but Pururava saw from the look in his eyes that Ikshvaku had won. There was no choice for the Rakshasa, Ikshvaku would not let him out of Avisari on any other terms. Pururava marvelled at his uncle's acumen. Despite all impulse, he did not kill the Rakshasa, instead, making an unwilling ally out of him. It was the true stratagem of a King, not the brash reaction of a boy seeking vengeance. Pururava promised himself that this was a lesson he would not forget. Later that night over dinner, Ikshvaku explained his actions.

"As the horrible Deva-Asura wars have taught us," he said, "War only breeds further war. Each time Indra slew Vritra, another took that name. Each time Surya fell, another rose to claim that title. And the wars went on. I do not wish to start a cycle of war between Rakshasa and Suryavansha that may one day take the lives of my descendants. I forgive Narantaka and the Rakshasas, even if I will not forget what they did to General Ardra. Let us put the shadow of Kamyakvana behind us and move on. We have decimated their population, leaving them a dying tribe of humanity. Let us not kick the enemy when he is already down."

But the King only revealed half the truth. He told no one of his real motive in keeping Narantaka alive. Finding the seal of Surya was important enough that avenging Ardra's death could wait. And Ikshvaku would lose his power over Narantaka if the Rakshasa knew what he needed. It was not the first time Ikshvaku felt alone as a King, trusting not even Haryashva or Drishta. He did not reveal Nivritti's true identity either. No one could spot a connection when a few days later Ikshvaku took on a second wife, an infant already in her arms. The boy was born of their love before marriage—that was the King's claim. Sarmi accepted it with grace, for polygamy was the way for the house of Marici and his descendants. In the years to come, only Haryashva and Maharshi Vasishtha would notice Ikshvaku's diligence in ensuring that his second wife and Narantaka never came face-to-face.

On the Lunar Side

"For a while there was peace in Ikshvaku's life, the kingdom was secure and the Rakshasas dismantled. Concentrated more on training his nephew Pururava, Ikshvaku failed to pay attention to his brothers—the others sons of Vaivasvat Manu. This would have grave consequences."

King Bhagiratha to Sudasa

Year 41, Seventh Era

King Ikshvaku surveyed his nephew proudly. Pururava had joined him as a promising boy of thirteen, born in the Lunar family of Maharshi Atri. But he was a man of eighteen now, taller and bigger than the son Ila had sent him. And he was every bone and sinew a Suryavanshi warrior, imbibed with all the skills of combat that were possessed by Ikshvaku, Drishta, Haryashva and Varman combined. Only two things could mark them out for the relatives they were. Their noses were the same, descended to both from Vaivasvat Manu. And the look in their eyes, the way they observed the world, gave them a brotherly aura that was hard to miss. The trait was picked up by Pururava in his five years, developed involuntarily through keen observation of his uncle at work. But in that similarity also lay the reason they would forever be of different lines. Ikshvaku's eyes were the burnt hazel of Solar blood, while Pururava inherited the clouded moon-grey of his Lunar inheritance.

"Plaksha calls to you now," King Ikshvaku said to his nephew. "I can almost imagine my sister waiting at the river-dock for your arrival. I do not begrudge your departure, dear nephew, but I shall certainly miss your company."

"As I will yours, uncle," Pururava responded. "We are connected to each other by blood, but I feel a deeper bond with you. You are not just my mother's brother, you are my friend and mentor."

"Are you leaving, Pururava?" asked Vikukshi, Ikshvaku's six-year-old elder son. Vikukshi was accustomed to Pururava's presence, infinitely more preferable to him than the Nripalaya's otherwise grim and austere aura. Who would give him horse rides on his back now? Who would sneak him more sugarcane once his mother declared that he had eaten enough? Most importantly, in a world where everyone seemed to favour his younger brother Nimi, who would take his side once Pururava was gone?

Pururava smiled at the worried look on Vikukshi's face. "Yes, but I will be back," he promised. "And you can visit me too, can you not?"

Vikukshi's eyes lit up. "Yes! But I will not bring Nimi with me."

The King chuckled. "You can go alone if you like. Will you travel through Kamyakvana and cross the rivers alone? Can you find Plaksha?"

Vikukshi gave it a moment's thought before replying confidently, "Yes."

"I've shown him the map a few times," Pururava explained.

The King raised his eyebrows in understanding. "And what is your plan, Pururava? Ila has sent reports of Gandharva raids on Plaksha. I can always send men with you, you know that."

"I do, uncle. But as I have often said, I would rather that you keep your attention firmly on Narantaka. His presence among us is sinisterly, and I know that he would betray you in a heartbeat."

"He very well might," Ikshvaku admitted. "Which is why I offer him no opportunity for betrayal. But I *need* him, Pururava. Rakshasa inhabitation of Kamyakvana may have been overthrown, but hundreds of Rakshasas are still alive. Many are part of small raider bands that have turned nomadic. Even more have crossed west of the Sindhu, from where they may return stronger one day. Narantaka is my only link to the Rakshasa mind. And I counsel you this, if there is a growing Gandharva threat then you must resolve it before it becomes what the Rakshasas are to us." It was a well-rehearsed explanation, one that Ikshvaku often gave in lieu of the real one—that Narantaka might be his route to the seal of Surya. Ikshvaku still had only Nivritti's word on this though, for nothing in Narantaka's revelations had hinted anything. The attempts to use Narantaka as an intermediary to broker peace had proved futile as well. The Rakshasa clans were in disarray, with no clear leadership discernible among them to negotiate with. And once word spread among them that Narantaka joined the Suryavanshi, he was useless as a mediator. Rakshasa hostility towards the Solar tribes was all the more pronounced, merging with their hatred for their traitorous ex-leader.

"Are peace and negotiation even an option with these tribes?" mused Pururava, breaking into Ikshvaku's thoughts.

"Let our experience of Kamyakvana not change our ways forever," said Ikshvaku. "There is no reason to assume that Gandharvas are as vicious or bellicose as Rakshasas. If there is a way to coexist with them in peace, then that is the way we must follow. This is what Marici once declared as well."

"Gandharvas are descended from Asuras as much as Rakshasas," Pururava countered. "I do not think they are much different, uncle. There is a reason we call these tribes Anarya."

Ikshvaku smiled, giving his nephew a piercing look. He wondered how Marici would counter that argument, and remembered a fable Vaivasvat once narrated. "Do you know the tale of Sarama and the Panis?" he asked.

Pururava nodded. "Then narrate it now," Ikshvaku said. "I think Vikukshi will enjoy the story."

"Sarama was a dog in service of Indra Deva, in an era long before ours," Pururava began. "Gifted to Indra by the ancient Maharshis, she was also his messenger, sending his word to friends and foes alike. Once, Indra sent Sarama to the Panis, a wealthy Asura tribe who lived across the Rasa river."

"Where is the Rasa river?" asked Vikukshi.

"We do not know," confessed Pururava. "Aryavarta was a different land back then, hundreds of years ago. Who can say where was forest and where river? But Sarama was familiar with the terrain, so she went to the Panis on Indra's bidding. They welcomed her, but mocked Indra, offering to make him herdsman of their cattle. She warned them that Indra could ravage their territories if he so willed. If they wished to be safe from such fury, they had to surrender their cattle to Indra."

Pururava paused, only to savour the keen expression on Vikukshi's face. Then he continued. "But the Panis confessed themselves to be ready for battle. Let Indra come, they said to Sarama. And yet she warned them. She admired their courage and bravado, but it would come to naught before Indra's might. But the Panis persisted, and warned her in turn that the path to their cattle was well guarded-hidden even. She insisted that nothing could stand hidden from Indra. Their fear of Indra aggravated at her admonitions, and they attempted to bribe her. *Stay with us, they said. Take some of our cattle even. Why would you run to and fro at Indra's bidding*? But her loyalty was unwavering, and despite the temptations they placed before her, she returned to Indra with their message—that they would not surrender the cattle."

"What happened then?" asked Vikukshi, afraid that the story was over before a satisfactory conclusion.

"Indra, Soma, Agni and several other Devas invaded the Panis' lands. They proved Sarama's warnings true, and the Panis lost both the cattle and their lives," said Pururava.

"And what does this tale suggest to us?" Ikshvaku asked. "Going by their actions, who was Arya and who Anarya?"

Pururava found no reply to that, never having looked at the tale of Sarama and the Panis in this manner. "Marici once sent a messenger to the Rakshasas," Ikshvaku continued. "Who narrated the same tale in a gesture of peace and reconciliation. But the man never returned, and Rakshasa hostilities never ceased."

"And I must send a messenger to the Gandharvas?"

"Why not? But not because we take this tale literally. That was Marici's one mistake. He took our prayers and fables as literal, accurate representations of history. But we cannot look into the minds of the seers of that age, and I suspect that Sarama and the Panis were never real."

"What does that mean, father?" Vikukshi asked, excited that there was a twist in the story.

"Sarama, Indra, Panis and the cattle are only metaphors, son," Ikshvaku explained, though his gaze was locked with his nephew's. "For their tale is that of day and night, and their eternal battle."

"I do not see the allegory," Pururava said, frowning.

"In this fable, Sarama is Dawn and Indra is the Sun," Ikshvaku said, smiling as he did so. Pururava could not tell whether he was being serious or making a tale for Vikukshi's benefit. "The cattle are the sun's rays, and at the beginning of the tale they are in the Night's possession. Thus the Panis are Night. To bring daylight, the Sun sends Dawn to get his rays back from the Night. This is a physical and natural phenomenon that took the shape of Indra, Sarama and the Panis. And the moral is this—nothing is what it seems. There are often hidden layers of truth, and the more we dig the more we perceive. In Kamyakvana I realised that Rakshasas had families as well. They reared children with the same love and affection that we do, and in the end were fighting only for their homes and the right to live. You must similarly assess the Gandharvas' true motivations, even if that finally leads you to conclude that they are enemies indeed."

Pururava nodded, appreciating the wisdom in Ikshvaku's sermon. Vikukshi followed every word, listening to his father with fervent ears. He knew that he could be King one day, but he had to be better than Nimi for that. Unless father decided to give it all to his elder son, which could happen, as mother once explained. Then the young boy had a sudden moment of insight far too deep for his age. "Will you also be a King, Pururava?" he asked. As if Nimi was not enough, would Pururava also be a rival to him?

Pururava looked to Ikshvaku, and a look passed between them that Vikukshi did not understand. "Yes," Pururava replied, still looking at Ikshvaku. "But not for a while. I must prove myself worthy of that title first, just as your father did many years ago."

Varman would accompany Pururava till Prasthala, from where traders could give him a ride on one of their carts. He knew the city's name to be a clever wordplay. *Prastha* was the word for stable or firm in Solar dialect, while *Sthala* meant a mound of raised earth. Prasthala was thus the Suryavanshi way of saying *Firm Place*, and they were sincere about it, too. The city had all the markings of a military outpost, large walls and soaring turrets dotting its skyline. This was once Varman's hometown, before he fell into the company of Vaivasvat Manu. Nowhere else in the Suryavanshi kingdom did he command so much respect and authority. They were led through some of the city's less crowded lanes, and a few alleys Pururava was sure only Varman's men knew about, to reach its southern gates. Here Varman bade him farewell.

"The next time we meet, you will be a King," said the bulky veteran.

"To you I will always be a shishya," Pururava replied. "I would not be the warrior I am without you."

Varman gave Pururava a terse nod and pointed him towards the awaiting cart. Pururava bent down and touched his mentor's feet.

The traders kept to themselves during the journey, seemingly disinclined to taking too many breaks. This suited Pururava just fine. He was no stranger to the route, having travelled it a number of times before. The Shatadru river cut roughly midway between Prasthala and Plaksha, and near the crossing it scattered into several rivulets before regrouping and flowing along its route to meet the Sindhu at Vitabhya. This made for a relatively easy crossing point. The rivulets flowed through dozens of islands and around small patches of land, over which both man and beast could cross to the other side. Soon after that the Sarasvati would come into view, and on the other bank lay Plaksha. Situated at the base of the Himalayan foothills, Plaksha was surrounded by clumps of fig trees on two sides. The fig tree was called *plaksha* in the Lunar dialect.

It was home to the small but venerated Atri school of rshis, still under the tutelage of its founder, Maharshi Atri. As Pururava approached his place of birth from across the Sarasvati, it looked as peaceful as it once was in his childhood. But trouble was afoot now, and Gandharva raids were slowly beginning to take their toll on the inhabitants of Plaksha.

Plaksha

"Plaksha was founded by Tapin Soma, and in the final Deva-Asura wars it was his base of operations. Through several generations it descended to Atri Somi, who you know as one of Aryavarta's first Maharshis. It is the oldest known town in Aryavarta, the first to be established along the Sarasvati."

King Bhagiratha to Sudasa

"Gandharvas prefer not to be violent, if they can," said Ila. "They come in the night, stealing cattle in perfect stealth. We've kept men on guard, but the Gandharvas are able to sneak up from behind and press a peculiar herb to their noses. It causes unconsciousness within seconds and lasts for a few minutes." Like Yakshas and Rakshasas, Gandharvas were descendants of the Asuras. Their rituals and culture was far removed from the Arya way, and the new era had cast them into conflict with the Lunar tribes over land and cattle.

"And when there is violence?" Pururava prompted.

"Then they fight vicious and brave," said Devapi, Ila's trusted lieutenant in Plaksha. Born to one of Maharshi Atri's daughters, he was cousin to Pururava. "But their weapons are primitive, made of only wood and stone. Of metal they know nothing. Their threat to us is marked by their strange control over mountain wolves. The wolves guard them at all times and seem to understand their calls. Some of the bigger ones even tolerate Gandharvas riding them. And the men here are no warriors. We are farmers, potters, fishermen and seers. We are not adept at defending ourselves against them."

"Have we been able to capture one of them? Have we tried to broker peace?"

Both Devapi and Ila shook their heads in the negative.

"Ikshvaku has been kind enough to send 500 horses with me," Pururava said. "Bred from the finest mares of Kapisa, these beasts fear neither wolf nor leopard. Next time the Gandharvas come raiding, I want to capture one of them." The discussions with Ikshvaku were still fresh in his mind, and he wanted to talk to the Gandharvas before taking any drastic steps.

Ila nodded. "There is another matter to discuss, my son. Reports filter through from Yamuna and Ganga of human settlements among the marshlands and forests. If it is possible to establish towns and villages along these rivers, then we may consider the option of migrating."

"Especially since these lands have caught the attention of Gandharvas," Devapi added.

"And what will stop them from following us along the Yamuna and Ganga, once they have Plaksha?" Pururava challenged. "No, we must deal with the Gandharvas one way or the other before we think of moving our homes."

"Unless we decide to do both at the same time," said Ila. "I can lead an initial band of explorers downstream while you take over control of Plaksha, my son. You are a trained Suryavanshi warrior, born in the line of Atri the Lunar. The Somavanshi kingdom is but awaiting your claim."

"There is no claim, mother. I do not wish to take the title of King before I have proved myself worthy of it."

"But Ikshvaku was crowned at fifteen!" Ila countered.

"I am allowed to be different," Pururava said decisively. "Uncle Ikshvaku became King, and *then* thoroughly justified that title. I wish to earn it unambiguously *before* I take the throne."

Ila sighed. Her son resembled her brother in his resoluteness. She could see from his eyes that nothing she said would change his mind. Her little boy had returned a man, and the last of her maternal authority over him would soon fade away.

But then Pururava folded his palms in a namaskara. "And so we will do exactly as you suggest, mother. I will stay in Plaksha and form an army that can counter the Gandharva threat. You will lead a group of volunteers down the Yamuna, to find lands where we can establish towns. And when we are successful in both endeavours, then I will fulfil your desire to see a Somavanshi King."

"And will you tell her of your plan now, to visit Trigarta and Madra?" Devapi asked.

Plaksha, Trigarta and Madra—three cities that could together claim to be Aryavarta's most ancient. Once they were but sisters to each other, ruled by the sons of Tapin Soma. But the brothers' love did not survive to their descendants, and in time the sister cities were wrenched apart. They grew insular, three islands of civilization along a river that was otherwise unfamiliar to human settlement—the Sarasvati. And in such fashion they survived when the Solar tribes of Marici found their way into Aryavarta. Kashyapa was the first Suryavanshi to visit all three cities. Through him, knowledge of them passed to the Suryavansha, and through Ikshvaku it came to Pururava. Pururava never heard the tale in Plaksha of course, for no city ever spoke the name of the other two. Such was their bitter separation.

"I would not entertain such a desire," commented Ila sternly. "Trigarta and Madra are dark cities, coated with the grime of metal and ore that we know naught of. No man of Plaksha has visited either in centuries."

"Yet they are but a few days' travel downstream," Pururava said. "Other men have visited them and returned to tell the tale. Ikshvaku is one such man."

"And do they not confirm the worst? Are Trigarta and Madra not inhabited by Asuras surviving into the Seventh era?" Devapi asked.

"Not in the least. The people of these cities are but our kinsmen, fellow Somavanshi if you can call it that. They are descendants of Soma much like we are."

"Impossible! They would have visited Plaksha with grain and cattle were that the case."

"And is it not possible that they too harbour the same delusions about us as we do of them?" Pururava challenged.

Devapi opened his mouth to speak, but found no reply. Ila asked hesitantly, "What does Ikshvaku say of Trigarta and Madra?" But she knew her brother well, and knew that Ikshvaku's opinion would only be from the objective analysis of things that he learnt from their father.

"He calls them cities of endless toil. He confirms that they are devoted to the arts of metal, of bronze, copper and others we have yet to encounter. The Suryavanshi trade with them freely, stocking much of their weaponry through selling grain and cattle to them."

"You will have to convince the Maharshi," said Ila, speaking of her father-in-law. Maharshi Atri was as hostile to Trigarta and Madra as any citizen of Plaksha.

"So I will," said Pururava resolutely.

To the denizens of Plaksha, Maharshi Atri was the only Maharshi of any consequence. They knew little of Kashyapa, and lesser still of Vasishtha, both of who were born of Solar blood. But Atri was one of them, born in the house of Soma himself and thus heir to Plaksha's ancient, ruling family. Lunar genes were not inclined to breeding the warriors and monarchs that Solar genes were. Atri's was a spiritual clan, devoted to the matters of mind and consciousness. But they were administrators as well, and despite their inclinations the tribe looked to them for leadership. That leadership was adopted by Atri's elder son, and then by the son's widowed wife. Now their own son was of age, only recently returned from an arduous military training among Solar warriors. He could be King if he wanted. Instead, he wanted to visit the dark cities of a Lunar past.

"It is not in my nature to tell people what to do," said Atri. At eighty one, he looked old and weary. Yet his eyes were as alive as ever, and he spoke with a clear speech. He was well on the spiritual path when he encountered Kashyapa, decades ago. Together they searched for and took tutelage from the enigmatic ascetic Bhrigu, emerging from his teachings as the first Maharshis of Aryavarta. Kashyapa had only the one pupil—Vasishtha, who became a Maharshi himself. Atri founded a school, sharing his knowledge with all who were willing to learn. Even Pururava was once a student, but not anymore. "You have not been my ward for more than five years now," commented Atri. "Yet I will seek to dissuade you from visiting the dark cities. Not as your forefather, and not as a Maharshi. But only as an ageing fellow tribesman."

Pururava did not wish to argue against such a genuine entreaty. "I cannot bring myself to go against your wishes, grandfather. But I will try to change your mind nevertheless. Tell me of the dark cities. Tell me why it is unthinkable for a citizen of Plaksha to go to Trigarta and Madra."

Maharshi Atri was silent for a while before he began. "Plaksha, Trigarta and Madra were once one," he said. "There were no cities then, nor towns or villages. Civilisation was a vast, unbroken tapestry of humans interacting and co-operating with each other. All of them were semi-nomadic in the least, and for others nomadism was the only way of life. At last, the people came to be ruled by three great clan heads who were sons of Tapin Soma. Their's was the last great civilisation of the Sixth era, before the age grew old and Marici led the Suryavanshi back to Aryavarta. But much before him, came the darkness."

"The dark ages were over when the last Devas defeated the last Asuras," said Pururava, though he knew that Atri would proceed to prove him wrong, or ignorant.

"Yet light did not flash across the skies when Vritra was finally slain," said Atri dryly. "Darkness remains for a long time once it finds a place in the societies of men. It takes luminaries to shine the way again. They did not appear till the Solar tribes returned to Aryavarta with men such as Kashyapa, Vaivasvat and now, Ikshvaku. And during that darkness our forefathers saw depths that they never imagined. The descendants of Soma's last sons grew hungry for power. Battles were fought so devastating that little from that age has passed to us. But we know this-Soma's direct line found refuge here, in Plaksha. The rebels established their homes in Trigarta and Madra. You and I are sons of that line, Pururava. I say this from fact, not pride. It will be an insult to our forefathers if we step foot in enemy lands now."

"Yet if we go back far enough," countered Pururava. "Then we share a common ancestor with them. Is it not an insult to Tapin Soma if we never try to repair our bonds?"

The young boy made a valid point, and even a Maharshi could be humble enough to admit that. But Atri would not surrender so easily. "What of the Gandharva threat?" he asked. "Your clan-duty is to concentrate on thwarting their raids."

"For which I have taken adequate steps. In a day or two we will be visited by Haryashva, an Ashvak who is friend to uncle Ikshvaku and guru to me. He will train our men better than I ever could, and his knowledge of horse warfare is renowned in Suryavanshi lands. With Haryashva to protect Plaksha while I am gone, you have nothing to worry about."

"So you are determined in your decision to visit the dark cities?"

"Have I not convinced you of the wisdom in doing so, grandfather? Trigarta and Madra have metals that can forge us weapons. Their ploughs and axes will help us settle along the Yamuna and Ganga. And if we are to expand along the Sarasvati, then we need our boats to sail downstream without their interference. The past era, the Age of Devas, is over. This is the Age of Aryas, and all tribes of men must cast a new destiny for themselves."

The House of Marici

"I wear this seal around my neck today because of Ikshvaku's unparalleled resolve, his single-minded focus on finding it no matter what. And Narantaka was eventually proved indispensable in that quest."

King Bhagiratha to Sudasa

Year 44, Seventh era

Sakala. He was only a boy the last time he was here, young and aloof about the world around him. But the twelve years since then had carved Ikshvaku into a hard, grim ruler. A dense beard covered his dark face, and he looked older than his twenty-six years. Yet, as he stepped into Sakala and walked its narrow alleys, he felt like the young son of Vaivasvat Manu again. A ward in training, descendant to Surya, and son to Manu. He tried to remember himself back then, the young boy of his memories was certainly not him, naive and inexperienced as he was. When did he truly become the Ikshvaku he was now?

Vaivasvat Manu observed his son in silence, enjoying the gentle breeze that flew over the Shatadru and cooled Sakala every evening. Ikshvaku's hands were callused with numerous cuts, and even though he tried his best to hide it, his right ankle suffered a limp from an old injury. Manu suspected it was from his early battle against the Yakshas, and wondered whether it was the only lasting wound his son nursed. He looked as battle-hardened as a man twice his age, and in his eyes was the perennially dark look of a soldier scarred from the brutality of war. Manu took a deep breath and said, "Perhaps it should have been me."

Ikshvaku frowned. "I do not understand, father."

"I should have claimed kingship for myself," Manu said. "And once it was even offered to me, though I never told you this."

Ikshvaku looked back out to the river. "I suspected as much. When I think of you and Varman as young men, forming militias in towns and villages in response to Rakshasa raids, you were already doing the work of a King. It stands to reason that someone would have suggested you make it official."

"But I thought of Kashyapa's abdication," said Manu. "And realised that I could not reclaim what my forefather disowned. Our family walked away from what was both our right and our responsibility, and I had to live with my grandfather's decision. That was to be Marici's fate."

"You never shared these speculations with me," Ikshvaku said, but there was no accusation in his tone.

"It was a deliberate omission. A father must always play a delicate balancing act. On one hand he must be a good mentor, a reliable guide that the son can fall back on. On the other, he must take care not to carve the son in his own image. He must allow for the individual to take his own path, for every parent must learn to let go at some point. I often feel it is easier for mothers. Their love can be unconditional, blind even. Not for them are the doubts, frustrations and regrets of a father. But who am I to comment on such matters."

"A better father than most," Ikshvaku said.

Manu smiled, accepting his son's compliment. "I wonder how Marici would have felt, when Kashyapa declared his desire to abdicate rule."

"It would have broken him," Ikshvaku speculated. "Solar unity was achieved after decades of hard work, Marici gave it his entire life. To see a son so casually discard that would have been unbearable."

Manu patted his son amiably, trying to lift the mood. "Come now, don't look so glum. Let me interest you in a story on Marici, or have you grown too old for that?"

Ikshvaku smiled, and for a moment he looked like Manu's young son again. But then his expression darkened. "For Marici, I could never be too old. But I must tell you some things first."

Manu noted a look of extreme conflict on his son's face. "What is it, Kshauva?" he asked, using Ikshvaku's childhood name.

It pained Ikshvaku to hide the true reason why Narantaka and Nivritti were in Avisari. It pained him to hide it from Sarmi, Haryashva, Drishta and Varman. But hiding it from Manu hurt the most, and it had finally become unbearable. "Six years ago, when we captured Narantaka, I also captured his wife and son," began Ikshvaku, the words coming out rapidly now that the decision to speak the truth had taken hold of him. "But I was alone when I came upon them, and I was able to bring them to Avisari as Nivritti and Nimi."

Vaivasvat Manu's frowned at the revelation. "The Rakshasa's family as your own!" he exclaimed. "What madness would make you take such a decision?"

"The seal of Surya, father. I need to find it. It is not madness, finding it is the single greatest act I can commit as a Suryavanshi. When I captured her, Nivritti speculated that Narantaka might know of the seal's whereabouts, even if he may not know of its importance."

"And you believed her?"

"Not entirely, at least not initially. But over the years I've come to understand Narantaka and glean much from him. I daresay, father, that I now understand the Rakshasa mind even better than you do." That was not an idle boast to make, for Vaivasvat had spent his life intimating himself with Aryavarta, its people and its rivers.

"And what is it about them that I am missing?" asked Vaivasvat.

"Their motive," replied Ikshvaku. "Close to a century has passed since we first entered Aryavarta and encountered them, its *indigenous* tribes. But we are no closer to understanding the true reason for their hostility towards us. We may speculate, as we often do. But every guess has been proven wrong by their relentless belligerence."

"Until now," Manu prompted, eager to learn Ikshvaku's insights.

"Rakshasas are voracious collectors of metal and gold," Ikshvaku began. "But before Marici led our ancestors to Aryavarta, all they could acquire were the odd tools and trinkets from Trigarta or Madra. The Solar tribes arrived with weapons and artefacts more glorious than any Rakshasa had ever imagined. Sharp cuts, precise shapes and gold embossing attracted them to us—and that was the true reason for their unending raids. The Rakshasas took our cattle, wood and women too, but they were actually after the weapons and relics. It stands rooted in a much deeper, primal sentiment; envy. The Rakshasas envy us, and how could they not? We call ourselves noble and dress like it. To them, we appear haughty and self-righteous.

We look down upon them from our horses, and carry with us all the apparent prosperity of human life—cattle, metal, wood, tools, horses and weapons."

"Envy," Manu mused. "And how does this connect to the seal?"

Ikshvaku answered that with a question of his own. "How did Marici die, father?"

Manu frowned. "I don't know," he confessed. "I never thought of it. I simply assumed that he died of old age."

"That's partly true," said Ikshvaku. "But I speculate that Marici also died of a heart attack, bruised from the psychological trauma inflicted on him."

"Kashyapa's abdication?"

"No. The theft of the seal of Surya," said Ikshvaku. "After talking to Narantaka for many years now, warily circling around the relevant tales, this is the sequence of events I have woven—Marici died just a night after a Rakshasa raid had run through the village, did he not? In that raid, unknown to him then, the seal was stolen by a Rakshasa. Surely the Rakshasas had seen it on him before and coveted it. He discovered the theft later, when the raid was fended and order restored in the village. The shock caused a heart attack, and no doubt he was weak from grieving at Kashyapa's abdication. That's why the seal was never found at his funeral, and we were led to the mistaken belief that only a Suryavanshi could have stolen it."

Manu took a deep breath, thinking over Ikshvaku's plotting of events. He knew his son possessed an intelligent, shrewd mind. But could Narantaka's not be wilier? What tales might he be spinning to keep himself alive? "Where is the seal now?" he asked.

"If only I could ask Narantaka that directly," said Ikshvaku. "But he still does not suspect what I am after, and I wish to keep this status unchanged. But I know that at some point the seal came in his possession. He has hinted that he had it transported west of the Sindhu-in the keeping of a distant but trusted relative. I know it's the seal, father. His description of it matches yours."

"When do you march west?" asked Manu, realising that that was Ikshvaku's plan.

"The preparations have already begun," replied Ikshvaku. "I have sent scouts ahead to chart the region and report to us, before we take the entire army west of the Sindhu. At some point Narantaka will suspect my true motive, if he does not already. But till then we will march in the guise of an expansion campaign. The land west of the

Sindhu was home to our people, between the times of Aurvan and Havishmana. It is only natural that the Suryavanshi kingdom lays a claim to it."

Manu looked at his son with pride, his lips curving in a faint smile. "It is no longer possible to see you as a young boy," he said. "It is said that children are always children to their parents, but I now see that you have outgrown me as a man. In your determination, your devotion to your tribe and family—you possess a passion I cannot match. How large will be the shadow you cast on other men by the time you are the age I am now. But your shadow already looms over a few, and they are your own brothers. You have never even met them, my son, and yet they have heard so much about you. You are their eldest, and one who became King at the age of fourteen no less! Talk to them, share with them some of your innate wisdom. Do it before they deify you to the extent that they start envying you."

And so Ikshvaku met his brothers for the first time—the other Manavas, or sons of Manu. Pramshu, Sharyati, Nabhaga, Karusaka and Narisyanta. Ikshvaku did not know what to make of them, so wide was the age gap between them. Yet they resembled Vaivasvat Manu in parts, and thus him as well. Their meeting was short and awkward, either side looking to keep it curt and brief.

"Can we not accompany you to Avisari, brother?" asked Pramshu. "Pururava was trained there once."

Ikshvaku studied his brothers. The eldest three—Pramshu, Sharyati and Nabhaga, were ten years old. And though they were born of different mothers they spoke with one voice.

"Not yet," Ikshvaku replied. "Pururava joined us when he was thirteen." He did not know what more to say. There was no connection between them, only a vague awareness that they were born to the same father.

"Pururava is a Lunar," said Nabhaga, and Ikshvaku perceived wisdom in his young eyes. "But we are Solar, and Manava even. Did your own training not begin at the age of seven?"

Ikshvaku was in no mood to argue with boys. But the look on Nabhaga's face told him that he had to give a satisfactory response. "Training Pururava was a debt I owed to my sister, to *our* sister. I would not be a King were it not for Ila. But you must bide your time. You are young, half the cares of this world unknown to you. Enjoy that state as long as you can. It is a pleasure I missed out on," Ikshvaku said sincerely.

Pramshu was ready with a response. "Vikukshi is nine. Will you keep him away from the sword as well, next year?"

At that, Ikshvaku was unable to hold back a smile. Pramshu's confidence gave him a glimpse of something he was forgetting more and more—his own childhood. "There is no law stating who is to ascend the throne after me," he said, looking to them all. "And maybe one day our lands are so vast that there can be more than one. All I ask is for you to have some patience. Allow your elder brother to pave the way a little more for you."

But he knew that there was little truth in his words. The Solar tribes needed a singular ruler. He had scarcely given thought to the idea of his succession, even though Drishta and Vasishtha were ever persistent with the proposal of primogeniture. But Ikshvaku was sure that the capability of rule could not be decided by something so incidental as being born the eldest. This brought with it the awareness that his brothers could contest his right to be King on the same grounds. But for now, they fell silent after his request for their patience, bidding him farewell like well behaved younger brothers ought to. But for how long?

Enemies Within

"In the course of his life, Ikshvaku made many enemies. But not all of them were other men. Some were internal, rooted in his heart and troubling his convictions. Maharshi Vasishtha's famous Lament of Existence was one such enemy."

King Bhagiratha to Sudasa

Year 45, Seventh era

"When did Creation begin, who can know?" chanted Maharshi Vasishtha, his enunciation perfect. "For even the Gods came afterwards, did they not? Perhaps Creation came from itself, and perhaps not. The Mighty One above, perhaps he knows? But perhaps even he does not!" This was the seer's newest composition, its phonetics and metres lending themselves to a sonorous intricacy only he could have designed.

Ikshvaku speculated on the words, perceiving an agnostic tone to them that was quite unlike the Maharshi. "What is this prayer called, Maharshi?"

"Nasadiya Sukta—the Lament of Existence," Vasishtha replied, his voice sombre and deep. "The prayer expresses my grief, my lament at never being able to know the true nature of our lives."

It was a rare for the Maharshi to confess limitation in his knowledge, and rarer still for him to be melancholic. "Our lives are governed by the Cosmic Order," Ikshvaku said, repeating something Manu had taught him. "It defines the nature of life and death, of being and not being. Adherence to the Cosmic Order is the true nature of our lives."

"Yes, but what is this Cosmic Order?" Vasishtha said, not expecting his young King to respond. "Where does it come from? Who or what instituted it?"

"God, The Primeval Being," Ikshvaku said. "The First and Foremost. He who breathed life into this universe and set it in order."

Vasishtha smiled, eyeing Ikshvaku shrewdly. "You are wise enough to spot the essential fallacy in that logic, dear boy," he said. "What breathed life into the Primeval Being? And what caused that life-breathing force to exist in the first place? The upwards spiral of causality in this scenario can never end."

"But even if everything has its own cause, why does the chains of causes exist in the first place?" Ikshvaku countered. "The Primeval Being is the First Cause, the one who started it all. However high on the spiral He may be."

"And yet we do not know exactly how high that is," Vasishtha stated, looking to settle the debate for now. "The one we know as the Primeval Being, is he really the axiomatic First Cause? Or is he but another stage in the hierarchy-the highest that we can perceive? And this is the Lament of Existence, King Ikshvaku. We can never really know, no matter how hard we try. Perhaps the ones we call Gods know, perhaps the Primeval Being knows, or perhaps even he does not. For all the order, joy and sorrow in our lives, we know but nothing about its meaning or purpose."

Ikshvaku fell silent, contemplating the Maharshi's lament. He did not agree with it, uncomfortable with its dismissive and fatalistic tone. It threw into question everything he had dedicated his life to, for if nothing could ever be learnt or gained then what did duty mean? What did loyalty to the tribe mean? What did it mean for him to become a King but be ignorant of the reason for existence itself? Yet he knew that Vasishtha would not respond to such queries, at least not until Ikshvaku had meditated on the prayer itself for long enough. Years of experience had taught him that when Vasishtha composed a new prayer it was certain to be of great import. "I suggest we transmit this prayer to other schools," Ikshvaku said. "Maharshi Atri must be informed immediately. As soon as you can assign rshis to transmit the prayer, I will send them forth with riders."

"I will begin teaching them immediately," Vasishtha said. "But it will take time. The complete prayer is long and complex, and only memorising its meters will not suffice."

"I have no desire to hasten you, Maharshi. And we certainly have other pressing matters to attend to. Haryashva has returned from his visit to Vitabhya. I would like your presence and counsel."

"You always have it, my King," Vasishtha said.

The King and his Chief Minister, for that was Haryashva's official title now, met like the old friends they were, in an affectionate and tight embrace. When they withdrew, Haryashva said without preamble, "Vitabhya's loyalty belongs to Prince Pramshu. The boy's maternal uncles have been fostering resentment against you, reminding the people that the blood of Manu flows in him as well. I talked to people on the streets who spoke of Pramshu as the king-in-waiting."

"Vitabhya is not happy that its Suryavanshi princes are being ignored," Vasishtha observed. "And Avisari is too far away for the people's loyalty to remain unwavering to a distant King."

Ikshvaku smiled without humour. "Spent more than a decade ridding our people of the Rakshasa threat, and this is what we get in return."

"The situation is not so dire," Vasishtha said. "The sentiment at Vitabhya has not spread anywhere else yet."

"And how do we deal with it, Maharshi?"

"Bring your brothers here to train, the way you trained Pururava. And provide them with their own colonies, once they are of age."

Ikshvaku nodded. "Send for Narantaka," he said to the Chief Minister.

Haryashva eyed his King warily. "What are you planning, Ikshvaku?"

"Only something that I've delayed far too long. It is time to begin the next theatre of battle, my Chief Minister. We shall take our armies west of the Sindhu." He did not share the real motive, of course—finding the seal of Surya. That was a secret he shared only with his father.

"Is such a campaign necessary?" the Maharshi asked. "There are enough lands between Sindhu and Ganga, and we need not look westward."

"I will not encroach upon lands that belong to the Lunar tribes," Ikshvaku said. "East of the Sarasvati belongs to them, and if my brothers are to receive colonies then we must look to the west."

"We know little of that land," Haryashva said, thinking aloud. "And lesser still of its people and their ways."

"That is where Narantaka becomes critical," Ikshvaku said. "Do you remember how many Rakshasas we banished from Kamyakvana, commanding them to cross west of the Sindhu? Whatever obstacles we face there, they will form a strong part of it. Narantaka is my only window into their alien world."

The spy crept through the darkness, his silhouette visible in the fog before he stepped into the light. His features were unmistakably northern-flat nose, sharp eyes and wide jaws. He faced the Solar princes boldly, no customary respect in his eyes. Prince Pramshu looked at him and asked, "What is your name, spy?"

The spy's lips curved in amusement. His master had warned him that the princes were just boys. The eldest one could not be more than twelve! "A spy has no name, young prince," he whispered. "And even if I had one, it is not important."

"What is your master's name then?" Nabhaga asked shrewdly. "For months he has been communicating with us through you. But before we join him in this rebellion, we must know his identity."

The spy's eyes narrowed. This one was clever, getting straight to the point. "Look at me, young prince," he said. "Do I look like a man who would reveal his master's name? A spy such as that would very soon be out of a job, and possibly his life as well."

Nabhaga waved the spy's comment aside. "What does your master propose?"

"He will aid you in taking control of Avisari, provided you are able to rally the warriors of Vitabhya and Harayupa against Ikshvaku. Hundreds of men in his service will add their strength to yours, outside the walls of Avisari."

"Vitabhya will not be a problem," Pramshu commented before Nabhaga could reply. "But Harayupa will be difficult. Ikshvaku's hold over that city is strong."

"My master is aware of this, which is why he is in no hurry. Besides, you are only boys. The rebellion must await your growth to adulthood."

"Which also gives your master more time to gain Ikshvaku's trust, to enter deeper into his circle of counsel," Nabhaga suggested, trying to pry information from the spy.

The spy raised his face proudly. "I cannot presume to know my master's mind. But his actions are no different from yours."

Prince Pramshu took a few menacing steps forward, hand going to his short-sword. "Watch your words, spy," he warned.

The spy appraised him with one eyebrow raised. "Careful, young prince. There are no instructions preventing me from harming you, and do not think I will hesitate before slaying children. You are all traitors now, your crime no less than that of my master. You cannot back out of this, for you do not know what he may reveal to the King. Prepare yourselves for this rebellion, stoke bitterness towards your elder brother. And when my master is ready, he will send for you."

"We come at no one's bidding!" Pramshu roared. Nabhaga put an arm on his shoulder and said, "The attack on Avisari will be at the time of our choosing."

The spy shrugged and nodded. "I will deliver your message, but I do not think my master will like it." He retreated into the fog, quickly vanishing in the haze.

Sharyati had remained silent so far, letting his brothers take the lead. Now he spoke, his voice far too deep for a twelve-year old. "We have condemned ourselves, my brothers."

The Hunt Begins

"Primogeniture, the right of the firstborn son to be ruler after his father. History often blames Ikshvaku for refusing to make it law, but would his brothers' have acted any different then? Would they have accepted his elder son as King simply because of a law?"

King Bhagiratha to Sudasa

"True blood lust is not known to you and your men, King," Narantaka declared. "A man is either born with it or he is not, but none can be trained to develop it."

"What is blood lust to you then?" asked Ikshvaku. He respected the Rakshasa way of war—brutal, fearless and untiring. The campaigns in Kamyakvana had given him enough exposure to it, and now he wanted to take the best from it and bring it to his own men. This was the latest of many discussions with Narantaka over war and combat. Every discussion was a way for Ikshvaku to learn more of the seal's whereabouts. Yet the tense cord of suspicion and wariness was forever strung between them. And then there was guilt within him as well. Narantaka's wife and son lived under the same roof, in reality only a few chambers away from him. Why did Ikshvaku not unite the family? Would it not earn him Narantaka's eternal goodwill? Perhaps the Rakshasa would willingly share the seal's location then? But as things stood right now, if anything happened to Vikukshi then Nimi would be King after Ikshvaku. Did he really want that—the son of Narantaka on the Suryavanshi throne? Nimi did not know of his true origins, and his mother had mercifully kept the truth from him. But if Narantaka ever learnt the truth…

"Capture a man and bind him, tie him to a post so he is at your complete mercy," Narantaka continued, cutting into Ikshvaku's musings. "Now torture him, claw and tear him till his very skin is ripped off. How would this man react? Most break at the treatment, begging for mercy, freedom or even death. But every once in a while there comes a man who stays doggedly determined. He may even laugh through it, unbelievable to those of us who can imagine his pain. You see, this man has already seen death. He knows what lies beyond and sees no fear in it. He has seen enough darkness in his past, that the pain you inflict on him pales in comparison. What if you now set this man free with a weapon in his hand, and unleash him on his captors? Then you will see what blood lust really is. It is a state of intoxication, where you are not really human anymore but a vicious beast that has caught the scent of blood and knows nothing else. It is borne from our primitive and hidden past, from the times when we were still animal and not yet fully human."

Ikshvaku nodded in thought, taking a deep breath as he recalled some of the fiercest warriors he fought in Kamyakvana. There was no doubt that several of them were the sort of men Narantaka described. But he felt a note of pride too—he had faced each of those Rakshasas and come out alive, even as a boy.

Narantaka sensed his thoughts. "Yet blood lust is not an assurance of invulnerability," he said. "It is a tool that is wielded well by some and not so well by others. It breeds both lions and hyenas, after all."

Animals that the Suryavanshi were not familiar with—Ikshvaku had heard Narantaka speak of them before, and despite the descriptions he could form no image of them in his mind. Their habitats began far south of Vitabhya, ranging west of the Sindhu into unchartered lands. But soon he would finally lay his eyes upon a lion on the hunt, and Narantaka was crucial to these plans.

"We are marching west of the Sindhu," Ikshvaku announced suddenly. "The time has come for me to expand my kingdom. What do your people call that land?"

"Harivarsha," said Narantaka, not reacting to Ikshvaku's declaration. "A name that survives to us from the Fourth era. Our traditions remember it as a place where the Devas Trishika Indra and Virasa Surya massacred thousands of Asuras."

Ikshvaku shifted uncomfortably. The Fourth era was a dark period in the Age of Devas, replete with stories of atrocities committed by the

Devas against innocent and unarmed Asuras. Deva traditions, and consequently those descended to the Aryas, carried only a passing mention of that era. The Solar tribes learnt its details from Maharshi Kashyapa, who learnt it from his mentor, Bhrigu. "I have no intention of committing those crimes," said Ikshvaku. "As implausible as it sounds, my expansion will not be of conquest." He left it at that, knowing that Narantaka would not be convinced. But nevertheless, it was true, Ikshvaku's sole motive was the seal of Surya.

Prince Pramshu's body gleamed in the sunlight, basking in the glory of Surya, his patron deity. The Suryavanshi army would march across the Sindhu from Vitabhya, 12,000 men following Ikshvaku's whim. Pramshu did not really know his brother well, and he did think it was unfortunate. Ikshvaku had always kept his brothers at an arm's length, separated by the Sindhu's entire span between Avisari and Vitabhya. In his twelve years Pramshu had met him only once, and the encounter had been brief and cold. Ikshvaku belonged to the north, and thus his control ended there. This was a view shared by a large part of Vitabhya's populace. Some of them stood behind Prince Pramshu now, observing Ikshvaku's contingents cross the river on their boats. Hundreds of horses, thousands of men, countless swords and shields. How many of them would return? And whatever pitiful force did make it back, Ikshvaku would not be among them—this was part of the deal Pramshu and his brothers had made with the unknown traitor of Ikshvaku's party.

"We must prepare, my Prince," said Anuvesha, uncle to Pramshu on his mother's side and secretly the chief instigator to Ikshvaku's brothers. "The men are ready, we only await Ikshvaku's complete departure."

"*King* Ikshvaku," Nabhaga corrected.

"King Ikshvaku," Anuvesha agreed. "It will take till nightfall for the entire army to cross. His advance party would have made camp some distance away. We must begin by then, as timing is of the essence."

Pramshu nodded, his gaze turning to Sharyati. He was the party's reluctant member, an unwilling participant in the rebellion against Ikshvaku. "Are you with us, brother?" Pramshu asked.

"I am," Sharyati said curtly. He kept his opposition to himself. In public, it was not well to show a rift between the brothers.

"Then let us begin," Pramshu said, his teeth clenched with determination. "Tell the men to begin their march to Avisari. As Ikshvaku loses his life in the west, we shall take his capital."

Harivarsha

"Narantaka never did suspect Ikshvaku's true motives. The seal of Surya was hidden somewhere in Harivarsha only because he saw it as a valuable trinket. But if he knew what it was, what it represented, surely he would have had it destroyed."

King Bhagiratha to Sudasa

"The men say that Haryashva can best you," shouted the soldier, the others cheering him on. "But I refuse to believe that, my King!"

Ikshvaku laughed in mock exaggeration, sweat and dust coating his muscular, tanned body. "And I thank you for that, Bahuka!" he said. He knew the name of every commander in his army, each man among the hundreds. "It is a rumour, spread no doubt by Haryashva himself!"

The soldiers cheered and roared, chanting the name of their King. It was a weekly practice—the King wrestling volunteers in unarmed combat. The reward was that a victor could get Ikshvaku's throne, though none ever came close to claiming it. Ikshvaku egged his men on, raising his arms and gesturing for them to bring Haryashva out. Three men had come forward today, each a spirited combatant. But Ikshvaku was only getting warmed up, and it would be fun to match his strength with Haryashva.

The Ashvak was pushed forward into the circle, appropriately washed in oil. He was a stocky, muscular man who relied on the brute force of his upper body to crush wood and bone alike. Ikshvaku smiled and casually stretched his arms in exercise. "This time you go too far, my friend," he shouted above the din.

"I don't think so," Haryashva replied, playing along while he stretched his limbs. "It's time we disprove the notion that no man can better you! You and I in unarmed combat, finally."

Ikshvaku laughed and lunged, moving away at Haryashva's parry. The soldiers roared in delight. King Ikshvaku and Haryashva's friendship was the stuff of legend, inspiring loyal bonding through the ranks in imitation. They knew that Haryashva had volunteered no boast, but the move was made and the Ashvak had to oblige the warriors as much as the King did. Urged by the men, the friends locked themselves in combat, muscular arms grappling and slipping over each other. Ikshvaku let the game go on for a while, the soldiers needed to have their fun after all. But the conclusion was foregone, and before long the King had his friend pinned to the ground.

"Yield?" Ikshvaku asked.

"Yield," Haryashva said grudgingly. The soldiers cried out in mock jeers, booing the Ashvak for his tame loss. Ikshvaku smiled and helped him back to his feet. He signalled an end to the day's events and none complained, for the final fight was enough to satiate their need for rest and entertainment. King and Ashvak walked to the bathing tanks together, continuing their banter for a while before Haryashva brought it to serious matters.

"You trust the Rakshasa far too much," he said for the umpteenth time.

Haryashva had still not come to terms with Narantaka's presence among them, and sometimes Ikshvaku wondered why he did not confess the truth to his closest friend. Perhaps it was his own guilt, knowing that the decisions he had taken would be questioned by Haryashva most agitatedly. "They said that about you too, when you first joined us," Ikshvaku said, giving his friend a dry smile. "But I do not trust Narantaka the way I trust you. I keep him at an arm's length."

"Even that is far too close. Narantaka is among our men day and night, learning our ways, our strengths and our weaknesses. And he talks to the natives in strange tongues, who knows what he truly says to them?"

"But what of the information he gives us?" Ikshvaku countered. "His familiarity with this terrain and its people allow our army to pass through most areas without a battle or raid. He speaks with the locals and brokers peace, trade and even an exchange of rituals and prayers. And do you not appreciate his latest suggestion?"

Six months after the Suryavanshi army roamed the land idly without direction, Narantaka proposed a novel expansionary tactic. Ikshvaku was to select his finest stallions, young and powerful, and allow them to scanter across the land. A contingent of soldiers would follow the horses from a distance, and claim all territory they ran across in the name of the Suryavansha. Narantaka did not expect the natives to submit easily, but population here was surprisingly sparse. Most of the settlements they came across were home to isolated bands of Rakshasa traders and miners, and Narantaka easily negotiated mutually beneficial terms with them. There were dozens of nomadic tribes though, all as seemingly proficient with the horse as Ashvaks. Most of them had no conception of territories, settlements, farming and the like. But some of these tribes spoke of a far south-western city, built like a fort with farmlands like no city of Aryavarta—Uruk, ruled by King Enmerkar. But Uruk sounded too far away for its military to be roaming these lands, and it took Ikshvaku many restless nights before he was able to determine from Narantaka that the seal of Surya did not reside there.

The people of Harivarsha spoke dialects phonetically similar to the Prakrits east of Sindhu, albeit with small differences like using *ha* instead of *sa*. Sindhu was Hindhu to them, and the Sarayu river was Harayu. Ikshvaku set some of his best bards to record all information on history and geography, intending to send it to Manu for analysis. His team of architects designed a simple garrison that could be constructed swiftly with just a few pieces of wood and stone. The garrisons were established at regular intervals along the Setumanta river's western banks, and more still were being constructed along its tributaries. The river's waters were not salty, and Narantaka informed Ikshvaku that the Setumanta never met the sea at all, draining all of its waters into the Arkasatala lake. Indeed, the river's water tasted different from what the Suryavanshi were used to. Many got sick, unable to avoid the nauseating effects of foreign water even after boiling it. The terrain itself was harsh and hostile, peppered with stark peaks and jagged ravines. West of the Setumanta were the water basins it shared with the Parasi river. The basins provided fertile grazing grounds for horses, and countless wild herds were found. Narantaka suggested that it would offend the native nomads if Ikshvaku tried to domesticate these horses, and so the King desisted despite opposite counsel from Haryashva and his band of Ashvaks.

The Rakshasa walked up to them now, his expression grim. "There is something..." he said hesitantly.

Ikshvaku turned to him. "What is it?"

"Something has happened among the captured tribals. It would," he paused, trying to find the right words, "Surprise you."

Ikshvaku raised his eyebrows. Four days ago they had come across a band of hostile Rakshasas. Ikshvaku allowed Narantaka to attempt a negotiation, but the Rakshasas were equally hostile to his overtures. "Either flee, King, or fight these Rakshasas right here," Narantaka had summed up. The Rakshasas took two nights before surrendering, and Ikshvaku held them captive till he could figure out what to do with them. "What's happened?" he asked.

Again Narantaka hesitated, choosing his words carefully. "There was a dispute between two of the captives. One of them has killed the other."

Ikshvaku frowned. "Killed? He murdered another?" This was a crime virtually unheard of in Suryavanshi lands. Men brought their conflicts out in the open, presenting both stories to their chief for his final decision. In more hostile scenarios there would be a public duel, where both men were prepared to lose their lives and took the decision willingly. Moreover, every Solar man or woman was related to the other by some measure, and they could trace a common ancestor in the form of Aurvan Surya. In Suryavanshi life, murder was equal to fratricide.

"Yes," Narantaka said. Then he added, "I know this is new to you."

Ikshvaku was at a loss. Battle was different, battle had rules and reasons. Even prisoners of war had their rights. But to wilfully take the life of another was unthinkable. "Are you saying that murder is not new among Rakshasas?" asked Ikshvaku. It was unknown in the Solar tribes' entire history.

Narantaka nodded. "It does happen, yes. We do not think much of it," he said nonchalantly.

"This is a black act, Narantaka, an unpardonable deed." Ikshvaku did not know what else to say.

"I will have the offender executed."

"No!" Ikshvaku said firmly. "That is no better than murder, and I am no dispenser of justice. I do not understand the ways of people here. These Rakshasas and horse-riders are alien to me, just as much as I am to them. What do you suggest I do?"

"Set them free," Narantaka said without hesitation. "They might return one day and attack your men again, but so what? This is a ragged bunch that will as easily fight within itself as charge at your Suryavanshi. If and when they return, they will be easy practise for your soldiers."

Ikshvaku considered the proposal. He wanted to claim territories without force or aggression. He wished to allow the natives their cultures and freedom. How could he complain then, if violence and conflict *was* their culture? He thought of the seal of Surya. How would these natives have reacted to that relic strung on his neck? Would they have known its significance, or recognised it even? But then he remembered something Manu had once said. *Idols and artefacts do not define us. Our actions do. Our decisions do.* "Very well," Ikshvaku said finally. "Let them go, but make sure they leave without armaments. And tell them that if they ever turn hostile towards us again, I will not be so kind."

As he watched Narantaka nod and leave, Ikshvaku wondered whether he was any close to finding the seal. Narantaka was growing different of late, or rather returning to the reticent, secretive Rakshasa that Ikshvaku had first captured and turned into a reluctant ally. Several times Ikshvaku or his men had spotted Narantaka conversing with the locals and captives in secrecy, their heavily-accented dialect and low whispers making it impossible to know what they discussed. This wasn't enough to daunt Haryashva though, who managed to both hear and understand enough to confirm that Narantaka was planning something sinister. But was that Haryashva's own prejudice playing a part? Or was Ikshvaku so driven by his quest for the seal that it blinded him to the threat Narantaka's presence posed?

"Do you sing their prayers too? Do you dance naked around their fires?" The malevolence in the Rakshasa's tone was unmistakable.

Narantaka sighed. He had played this game before. "I sing no prayers, and even they do not dance naked around fire."

"See how he defends them!" the Rakshasa said to his companions. "He is not one of us."

"And I don't claim to be," Narantaka replied quickly. "Your kind and mine are nothing alike, we are united only by the title these Suryavanshi use for us."

"And what are you then?" the Rakshasa challenged.

"I am Narantaka," he roared, raising his voice. "I once led the 6,000 Rakshasas of Kamyakvana, of which there are only a few hundred left, and I lead them no more. I lost to Ikshvaku and his Suryavanshi armies. But the Asura deities saw fit to give me another chance, and here I am today—in the only place where I can gather men and women for my rebellion. Or so I thought, clearly I was wrong."

"You hide your intent behind too many words," a Rakshasi growled. "Speak plainly, Narantaka of Kamyakvana."

"Ikshvaku sets you free with a warning—do not return with arms against him again. But that is because he sees you as a scattered bunch of tribals, no match for his trained and well-equipped armies. What he does not account for is the possibility that you may gather, that you may swell in numbers, or that you may even arm yourselves against him. My intent is to facilitate this possibility."

The Rakshasi stepped forward, and with a flash of insight Narantaka realised that she was the leader of the group, the matriarch. He assessed her differently now, perceiving the power and aura she commanded. "You propose to unite the tribals of this land, to arm and train them?" she asked.

Narantaka laughed. "Certainly! And I am in the perfect place to make this happen. I can take the message across this land. I can help you steal weapons, and bring to you Suryavanshi fighting techniques. I was once a leader of rebels, maybe I still am."

"You are a snake," the first Rakshasa growled. "You whisper and connive. You are not one we can trust."

"Then don't," Narantaka replied with indifference. "You are free nevertheless. Sooner or later, I will find a group that sees merit in my proposal. Where one can be found, more will be."

"And what are your motives?" the Rakshasi asked. "What do you want to build here?"

"A nation of our own," Narantaka replied, as if that was the most obvious thing in the world.

"This cannot be altruism or kindred spirit," the Rakshasi said. "People like us are not known to possess such sentiments. So I still do not trust your motives, Narantaka. All this, to bring vengeance upon the Suryavanshi? Upon this King Ikshvaku? To avenge the death of thousands of your people?"

Narantaka allowed himself an evil chuckle. "I care not for the dead," he said. "Except for two, my wife and son."

"What of them?" the Rakshasi asked, though her tone was devoid of any genuine interest.

"They're dead," Narantaka said, making a long story short. "And Ikshvaku is to blame. That I can neither forget nor forgive, and I will bring destruction upon the Suryavansha for this transgression. But Ikshvaku has an army and a country. To begin with, I need that as well."

It took another year for the messengers from Avisari to finally catch up with Ikshvaku, and the news was grim. His younger brothers had rebelled and captured the city, commanding the loyalty of Vitabhya's entire fighting force and some of Harayupa's as well. He had stepped into Harivarsha to expand his kingdom, so that one day it could accommodate the ambitions of all his brothers. Now Pramshu and Sharyati held Avisari while the remaining brothers hunted for his wives and sons. But the rebellion had to wait, and Ikshvaku turned his attention back to Harivarsha.

"We are in firm control of Setumanta and its tributaries," Haryashva said. "The barracks are strong enough to repel any Rakshasa raids."

"The real challenge will be south of the Lorikdanai river," Drishta commented. "A barren land with no rivers to feed its thirst. I never knew how vulnerable Vitabhya truly is from an attack coming in from west or south-west."

"There is no need to venture south," Ikshvaku suggested. "I wish to cross the Parasi river and explore beyond the Sarayu. Our forefathers might have taken the same route in reverse on their way to Aryavarta." The truth was that Ikshvaku had by now pieced together a theory that the seal of Surya was somewhere along the banks of the Sarayu river.

"I agree," said Haryashva. "We must stay along the rivers, why venture into barren and harsh lands?"

"I agree as well," said Drishta. "But the south will remain a challenge. We know that various Rakshasa bands roam nomadic there, and nothing stops them from turning to Vitabhya one day. Before we return east of the Sindhu, we must tackle their threat."

"Indeed," observed Ikshvaku. "And what of the rebellion?"

Haryashva scoffed with disgust. He was long suspicious of Ikshvaku's brothers, even suggesting assassination in his early years with the Suryavansha. Now the worst of his fears had come true. "We can send a few contingents back," he suggested. "Let them gather Ashvaks at Kapisa and march on Avisari."

"More men can be rallied from Prasthala, Harayupa and Kashyapura," Drishta added. "I can lead the charge if you command it, my King."

"No," said Ikshvaku with force. "I will spare no men from my current endeavours. From where we stand right now, Pramshu and the others' presence at Avisari is of little consequence to us. My family is safe, and my territories will be there when I return. Till then, let the boy enjoy playing King."

Gandharva

"The love story of Pururava and Urvashi is popular, heavily embellished and modified. But the true tale of their first encounter is a grave one, its circumstances dire. Some even suggest that Pururava married for political reasons, gaining Apsara warriors in his war against the Gandharvas."

King Bhagiratha to Sudasa

Year 47, Seventh era

Devapi surveyed his blade yet another time. "This batch is certainly better than the previous," he commented. Led by Pururava, he walked deeper into the forest, lines of soldiers following a few steps behind them.

Pururava nodded in agreement. "The Trigartans have a new melting technique. It makes for a more robust and stable sword."

"What of the shields? Our men still do not have the strong arms of a Solar warrior. Many are unable to fight with the shield in one arm."

"I know, which is why I decided not to carry them for this battle. But it's a problem we will solve later, with Haryashva's help. Now turn your mind to the forest ahead, cousin. With Ikshvaku away in the west, we have to fend for ourselves."

"What of these Manava brothers?" Devapi whispered, unable to maintain the sort of solemnity that usually preceded a battle. His was the simple farmer's mind, and the sheer horror of blood and death was still far from his imagination despite the experience of a few battles. "King Pramshu claims that King Ikshvaku is dead."

"There is no King Pramshu," Pururava said, trying to peer through the darkness. Intensive scouting of this part of the foothills had revealed a dense Gandharva presence, and eradicating it would go a long way in securing Plaksha from further raids. "There is only King Ikshvaku. And he will deal with his brothers as is appropriate when he returns."

"But there are those who say that Pramshu is a better King. He is a man of peace who seeks not war and death like Ikshvaku."

Pururava scoffed at his cousin's ignorance. "Do you know why Pramshu can afford to play at peace? It's because Ikshvaku has taken care of the Rakshasas for him. Pramshu needs to fight no wars because Ikshvaku does that for him!"

Devapi could not respond, as just then the forest exploded in a cacophony of noises and screams. Wolf eyes gleamed menacingly from the darkness, and Gandharvas swooped in from the trees with broad spears in their hands, catching several of his men by surprise. Pururava roared in indignation and jumped into the fray, slashing his newly forged sword in the sequences Varman had taught him. *You must experience serenity when you fight, Varman had once said. Think of the thing that calms you most, that which gives you solace when all else fails. Find it and stay with it while you take lives dispassionately. It's the only way to deal with the insanity of war.*

Pururava thought of his mother, remembering her infectious smile and untiring love. Her initial expedition down the Ganga had found several new Lunar settlements, the last of which was named Pratishthana. Her words, delivered to him when she first returned from the expedition, were forever fresh in his mind. *It is a sight to behold, my son. The waters of Yamuna and Ganga fight with each other, their dividing lines clearly visible. Then as you row further downstream you can see the Ganga slowly winning, its waters conquering the eddies till the Yamuna's darker hues are visible no more. By the banks of this confluence I have settled my people, your people. You must visit it as soon as you can.*

He allowed the image of his mother to accompany him for a while, but soon the blood and grime around him began to weigh heavy. He was taught that when the battle ran deep every stroke and slash either saved your life or took that of another, and a soldier easily gave into battle lust and instinct. The high of war was compared to that of the Soma plant-war being intoxicating to men with sword and armour. When his training was complete, Varman had proudly announced to Ikshvaku that Pururava would be a warrior full of glory and valour.

He felt none of that though. Every weary breath he took brought stench and dust to his lungs, and more muscles ached in his body than he thought he had. Fresh batches of gristle and blood splattered across him with blinding frequency. His eyes stung, and rubbing them with his bloody, grimy hands was of no help. Even the many cuts and bruises upon him were beginning to hurt. The daze that was setting in on him was fatigue, not battle lust. But despite the exhaustion he was able to admire his sword and the Trigartan metal that formed its blade. His visits to Trigarta and Madra had proven successful, and Plaksha now traded with them as much as Prasthala or Vitabhya did. Metal, sword, axe and plough flowed upstream to Plaksha, fuelling Pururava's campaigns against the Gandharvas. In return, cattle, goat and grain were sent downstream to the people of Trigarta and Madra. The cities were fiercely independent though, not inclined to political alliances of any sort. And despite their denial of it, Pururava suspected they had a treaty with Gandharvas, keeping them safe from the raids that plagued Plaksha. It was certainly strange—Trigarta and Madra were both located right opposite Khandakvana, only the Sarasvati's width separating their fires from the forest's darkness. By all means they should have been easy targets for Gandharvas, yet there was no confrontation. He could get trade from the Trigartans and Madrans, but he could not get more information on this subject. They were a terse and wary people, drawing a deep divide between themselves and outsiders. No foreigner could make a home there and become one of them.

The howls of the wolves pierced through roars of men as both clashed in a bath of crimson rain, bringing Pururava's attention back to the battle. Gandharva wolves were vicious creatures, deeply loyal to their masters and ruthless to the enemy. Ashvak stallions were able to keep them at bay, but only for a while. The wolves were remarkably intelligent, swiftly able to coordinate their efforts to bring down one horse at a time. Pururava loathed sacrificing his horses in this manner, but it was the only way he could distract the wolves long enough to kill them with archers and spears. While Pururava's men were busy with wolves, the Gandharvas bounded from tree to tree and jumped down in great swoops, using the momentum to drive their spears through the copper armour of his soldiers.

They were courageous, there was no doubt about that. Pururava took on Gandharvas half his size who charged at him with no fear. Though outnumbered, they knew the terrain and used it to their advantage. But gradually the tide turned in the Lunar tribes' favour. Dozens of Gandharva companies turned tail and fled into the mountain vales. Devapi warned Pururava that they would return in a few days with more behind them. To address this, he set his horse-riders to one purpose—hunt down and kill every fleeing Gandharva. Man, woman or wolf.

But there were still many Gandharvas about, those who bravely chose to fight even while their kinsmen fled. Two Gandharvas came at Pururava together, their spears pointed firmly at him. He turned to face the oncoming attackers and braced himself. As they came close, he charged and crashed against one as hard as he could, pushing him away. While the Gandharva reeled and recovered, Pururava slashed his sword, firmly lodging it into the waist of the second one. For a moment, he thought he saw surprise in those dying eyes, before the first Gandharva charged at him again. He easily evaded the spear and thrust his own sword straight into the Gandharva's throat. Blood spurted from the Gandharva's throat as he fell and joined his companion in death.

Pururava looked around and glanced upon Devapi finishing off a Gandharva, removing his sword from the slain one's gut. Elsewhere around him his men were walking the battlefield, tending to their injured and finishing off wounded enemies. The sound of horses distracted Pururava, and he turned around to find the source. Two Gandharvas had mounted one of his horses, and a third one another. Before the soldiers closest to them could react, they charged the mares and sped away, but in the opposite direction, towards Khandakvana. Without realising it, the high of battle was now upon Pururava. He longed for more blood, and mounted a stallion of his own to chase the fleeing Gandharvas. Behind him he heard the hooves of a following horse, and knew by instinct that Devapi had given chase as well.

"We should turn back now," Devapi suggested. "They're bound to turn around, the men will catch them then."

But something didn't feel right, even Pururava's horse sensed it, twitching and clacking agitatedly. "No," Pururava said. "They're not turning back, I know it. They're headed into Khandakvana."

"There's still open country between here and the forest," Devapi said. "They won't risk that."

Yet something told him that they would. So he kept the pursuit and Devapi followed dutifully. In the distance on either side, they saw the glistening waters of the great rivers, Yamuna and Sarasvati. The rivers disappeared from time to time along the way, curving between the foothills of the great Himalaya and being engulfed by random streaks of trees. Pururava knew that the entire land had been a dense forest once, and Khandakvana was a vast jungle that extended from just above the Vindhyachala mountains all the way to the trans-Himalaya. Around the myriad lakes and ponds in that forest, the Devas and Asuras had fought their wars, hundreds of years ago. Then the trees receded, rivers turned the land fertile, and the last Devas and Asuras died off. Now their descendants waged the war they had ended. The Solar sons of Aurvan Surya battled Rakshasas, while the Lunar progeny of Tapin Soma engaged with Gandharvas.

The Gandharvas they chased obviously knew the land as well as they did, if not better. They bounded left and right, doubled back in circles and made false trails that led to a clump of trees or disappeared as they turned back. It made progress slow and stuttered, and Pururava was getting impatient. After more than four hours, the sky was turning a faint orange. Pururava's legs hurt, and he knew his horse was tired too. The trail led them to another cluster of trees. From here on, the jungle continued to get more dense till it covered the entire land between Sarasvati and Yamuna.

They stopped and dismounted, bending to see depressions in the grass and pick the next trail. "Let's end it here," Pururava said finally. "They're definitely inside Khandakvana now, there is no way we can pursue them."

"I agree," Devapi said. "We can rest here awhile. I have a pouch of fresh fruits with me."

"I'm not hungry," Pururava said, distractedly. Then, realising that he should appreciate Devapi's foresight, he added softly, "But give some to the horses. They must be ravenous, and the grass here is sparse."

Devapi obeyed, and Pururava idly ran his fingers through the glade. Then a faint, distant melody floated to him. He looked about alert—where was that coming from? He strained his ears and the melody became clearer, floating with the breeze. His eyes met Devapi's, and they nodded, confirming that they both heard it. There were no villages or settlements here, and the melody was unlike one they ever heard of. This was not the sound of a flute or wood drum. Devapi gestured towards the forest, and Pururava nodded nervously. With hands on their swords they moved closer in, towards the source of the music. By the time they came to a clearing the sun was well on its rise, and its bright rays were piercing through the trees in shallow beams of light. In the middle of that clearing was a pond, shining under the rays. By its side Pururava found the source of music—and the Gandharvas he pursued. The horses they fled on were nowhere to be seen, and two of them lay on the ground by the pond. The third one, wrapped in robes similar to the others', played the strange instrument emitting dulcet waves of melody. Pururava's attention went to the instrument first, a long and slender piece of wood that was oblong at one end. Thin, barely visible strings ran from one end of it to the other, and the Gandharva was running its fingers through them with a fluid, hypnotic ease. Pururava moved closer. At the sound of his approach the Gandharva stopped abruptly and stood up, looking nervously between them and the apparently unconscious companions nearby.

A strange discomfort came over Pururava when the music disappeared, as if something beautiful was instantly sucked out of the world. The last string the Gandharva twanged resonated within him longer, echoing from one ear to the other and back. Suddenly, he regretted stepping closer, he should have stayed at the clearing's edge and continued to listen. That was when the Gandharvi spoke.

"You have come to kill us," she stated flatly.

Pururava could not find his voice. His ear still craved the music, and yet a part of him wanted to listen to this Gandharvi talk.

"Do it then," the Gandharvi urged, a pleasant lilt in her voice.

Already he knew that he could not, he would not. Pururava noticed her chest, the wide curve of her hips and the slender legs beneath her robes. Her face was hidden, but she was unmistakably female—he could not raise his blade against her.

Devapi sensed the change in Pururava's intent, or perhaps changed intent himself. "Relax, Gandharvi," he said softly, and added, "We will not hurt you."

A voice inside Pururava told himself to take charge. He was the commander here, and he was acting like a tongue-tied fool! He stepped forward and said, "Are your companions injured?"

"They are," the Gandharvi replied hesitantly.

He stepped closer to inspect, and the Gandharvi backed off in alarm, her eyes widening in fear. "Fear not," he said, voice firm but gentle. "Yes, we have been chasing you all night. But now that I see you, now that I have heard your music and your voice, I cannot cause you any harm."

He saw a trace of relief blink across the Gandharvi's eyes, mixed with uncertainty. She opened her mouth to say something, then stopped. He stepped in closer to catch a glimpse of her face, and she looked up at him. The sun fell directly on her face, and as she looked up her hood fell back, allowing her velvet-black hair to fall out. Pururava sucked in a deep breath, never had he seen a woman of such beauty. The women of Sringara were fair, and the women of Kapisa surpassed them, but this Gandharvi's beauty astounded him. Her skin was the colour of creamy milk, and there was a dark hue in her eyes, her nose sharp and distinct.

"Will you help me, Lunar warrior?" she asked.

"I will," he heard himself say, still enamoured by the Gandharvi's beauty. A strange thought occurred to him now, one that had never been pertinent before. He thought of a wife, of children and a family. It came from deep inside him, the decision that he wanted this woman for his companion. "What is your name, Gandharvi?"

"I am named Urvashi of the Apsaras," she replied shyly.

"Apsaras?" Pururava repeated. "What tribe are they? Are you not a Gandharvi?"

Urvashi shook her head sideways.

"Then how were you among the Gandharvas we attacked?" he asked. "And where are the Apsaras from?"

"I was a captive of the Gandharvas," Urvashi replied. "We were originally a travelling party of nineteen Apsaras from beyond the Twin Lakes."

Devapi gave Pururava a questioning look, who explained, "The lakes of Rakshastala and Mansarovara."

Urvashi opened her mouth, then stopped herself again. "Speak your mind, Apsara," Pururava said.

"What is your name, Lunar warrior?" Urvashi asked.

"I am Pururava Aila. This here is Devapi Atreya, my General."

Urvashi's eyes widened in recognition. "You are loathed figures among Gandharvas," she said confidently. "I heard them curse you many times during my captivity."

Pururava took pride in her compliment, though anything she said sounded as accordant as her music. "No harm will come to you," he reassured her. "But your companions are injured, let me tend to their wounds."

"You are a healer?" Urvashi asked in surprise.

Pururava smiled at her simplicity. "No, Apsara, I am not. But I know enough about wounds to try to help them. It could give them enough time till we bring them to the real healers."

Urvashi smiled widely, looking even more beautiful. "See to them then, Pururava Aila. They are only boys, my brothers. My parents charged me with their protection. Please help them." With that she fell at his feet.

Pururava backed up and spread out his arms. "No, Urvashi, you need not do that. And it does not befit me to have a woman touch my feet."

"But you have offered me and my brothers your protection," Urvashi said, clearly at a loss. "We are your slaves now, you may do with me as you wish."

Pururava bent forward and picked her up. Her robe skins were torn and tattered, and when he gripped her arms his skin touched hers. For the first time in his life, Pururava experienced lust. He wanted this woman. But Ila's deep sense of dignity had descended to her son as well, and he knew that there was a right way to do this.

"There are no slaves among us, Urvashi of the Apsaras. People are not treated with such dishonour in Aryavarta. And with the beauty that you possess, there is only one thing I desire to do. If you are willing, I would like to make you my wife."

Sons of Devas

"The term Dasa was coined by Ikshvaku, it was his name for the people of what-was-then Harivarsha. They tested his resolve and patience like nothing had before. Indeed, for four years after the Suryavanshi army returned from Harivarsha, Ikshvaku was not there to lead his men."

King Bhagiratha to Sudasa

"I pray to Vritra, and Ouruna and Mittara," said the priest proudly. "Surely you pray to them too?"

"To Varuna and Mitra perhaps," offered Ikshvaku. "But they are low in our hierarchy of deities, and only our enemies pray to Vritra."

The priest looked offended at that. "Then I am your enemy too, for Vritra is supreme to me."

Ikshvaku placed a reassuring hand on the man's shoulders. "It will be a dark day when we wage war simply because of belief in different deities. I only mean to say that worship of Vritra is unknown among my people, though he is important to Rakshasas, who we consider an enemy."

"Ra-ksha-sa," said the priest, sounding out the new word. "Raksha-sa," Ikshvaku corrected, and the priest pronounced it again. It was not a part of his dialect, nor that of other dialects in his land. These men from across the Hindhu river carried strangeness with them. Strange customs, strange beliefs and strange sounds. At least they prayed to fire, constructing elaborate altars that were not too dissimilar to his brick arrangements. And their bearing suggested that they could be the men he had been waiting for. "Who are Raksha-sas?" he asked.

Ikshvaku thought for a moment. He had to choose his words wisely, or the entire game would be up. But the priest's knowledge of history from east of the Sindhu was so bleak, so close to non-existent that Ikshvaku had no context to set for him. "Rakshasas are a tribe of my land," he said finally. "They prefer the darkness of forests to the light of land and river. They are our enemy-raiders, pillagers and thieves."

"Where do they come from?" the priest asked, curious.

"They are descendants to Asuras. Or perhaps you call them Ahuras."

"Ahuras!" the priest exclaimed. "Then they are my kinsmen, for I too am a son of Ahuras."

Ikshvaku smiled indulgently, deciding that it was time for the veil to drop. "I know," he said. "That's why Narantaka trusts you."

The priest was not the only one to frown at that. Drishta and Haryashva's brows furrowed as well. For four months they had charted the length of the Sarayu, guided by Narantaka to what ends only Ikshvaku knew. A few hours ago they came upon the priest in his solitary shelter by the Sarayu's western bank. Ikshvaku immediately sent a very agitated Narantaka on yet another scouting mission before beginning this discourse with the priest.

"I know of no man by that name," the priest said.

Ikshvaku nodded. "Perhaps you know him by the name Zarath."

Haryashva and Drishta exchanged a look. They knew Ikshvaku well enough to realise that their King was keeping a grave secret from them, one which they were yet to fully discern. Drishta's expression was pained, Haryashva's shrug nonchalant, as if to say *It's Ikshvaku, after all.*

"Yes, of Zarath I know. He is a kinsman."

There was no suspicion on the priest's face, nor any deception. It confirmed what Ikshvaku had conjectured about Narantaka, and it was time he reveal it to his men. Before turning to Haryashva and Drishta, he said to the priest, "Zarath has sent me for the relics. Will you bring them to me?"

The priest nodded and left wordlessly, and Ikshvaku began. "The seal of Surya," he said to them. "Have you never wondered where it is? You, uncle Drishta, mighty son of Havishmana just like me? And you, Haryashva, a man of adventure and thrill? Is that not why you joined us, all those years ago?"

"I think of it every day," said Drishta, looking offended. "But you are the one who goes about drilling the idea of duty into everyone. My duty was to follow the Suryavanshi King's command and impose his sovereignty. I have done well by it." It was rare for him to talk to Ikshvaku such, for the old uncle-nephew relationship had long been replaced by a formal one between King and loyal General.

"You rarely talked about it," added Haryashva. "I thought it unimportant to you. In the meantime, we were having enough adventures."

"It has consumed me ever since I learnt of it," Ikshvaku confessed to them. "Like a burning itch beneath the skin that you just cannot soothe. I do not know when secrecy became a habit, when those I trusted most were put at an arm's length. That is what addiction does, father once told me. Though he was talking about Soma-addled outcasts. Perhaps it applies to me as well."

Haryashva placed a reassuring hand on his friend's shoulder. Fifteen years had passed since he first met the boy King who called himself a son of Surya. Countless battles they had fought together, and many more they had to still. Whatever was troubling Ikshvaku, it had to be resolved quickly. "Out with it," Haryashva urged. "Is the priest returning with the seal?"

"If my conjecture is correct."

"And what is your conjecture?"

"That through a long twist of fate the seal of Surya came into Narantaka's possession, and in this priest's shelter it lies protected. You see, Narantaka is secretly a man of cult and worship. He idolises several Asura deities, including Vritra, but he has no surviving remnants of their existence. And so he started collecting ours, perhaps intending to melt and forge them anew in Rakshasa mould. Once I became King and the Suryavansha reunited into one army, Narantaka realised that Aryavarta was not a safe place to store them. He would have known that they were important Solar symbols, I imagine that the sun embossed on the seal of Surya is unmistakable. So he sent them to the one place he thought we would never look-Harivarsha."

There were many problems with Ikshvaku's theory, and double the amount of questions to ask. Drishta pointed out the most obvious flaw first. "It is Narantaka who has led us across Harivarsha, and brought us to this very spot."

"An argument I have carefully considered," said Ikshvaku. "But it is explained by the subtle but elaborate game we have been playing ever since he joined us. That he once possessed several Suryavanshi artefacts is known to me by direct confession, but everything else I have gathered through indirect lines of conversation. He mentions his family often, deeply regretful that he did not send them away to Harivarsha before it was too late."

At that Ikshvaku paused, a wave of intense guilt passing over him. Nivritti and Nimi, Narantaka's wife and son, were alive, even if currently in hiding from Ikshvaku's rebellious brothers. But that was a secret for another day, for if he gave Drishta and Haryashva the full dose here he would lose his credibility completely. "Which led me to believe that Harivarsha was where he would have sent anything important," Ikshvaku continued. "And he gave himself away when I declared my intention to march west of the Sindhu. The prospect excited him, for it would give him a chance to personally ensure that his treasures were still safe. Other things he said hinted that the hiding place was along the Sarayu, and he certainly has been far more nervous and sneaky recently than he has been for years. The behaviour inadvertently acted as a guide for me. The more nervous he got, the closer I was."

"I will not lie to you, nephew," said Drishta, his voice low and expression taut. "But it pains me that you kept me in the dark this long. This is not how a King treats the General of his armies, nor how a nephew his uncle."

Ikshvaku could not look into Drishta's eyes, suddenly feeling like a young boy again in front of the burly, boisterous cousin of his father. Then the sentiment receded and his conviction returned. "You can penalise me when we finish this, uncle, but for now let us see if I am right about all this."

"Yes, let us do that," replied Drishta. "But when this is over, and before you deal with your brothers, I will take my leave. I wish to retire, King Ikshvaku, for the world you create is too dark and devious for me."

Ikshvaku had no response to that, except the fervent hope that the seal's return to the Solar tribes would redeem him from all the secrets and lies. As they turned to the approaching priest, Haryashva added his query. "What is this business about Zarath? That's Narantaka's second name?"

"Rather, his first," replied Ikshvaku. "Zarath the Rakshasa earned the title of Narantaka when he began slaying hapless Suryavanshi farmers and cowherds." Then Ikshvaku stepped forward, unable to contain himself any longer. He had given his friends the explanation they deserved, or at least one that sufficed for now. A long nurtured dream, one that had guided him for more than a decade, could now come to fruition. He would lay his hands upon metal that was worn by Aurvan Surya centuries ago, and Havishmana Surya many generations after that. The priest brought before them a large, ornate box and opened it to reveal a dense clump of metal, gold and stone objects. Ikshvaku stared at them awhile, wondering what he would do if the seal was not among them. Then the feeling passed and he sifted through the objects, uninterested in what were otherwise quite important Suryavanshi relics in their own right. At the absolute bottom of the pile he discerned a chain, strung together by thick, twisted wires of metal. He pulled at it and followed its trail to hit upon a heavy, circular object. Breathing heavily, Ikshvaku pulled it out into the light.

There it was, the seal of Aurvan Surya. The circular disc at its end was heavy and fat, gold gleaming in the sunlight as it formed the shape of the sun and its rays on the disc's flat, scarred surface. Bold tears streamed down Ikshvaku's cheeks, and even Drishta's eyes were moist. Both Solar warriors were aware that this was a historic day for their tribe, and the moment was not lost on the unusually subdued Haryashva either. That was when the priest had the first inklings of suspicion. Were these men really sent by Zarath? They would come on decorated horses, Zarath had once said, looking noble and majestic in their bearing. They would be elite warriors of Zarath's mighty force, coming to claim his treasures on his behalf. That was Zarath's dream, creating a nation in imitation of the Suryavanshi and their Aryavarta. But the priest had no way of knowing that the men facing him were the originals, not imitations. Neither did he have a clue that the shaggy haired, unkempt Narantaka that Ikshvaku had hastily sent away a few hours ago was the young, handsome Zarath he knew. He considered unsheathing his dagger and making for the King's throat. But the two companions would kill him instantly, even if he succeeded. Zarath was a devout man, but he and his trinkets were not worth losing one's life over.

Wolves troubled him no more. His men had long ago learnt how to dispatch them swiftly, leaving only Gandharvas to deal with. Their hound-like, wimpy howls as they fled brought him grim satisfaction while he plunged his sword into the gut of a female Gandharva. Fighting Gandharvas was tricky business. They had both men and women in their ranks, and the women shared features with Apsaras that he now knew well. This particular Gandharvi had eyes that reminded him starkly of his wife, Urvashi. He hesitated for a split second while his sword was still lodged in, and she took the moment as an opportunity to swipe angrily with her left hand. A sharp piece of stone was tied to her wrist, and it slashed angrily across Pururava's face. Blood burst into his vision as a scar erupted, and Pururava finished the job by forcing his sword upwards and slitting her torso. Pain threatened to daze him, and he whirled around to see another Gandharvi charging at him with violent rage. Ignoring the blood dripping from his face, Pururava threw his sword straight at her. His aim was true and the blade sliced through her throat, beheading her even as the body continued its momentum and ran another two steps before dropping lifelessly. The Lunar chief walked over and collected his sword, bending momentarily to dress the wound on his face as best as he could in the circumstances. Then he stood back up and surveyed the scene around him. He clenched his jaws in grim resolution. Before the sun set on this day he would settle the Gandharva menace once and for all.

But it took the sun another complete cycle through the sky. The battlefield was a pool of corpses, lying in undignified and prone postures across the land. There was wolf flesh too, as well as horse tendon. Shields, swords and spears lay discarded, their owners on the journey to whatever lay beyond death. As the sun set and the moon took its place in the night-sky, it gave a fitting symbol to the rise of the Lunar warriors of Plaksha. They roared in the moonlight, imitating the wolves they had slain on these grounds. The beasts that managed to flee into the mountains stopped and stared back in their direction, the menacing sounds carrying to them and warning them to stay forever away.

No Gandharva stood alive for yojanas around, a paltry number managing to escape into the Himalaya or Khandakvana. He would deal with them later, but now Pururava surveyed his victorious men as they gathered around him and kneeled in obeisance. He appraised himself, noticing that he was coated in a layer of crimson-black. Did he look fearsome to them? Did he appear as the formidable Solar warriors he once trained under?

Devapi was among the kneeling men, and he looked up at Pururava. "With Soma the Moon as our witness, and slain Gandharvas as testament to our loyalty, today we declare you our King. Accept that title, oh Pururava."

"Rise, my friends and brothers," Pururava shouted, his voice carrying to every soldier. "We have put our lives on the line together today, fought the same risks as equal Aryas that we are. I humbly accept the title Devapi confers on me, but you will not bow to me today. Let the Somavansha find its King tomorrow. Tonight we celebrate as brethren and equals."

The men cheered in exultation, relief that the two days of heavy battle was finally over washing down their weary bones. But there would be no instant sleep on this moon-lit night. Tonight they would partake the finest Soma they carried, passing it around with the man who they would call King from tomorrow. Devapi walked over to his cousin. "Plaksha is safe, for now," he commented. "And now Pratishthana calls you, my King."

Pururava smiled and put a hand over his friend's shoulder. "You must learn to be obedient, Devapi," he said in jest. "There are no kings among us tonight, only equals."

For the longest time, Narantaka had only one goal-living the life of excess. Excess of women, brew, gold, plunder, food and anything else that found his fancy. But as Rakshasa-Suryavanshi confrontations increased, and especially after a boy rose to be King, Narantaka's life found a renewed purpose. But in the final clash he lost everything—family, tribe, and dignity. Why did he even continue to live, much less serve the same boy King in ridding the kingdom of Rakshasas? Because it enabled him towards the second goal—building a nation of Rakshasas to match that of the Aryas. Only when he had a kingdom as glorious as Ikshvaku's could Narantaka exact his revenge.

And revenge he would have, for despite all his excesses he truly loved his wife, and even more, his infant son.

But dread was upon him now. To maintain appearances, to sustain Ikshvaku's apparent trust in him, he had led the Suryavanshi straight to the priest, keeper of his treasure. Was that not the best tactic, to hide something in plain sight? But now he felt he could not be sure. Years of discussions with Ikshvaku ran through his head in hazy memory. The Solar King had so many queries, so many parallel lines of investigation. What all might Narantaka have unwittingly revealed? The Rakshasa decided that he could not take any further chances. He had used Ikshvaku's expeditions to scout the length and breadth of Harivarsha. Several secret alliances had been made, and he had to trust that they would hold true when he needed them. For now, it was time to reveal his true colours to the Suryavanshi King. Ikshvaku was too hasty in sending him away scouting, when they came upon the priest. Suspiciously hasty. Narantaka could not tell how much Ikshvaku knew, but surely he knew enough. Nothing else could explain the urgency with which Ikshvaku prevented Narantaka from even approaching the priest. And the old fool, on his part, did well not to recognise him and raise alarm. Narantaka used the opportunity to rally together several hundred warriors at short notice, enough to plunder through Ikshvaku's ranks and secure Narantaka's treasure before disappearing equally swiftly. The Rakshasa prepared himself, stretching his limbs before climbing on to the horse. It had been years since he engaged in any real, heartfelt battle. But he would enjoy seeing Ikshvaku's face when they faced each other as foes yet again. He would love even more to slice his sword across the man's arrogant neck. But whatever else he was, Ikshvaku was a formidable combatant. On this day, Narantaka would settle for the Ashvak, or even the ageing General.

"These are dark and black people, and these are not our people," counselled Drishta, speaking of the various local tribes of Harivarsha they had encountered. To Drishta they were positively Anarya, though Ikshvaku was not so sure. The General persisted. "Why do we spend more time here? We have the seal of Surya, which is why you led us here in the first place. Had you just told me, nephew, do you really think I would not have followed you anywhere? The seal means as much to me as it does to you."

Ikshvaku nodded at that, his jaw tightening. He opened his mouth to speak, but was cut short by the blaring sound of a trumpet, the alarm call. Two soldiers rushed into the shelter. "Rakshasa attack," one of them barked.

Ikshvaku clenched his teeth. "Narantaka," he said from intuition. Ignoring the priest as he tried to find a place to hide, Ikshvaku rushed out of the hut and war erupted into his vision. In a flash, he counted more Rakshasas than in any previous attack. Roaring in outrage, he jumped into their midst, but not before securing the seal. He never found pleasure in the act of killing, but now he felt righteous fury course through him as he slashed and cut. In the corner of his vision he saw his soldiers rallying together and felt pride shoot through him. This was the Suryavansha, and he was their King. The seal of Surya was returned to its rightful owner, and order would now be restored.

High on adrenaline, he cast his shield away and took on two Rakshasas together. Both were big, huge brutes, angrily swinging swords they had stolen from his men on previous raids. Snarling in rage, Ikshvaku pierced his sword straight through the gut of one and, with his bare hand, clasped the sword of the other. The blade easily cut through his palm, but before the Rakshasa could react he deftly slashed his sword upwards, slicing right through the Rakshasa's hand. The beast fell back in agony, and Ikshvaku hacked his sword through the head to complete the job before moving onto the next couple of Rakshasas, ignoring the deep gash in his palm. In a few hours, he felt as if he was transported back to Kamyakvana, such was the sheer number of Rakshasas around them. His arms burned with pain and tension while his legs moved as though he was wading in water. His men rallied well and overcame their initial surprise, but with the large number of enemy combatants, their task was taxing. Between fighting Rakshasas, he scoured the battlefield for Narantaka. Then he reminded himself that he was an ordinary warrior in battle, not a general surveying from a distance. *With the sword in your hand and enemies around you, you are but one man who needs to survive,* father had once taught him. He took a deep breath, trying to exhale some of the fatigue out, and plunged himself back into battle.

After what seemed like hours of cutting and hacking through Rakshasa lines, he finally found Narantaka engaged in a tense duel—with General Drishta! Ikshvaku roared from afar, his voice unable to carry through the din. He sliced faster, ending Rakshasa lives almost blindly as he raced to Drishta's assistance. The words of Haryashva, delivered so many times, ran through his head. Narantaka was a traitor in their midst, and finally he revealed his true colours. But even as King Ikshvaku transformed into a vengeful avatar of Surya himself, his charge was a few moments too late. By the time he came upon his uncle, Narantaka had sliced his sword across Drishta's torso and retreated into the melee.

Blood poured out of Drishta in waves, rapidly taking the life out of him. Ignoring the confusion around him, Ikshvaku knelt down and took Drishta's head in his lap. "He was a traitor all along," Drishta croaked, coughing out blood.

Ikshvaku helplessly pressed his hands against Drishta's body, trying to ebb the flow of blood. Drishta placed a tired, near lifeless arm on his nephew's shoulder. "It is useless, my son," he said. "It is time I join my forefathers with pride. My job in this world is done."

Those were General Drishta Rauruki's last words, and as life left him it seemed to take all will out of the King as well. Ikshvaku wept openly. His soldiers formed a protective circle around him, allowing their King to reveal a rare moment of vulnerability and pain. It was left to Haryashva to take command, and by nightfall they were able to repel the Rakshasa force, only a pitiful amount surviving to retreat. Narantaka was missing, and Haryashva ordered men to search every slain corpse. The sun began to rise by the time they tended to their wounded and dead, and General Drishta's pyre was lit. Ikshvaku looked lost and disconsolate. He refused to wash Drishta's blood off his hands, and remained on his knees throughout the funeral, feeling more defeated than he ever had before. The Lament of Existence came to him now, each syllable pounding heavy in his heart. And Maharshi Vasishtha's despairing words—*This is the Lament of Existence, King Ikshvaku. We can never really know, no matter how hard we try. Perhaps the ones we call Gods know, perhaps the Primeval Being knows, or perhaps even he does not. For all the order, joy and sorrow in our lives, we know but nothing about its meaning or purpose.*

The words rang true now, for what did gaining a piece of metal matter when it came with the loss of his uncle and mentor. How hollow it all seemed, when only a few hours ago it was the most joyous moment of his life. And perhaps even Drishta's. Life was nothing but a journey paved with such hollow victories. Is that what Kashyapa realised when he refused to rule the Solar tribes after Marici? Is that what Vaivasvat too realised, when he declined suggestions that he become King? From Aurvan to Marici, and in all the eras before the current, did all kings, Devas and rulers not see this futility? Or did they see it well and yet persist with their duty?

Haryashva sat down beside Ikshvaku, giving him silent company as he tried to come to terms with Drishta's death. "Dark and black people," Ikshvaku said at long last, echoing Drishta's words from earlier. Haryashva said nothing, lost in his own thoughts. "Uncle Drishta was right," Ikshvaku continued. "There is no reason for us to be here. Let us leave these lands to themselves, and the people to their fate. I name them *Dasa*-dark and black people. It is time we return to the right side of the Sindhu. It is time I give my men some peace and quiet."

"There is still one more thing left to do," said Haryashva, reminding him of the rebellion.

"Let my brothers be," said Ikshvaku. "Let them be kings if they want to. I am done with all this."

Haryashva said nothing, the two friends looking out to the distance. "Will you take the army back for me?" asked Ikshvaku after long silence.

"Where will you go?"

There was only one person who could help resolve the conflicts that raged within Ikshvaku. Only one man could put his storming mind at ease, and Ikshvaku had to finally meet that great personality. "I'm going to find my ancestor," he said. "Maharshi Kashyapa."

Many Suns

"Kashyapa was the most enigmatic of Aryavarta's early Maharshis. We have extensive records of Vasishtha and Atri, and both founded rshi schools. But Kashyapa survives to us only through prayers and fragmented tales. Long before Ikshvaku, he could have been Aryavarta's first King."

King Bhagiratha to Sudasa

Year 51, Seventh era

For four long years Ikshvaku scoured the Himalaya, sparing no thought for his kingdom, friends or family. The Suryavanshi empire he had built could have crumbled to dust for all he cared. He would not rest till he found the meaning of life itself. And for that he had to find his great-grandfather, Maharshi Kashyapa. Once, many years ago, Manu had narrated to Ikshvaku the tale of Kashyapa's abdication. And why did Kashyapa abdicate? Earlier, a simple answer had sufficed for the young Ikshvaku—deeply influenced by his mentor, the ascetic Bhrigu, Kashyapa had decided to pursue a spiritual path. But so many questions now needed answers. What was the nature of Bhrigu's influence? And what sort of answers lay on the spiritual path that could dismiss the Lament of Existence? Had Kashyapa found a deeper purpose to life, one that lay beyond even his pupil Vasishtha?

The Himalaya was Aryavarta's great, natural wall. In the current era, it was an incomparable border that ran from Aryavarta's north-west to far-east. But in the previous eras there was no Aryavarta, and the Himalaya was but a massive, impenetrable range running across Varaha Prithviya, the broad continent where the Devas and Asuras lived. In that endless stretch of landscape, near the end of the Sixth era, Aurvan Surya was born, roughly where Sringara stood today. Great seers prophesied him an even greater future, and Aurvan would later align with Maghavan Indra, Angra Agni and Tapin Soma to defeat the Asura clans once and for all. Their triumph ended a war that had raged for generations, across geography and time, since the Second era. Varaha Prithviya belonged to the Devas, and the Asuras could either run or hide. Most fled to the farthest reaches of the continent where no Deva tribe had ever roamed. But some chose to hide, and Varaha Prithviya's ample forests and landscape provided sufficient cover. Nowhere was this cover strongest but south of what Aurvan Surya called home. Long, winding rivers sped through dense, unending forests. Lush hills dotted this natural hideout, ponds and lakes merging with marshes and streams to provide more than sufficient cover. And then there was the Himalaya, with its tall, snowy and imposing peaks where none would bother to follow.

That would have been the end of the Asuras, for in a few generations they lost the capability for war and bloodshed that had so troubled the Devas for centuries. Primitive and isolated, their clans fragmented and then slept into dormancy. The mighty Asuras were survived by Rakshasas, Gandharvas, Yakshas, Vanaras and more. And on the other side, the victorious Devas should have emerged prosperous and advancing, the resources of Varaha Prithviya theirs for the taking. But history only knows of them fading into obscurity. Tapin Soma, who claimed descent from the Moon, disappeared into the Himalaya like many of his Asura enemies. Maghavan and Aurvan, Indra and Surya respectively, went to the western reaches of Varaha Prithviya and beyond. They too disappeared, no explanations surviving to future generations. But many of Aurvan's descendants remained in the boundless grasslands of central Varaha Prithviya, keeping with them both the memory and the title of Surya. Nomadic they remained for generations, till the death of Havishmana Surya prompted them to a change. Havishmana's grandson, Marici, led them back to Aryavarta, the birthplace of Aurvan Surya.

The title of Deva was discarded, as men and women of the future shed petty sentiments for the past. The title of Surya was given similar treatment, and Marici led his people to Aryavarta as a more moderately titled Mahajanapati-Supreme Clan Head. But the old memories and older ties did not entirely disappear, for the many descendants of Aurvan Surya were keenly aware of their heritage. Although they had scattered, nevertheless, they retained the consciousness of being one clan, the Suryavansha. They brought this with them when they returned to Aryavarta, but it was rudely shattered when Marici's son, Kashyapa, declined to take up rule after his father. Only one born of Aurvan and Havishmana's blood could take Marici's place, and so Kashyapa's abdication led to the Solar tribes' fragmentation into isolated city-clusters and sub-clans.

But Kashyapa did oblige one tribal duty and fathered a son called Vivasvana, who in turn gave to Aryavarta its great explorer and settler, Vaivasvat Manu. This was the vast history and heritage that Kashyapa had forsaken, and now Ikshvaku brought it back to him. Born only three generations apart in the same line, this was the first time they met. The Maharshi's meditative pose was like resolute stone, his spine erect as if sculpted from Himalayan rock. He opened his eyes when Ikshvaku entered the cave, and knew from intuition that this was his own blood walking in. After visiting hundreds of caves and the innumerable ascetics hidden within them, Ikshvaku too realised that this finally was Kashyapa himself. The seer looked supremely aged, yet he possessed a venerable aura. The Suryavanshi King fell at his forefather's feet, remembering the meeting with Maharshi Vasishtha nineteen years ago. He was a man of thirty-three, yet he felt like the young boy he was back then. "Kshauva," the sage said in a hoarse voice that clearly had not been spoken for years. "You carry my father's look. His gait, bearing and hair."

It was no surprise to Ikshvaku that Kashyapa perceived his identity without a single word being uttered. He kept his head lowered, unable to meet his formidable great-grandfather's eyes. What perception would pierce him if he did so, what inner demons would be revealed in an instant?

The seer detected the sentiment whirling in his descendant's mind, and felt a remote tinge of regret. He could have been a part of this man's life, guiding him and taking nourishment from his kindred youth. But all the years of life were now behind Kashyapa, and it was Ikshvaku's mercy to his retiring age that even a single meeting had been granted. "Only great labour can bring you here, beyond the highest peaks and countless caverns. What do you seek from me, my son?" Maharshi Kashyapa would grant any wish, were it voiced today by his dear descendant.

Ikshvaku sat down, crossing his legs like Kashyapa-heels over the knees rather than under them. "They call me the King of Suryavansha in the cities and towns of our people," Ikshvaku whispered into the cave, his voice echoing deep down its endless caverns. "Or at least they used to. It is a title I took for myself many years ago, claiming inheritance of Marici's grand dream."

Kashyapa breathed in a steady rhythm, his exhalations rushing through the walls like a gentle breeze. His was the Maharshi mind in constant consciousness of its prana flow, the routine journey of breath in and out of the body. And yet another portion of his awareness could extend to the outer world, partaking in it as if his full attention were devoted to it. Ikshvaku was aware of this art, having witnessed Maharshi Vasishtha practise it first-hand. It cast a strange aura of power around the practitioner, and he perceived it now in his great-grandfather.

"Nineteen years have passed since I became King," Ikshvaku continued. "And what a people we have become, Maharshi! From Avisari to Vitabhya, we are a tribe of irrigated towns, planned roads and profitable trades. We have conquered the river and forest both, emerging prime claimants to the bounty of Aryavarta. Yet, all this could have been achieved decades earlier by you, the young and promising son of Marici. I fulfil a dream for which you were greatly suited, ordained even. But it did not come to pass. I come to you for an answer to the queries that plague Suryavanshi consciousness. Why did you not wield Marici's inheritance? Why did you abdicate rule and take the spiritual path? Are we all fools then, fighting petty wars and growing perishable grains when there are higher roads to take? Your denial weighs heavier still on your direct descendants, and thus heaviest on me. Have I honoured Marici by affirming his ambition, or have I dishonoured you by reversing your abdication?"

Kashyapa's steady respiration continued, and Ikshvaku now looked into his eyes. Across generations, Kashyapa locked his gaze and found his father staring from behind Ikshvaku's face. His questions were Marici's come alive, accusations that a dead father could not pose to his rebellious son. "Bhrigu," Kashyapa whispered. "Maharshi Bhrigu, my guru."

It was supposed to explain everything, but Ikshvaku was far from satisfied. He waited for Kashyapa to continue. "I was seventeen years old when my father led our people into Aryavarta," Kashyapa began. "Marici was a stern, capable and formidable leader. The Solar tribes numbered thousands of men and women even then, and it was no small feat to convince those nomads to travel east and settle down. But then this version of the tale you know, do you not?"

Ikshvaku nodded.

"The tale you do not know of is my encounter with Bhrigu, and how that changed my entire life," Kashyapa said. "I still remember the first time I saw him. He was a lone light on the mountain across the valley, a madman dancing around fire in a cave seemingly impossible to reach. We were yet to cross the Sindhu into Aryavarta, and father planned to do so not too far from where Avisari stands today." Kashyapa paused and smiled in reminiscence, his skin cracking as if the muscles were frozen stiff from meditation. "Aryavarta was so new, its rivers and plains a mystery to us with our horses from the far north. And Bhrigu was most mysterious of the many strange sights we beheld. Of course I sought him out, I am fortunate to possess a curious and exploratory mind."

Kashyapa's eyes twinkled, and Ikshvaku gave an uncertain smile. How ancient Kashyapa was, but he was also a close forefather who could reveal the history of his own line.

"Agni, Vayu, Soma-these and other Devas were introduced to me by Bhrigu. We knew fire before him, of course. But we did not know Agni. We knew the wind, but not Vayu. And of Soma we had no clue, I assume because our ancestors forgot of the Lunar tribes when they turned nomadic. We lit the fire when we prayed, but we did not use it as the central pole of our rituals as we do now. These traditions were spread across your kingdom by Vasishtha. But they were transferred to him by me, and to me by Bhrigu. The journey he took me on was simply far more exciting and adventurous than the Solar life my father could bequeath to me."

"What about the responsibility you owed to the tribe, to Marici?" Ikshvaku knew that the question would not offend the Maharshi. Kashyapa would have settled such debates a long time ago, now Ikshvaku only wished to learn.

"I had to ask myself one question," replied Kashyapa. "Which you should ask yourself as well. When you are old and weary, all the years of your life behind you, who would you rather be? An explorer of the enigma that is our inner universe? Or a mighty ruler whose deeds will be remembered by countless generations?" Kashyapa did not wait for a reply and continued, "I concluded that there are higher responsibilities. I saw the search for my consciousness to be a stronger calling, duty to my soul more valid than my duty to Solar tribes."

Ikshvaku could not accept that Kashyapa had shed his guilt so easily. "How did you reconcile the opposition? How did you mitigate your internal doubts?"

"By knowing and accepting a singular truth—I did not wish to be ruler after Marici. I did not *wish* for power and authority. I desired anonymity. I desired the mountains, and company of men such as Bhrigu and Atri."

"You once said to Marici," Ikshvaku said. "That the wild tribes of Aryavarta could become our enemies, raiding our lands and robbing our cattle."

Kashyapa nodded, perceiving instantly that Ikshvaku learnt this from Vaivasvat Manu. He felt a distant sense of pride, Manu was a capable assimilator of history and knowledge.

"How could that not make you see the importance of a singular ruler?" Ikshvaku challenged. "Rakshasa and Yaksha raids had begun even by Marici's time, and in your early years you were a warrior. How could you leave the Solar tribes to their fate then?"

Kashyapa cast a grim smile, remembering the times. His memory of them was so vague now, and it was almost as if Ikshvaku remembered them more clearly than him. "Bhrigu," Kashyapa said again. "The answer to all questions is Bhrigu. He was a Yaksha himself, after all."

Ikshvaku frowned. He was not aware of this, and he doubted if even Manu knew it.

"Is it not a strange irony?" asked Kashyapa. "That the rituals the Solar tribes now swear by have actually come from a Yaksha? From Bhrigu I learnt that the divisions we draw among ourselves are superficial. Yaksha, Rakshasa, Suryavansha, Gandharva—all these and more are mere illusions, and the longer we abide by their boundaries the graver our disservice to the history of Aryavarta and its earlier eras. My father did try to make peace from time to time, but therein lies our biggest error. We live in a constant state of war and turn to peace-making only intermittently. Should it not be the other way around?"

It was a compelling argument, and came close to what a younger Ikshvaku himself felt about the Anarya tribes. But the biggest dilemma was yet to be resolved, and now he aired it. "When did Creation arise, who can know? For even the Gods came afterwards, did they not? Perhaps Creation came from itself, and perhaps not. The Mighty One above, perhaps he knows? But perhaps even he does not!"

Kashyapa frowned and made Ikshvaku repeat it, hearing it a further three times before declaring, "Vasishtha's composition."

Ikshvaku nodded.

"He always did have this streak in him," commented Kashyapa. "No amount of knowledge can ever really satisfy him. He remains a true sceptic."

"Then you are familiar with this prayer's tone, its despair?"

"Of course," said Kashyapa. "It is nothing but an expression of life's greatest dilemma. We are aware that our knowledge is not near complete, and can also perceive that it never will be. Who really knows when and how Creation arose? But how can anyone, when the act of Creation is not yet complete? What we call Existence is in fact Creation *still* at work, expanding its manifestations across the cosmos. Only when the act is done, when Creation withdraws its artefacts back into the black void, can one even contemplate upon its nature. And till then, all that life can do is participate with its full gusto. Life is the Creator *and* Created-both, and its duty is to survive till the end of Time. Then only can it coherently judge whether existence is a lament or a celebration. Only when life closes around you can you know whether your acts have been in vain, whether your duty complete."

Cast in this lucid argument, the Lament should have suddenly paled. But Ikshvaku's restive heart was not satisfied. "This does not explain the norms and order we seek to impose on ourselves," he said. "I have spent my life ruling the Suryavansha. You have attained the title of Maharshi. Whose experience is richer, and whose futile?"

Kashyapa studied his descendant, empathising with the conflict within him. "What is your fear, Kshauva?"

The confession was easy for Ikshvaku to make. "That my life means nothing. Everything I have done, everything I have achieved, has absolutely no significance in the larger scheme of things."

"You are right about that," said Kashyapa, not mincing his words. "In the larger scheme of things nothing we do can possibly matter. But that also means that we need not concern ourselves with the larger scheme. Return to the vital question I have posed: as a man of eighty, who would you rather be?"

"The ruler," Ikshvaku said, surprised that the answer came to him easily. "If I take the seer's path as you did, I would only pine with the regret of duties unfulfilled. Nor will I be able to forgive myself for letting lesser men take my place." The last sentiment was new to him, growing from a faint consideration years ago to a constant speculation in his mind now. His brothers' opportunistic rebellion had betrayed their true nature, and men as amoral as that could not lead the Suryavansha.

"Like my father," said Kashyapa, eyes glazed with memories he had not recalled for decades. "Always the first man to lead, the first to put his life on the line-the first Solar among thousands. I suspect that describes you as well. My father believed it came from our bloodline, descended as we were from Suryas. I am living proof that he might have been wrong."

"Perhaps you lead us down a different path, one that is as vital to our development as any," said Ikshvaku. "Which makes me ask—what answers have you found, Maharshi?"

Kashyapa smiled, his lips slowly curving wider than they had in years. "None at all, I must confess," he said dryly. "I am still searching, my son. I have several speculations of course, some more certain than others. But I have so much to learn still, and my only guru died many years ago. And yet I am certain that the path I have chosen is the best for me, for had I dedicated my life to the tribe like you, then surely I would have pined with regret."

"And the seal of Aurvan Surya," whispered Ikshvaku, delivering his final volley. "Your father's most prized possession. Did you never try to find it?"

Kashyapa's expression darkened, Ikshvaku had touched a nerve. "For years I secretly negotiated with the Rakshasas to return it to Vivasvana, but I was unsuccessful. I gave up after that, for the Himalaya was calling me."

"You knew that the seal was in possession of Rakshasas?" asked Ikshvaku, surprised.

Kashyapa frowned and nodded. "Who else would have stolen it? It went missing after a Rakshasa raid just a night before father's death."

"And over the decades it found itself in the hands of a Rakshasa called Narantaka," said Ikshvaku. "Who hid it away in the far western reaches of Harivarsha. I have found it, Maharshi, after many years of frustrating search."

Ikshvaku moved to remove the seal from his pouch, but the Maharshi spoke loudly. "No! Let it be, I do not wish to see it. It is a relic of my past, a reminder of the life I left behind long ago. I am heartened that it has found its way back to our line, but I have no desire to see or touch it."

Ikshvaku nodded, accepting Kashyapa's sentiment even if he did not really understand it. "I have not been King for four years," he said. "The Suryavansha is ruled instead by my brothers. They carry the blood of Surya too, but they are not men who can lead a tribe such as ours. I will have to fight them. Perhaps kill them." He did not know if he could really bring himself to do that, but cold fury was beginning to snake through his veins. The meeting with Kashyapa had brought him a closure he had long sought, and now he could return to life he escaped from. A life of blood, war and kingship.

"Do they not know that you carry the seal?" asked Kashyapa. "Have the men not seen it around your neck?"

"No. My finding of it coincided with the death of my uncle, General and mentor-Drishta Rauruki. That was when Maharshi Vasishtha's Lament of Existence finally dawned on me, and I found no recourse but to seek you out."

Maharshi Kashyapa frowned again. "You've been searching for me for four years?"

"Yes, and it has not been in vain, great forefather."

Maharshi Kashyapa was not moved. "Then these four years have been a disservice to your future-self, who will look at them as lost years. If you find no greater purpose in life than ruling the Suryavansha, then you must return to it. It is time you wield the seal of Surya, son. Wear it and observe the effect it has on people. Even I cannot explain the awe and loyalty it commands in those of Solar blood. I have never had the experience of wearing it, but I saw my father at close quarters. The seal has a powerful hold on our tribe, and its owner is implicitly a Surya in his own right."

It was time then for Ikshvaku to return, but much that he had achieved in the early years of his reign now lay undone. His brothers had captured his capital, his family was in hiding and his greatest enemy was alive and prospering in Dasavarsha, smarting from the loss of his accumulated treasures. But there was one last thing he had to do before he could consider his exile over. For four years he had possessed the seal, but his father had no clue of it. Duty demanded that he had gone to Manu the moment he found the seal and placed it in his hands. A deeper need had distracted Ikshvaku from that task, but now the need was fulfilled and he had to attend to his filial and tribal obligations. Manu had many sons, but Ikshvaku was the first and most loyal.

Even at the age of sixty-four, Vaivasvat Manu's beard was dense and black, his frame muscular and fit. He was a warrior, an explorer and settler, a man who established cities and farmlands. Ikshvaku fell at his feet before Manu picked his son up and pulled him into an embrace. "I have missed you, son," Manu confessed. "The sight of you alive and well after all these years is medicine for my heart."

Their eyes were moist, their faces joyous in the content reunion of father and son. The last vestiges of a young son had left Ikshvaku's eyes, and Manu now perceived him as an equal, or perhaps more. A King to a mere settler. "I have it," Ikshvaku whispered, his voice choked with emotion. "I have the seal of Aurvan Surya."

Manu stared, his face betraying no reaction. "I found it four years ago," Ikshvaku continued. "In Dasavarsha, which is the name I have given to the land west of the Sindhu, along a river called the Sarayu."

"I know, son," Manu said slowly. "Haryashva found me years ago, when he brought your army back to Aryavarta. He told me you found it, and of the quest that came upon you after Drishta's death."

"I am sorry, father. I should have come to you first. The seal belongs to you."

"It certainly does not," Manu challenged. "You found it. You returned it to the Solar bloodline. There is no contender for ownership. It is yours."

The assertion brought comfort to Ikshvaku, for it was important he had Manu's support. "But my brothers will surely contend," he said.

"Pramshu is but a boy," Manu said.

"A man of seventeen," Ikshvaku corrected. "As are Sharyati and Nabhaga. And young Karusaka is of an age at which I was King, father."

"Not all my sons are the exceptional man you are, Ikshvaku. And your brothers' fault is that they do not know this. They think themselves equal to you, but only because they do not really know you."

"If you are trying to defend them, father, then it is a little too late. My brothers occupy my home and refuse to vacate it. And the title Pramshu wears belongs to me. I have claimed it once in that city before. I will do so again."

"And what will you do with them?"

"I do not know," Ikshvaku answered truthfully. "My heart yearns to put my sword through Pramshu's gut. But my mind insists that I will be unable to do it. Which will prevail, father?"

"Only you can speculate on that, my son. My comments would be biased by the emotions of a father. I wish for their safety. I wish to see *all* my sons emerge out of Avisari alive."

"Will you not make me promise that it happens so?"

"How can I?" asked Manu, a defeated tone in his voice. "You have told me what your heart yearns to do. And I have always let you follow your heart, have I not, my son?"

Surya

"The war with his brothers is one of the darkest phases of Ikshvaku's life. Such reckless loss of life and limb, when the seal of Surya could have prevented it all to begin with. But it was true to Ikshvaku's nature, which was to test himself at every turn. He lived for challenge and conflict, and the rebellion provided that in renewing measure."

King Bhagiratha to Sudasa

Year 52, Seventh era

Haryashva gestured for the men to stop, perceiving someone move closer to them in the dark cover of the forest. For days he had suspected that they were being observed, but had so far allowed the unknown observer his freedom. But news from Avisari was that King Pramshu was preparing a large force for a single purpose—to hunt and kill every last rebel warrior in his kingdom. That included Haryashva and hundreds of other warriors still loyal to Ikshvaku. If the news was true, they could scarcely afford their presence to be known to any prying eyes.

"You are encircled now," Haryashva called out in the darkness. "We surround you from all sides, and it is better that you reveal yourself."

"An admirable perimeter," acknowledged the unknown figure, his voice oddly familiar. "But you forget that it is I who taught you this trap, Haryashva. And I also know how to escape it."

The figure stepped closer, into the pall of moonlight. He had obviously not cut his hair or shaved his beard for a long time, but Haryashva still had no trouble recognising him. His face lighting up in genuine delight, Haryashva pulled Ikshvaku into a fierce embrace. "You crazy fool!" he exclaimed. "You crazy, crazy fool! I might have simply shot you down."

"But you didn't," said Ikshvaku, returning the hug with equal vigour. Around them the men prostrated, delight writ upon their faces as well. Former soldiers, each of them had fought under Ikshvaku in Dasavarsha, they were now reduced to rebels without a cause. But their King had returned, their loyalties were vindicated. Calls went out into the darkness for the others to relax and regroup.

"Did you find him?" Haryashva asked. "Did you find Maharshi Kashyapa?"

Even though five years had passed since they'd parted, Haryashva's care and concern for his King was unwavering. Touched, Ikshvaku clasped Haryashva by the shoulders. "My dear friend, how joyous it is to see you. Yes, I found Kashyapa, and the answers I was looking for. I am back to reclaim what is mine. And I see that you have kept the fight up for me."

Haryashva turned to the gathered soldiers. "These men have stayed loyal to you when others parted. They have suffered the rebels' army upon them, when once they were the elite warriors of yours. All this while, I have constantly stated that you are alive and will return, and that you possess the seal of Aurvan Surya."

Ikshvaku nodded, feeling indebted to Haryashva and these soldiers. His flight from Dasavarsha after Drishta's funeral had been so swift that the men never got to see the seal. All they had was Haryashva's word. Emotion building inside him, he pulled out the seal and wore it around his neck. The gold on it glistened in the pale moonlight, and every man prostrated again, a current of awe and wonder passing through their ranks. This was the unmistakable souvenir of their shared ancestor, Aurvan Surya. Ikshvaku observed the effect, and recalled Kashyapa's words. If this was how other Suryavanshi would react as well, then he might not have to wage war against his brothers at all.

"Rise, my friends," Ikshvaku said to them. "You are my loyal elite, and I declare today that you need not kneel even to me. You are the first Solar warriors to lay eyes on the seal since Marici. I title you with my patronymic, and you shall hereby be called *Aikshvakus*. You will be the most feared group of warriors this world has ever seen. With the seal of Surya as evidence of my right, it is time for me to take back my kingdom."

"The men say that Surya rides at the helm of an ever-growing mass of armies," said Sharyati, Vaivasvat Manu's third son. "He burns everything in his path."

Nabhaga scoffed. "The men say many things, their declarations addled by fatigue, blood and brew. No doubt who they refer to as Surya is but a very charismatic and courageous leader."

"And who could that be?" asked Pramshu. "What if it is…"

"No," interrupted Karusaka, fifteen years old and growing quickly. "Ikshvaku is dead. Our secret partner ensured that."

"A partner we never met and still don't know the identity of," Sharyati pointed out. "And if the rebels are to be believed, then Ikshvaku never died in Harivarsha."

"It's been five years, brother," said Nabhaga in a tired voice. "Ikshvaku is dead, whether in Harivarsha or somewhere else. He could have died in a cave with Kashyapa, for all I care."

"Careful," warned Pramshu. "Maharshi Kashyapa is our forefather. You owe him some respect."

"What for?" challenged Karusaka on Nabhaga's behalf. Born to the same mother, the bond between them was somewhat stronger. "Kashyapa discarded what was both his duty and his privilege. He did his descendants no great service."

"We are getting off the point," insisted Sharyati. "This amassing army with a mysterious leader at the helm is our most pressing concern. And all debates can be settled when we have his head."

King Ikshvaku had returned a changed man. Haryashva could see it in his eyes—they'd turned dark and grim by whatever he had encountered in the four years of self-imposed exile. Haryashva had said nothing when Ikshvaku took their leave in Dasavarsha, departing in the middle of the night. He accepted Ikshvaku's decision both as a subject and a friend. In Ikshvaku's absence he had kept the fight alive, troubling Pramshu's armies and cutting off their supply routes, year after year. Now he deserved some reciprocity from his friend, and Ikshvaku's latest decision just did not make sense.

"Why do you not reveal the seal to all?" Haryashva asked. "The men will not rally under Pramshu with the seal of Aurvan around your neck. You can end this before it even begins."

"This began six years ago, my friend," said Ikshvaku. "When my brothers betrayed me, all the men who switched sides, all those who forgot who their true King was—I can forgive them for the lapse in loyalty when I was absent. But now that I am returned, will they rally under me again? Can I rule again, without the seal? I need to answer these questions." There was no mirth in him anymore, no heartening moments where the King was just an ordinary man. He ordered his troops and formulated strategies in terse conversation, speaking of his brothers only as "the rebels" and not taking any of their names. They charted a course straight for Avisari, capturing the town of Navapari on the way and effectively removing any possibility of aid coming from the south. The army grew in numbers as they marched, for many warriors did indeed fall back into his army when they saw that he was alive and returned. They warned Ikshvaku that while the journey to Navapari had been mostly conflict free, Avisari would be a different matter altogether. It was protected by Pramshu's most loyal contingents, those that supported him in the original rebellion. Before long, Ikshvaku's army was at the gates of Avisari. The sons of Manu were going to go to war.

"Three contingents of 1,200 each to approach Avisari from three sides," Haryashva said, assuring his King that numbers were on their side.

Ikshvaku nodded in approval. "Avisari is a good city to defend. We know its strengths and its weaknesses. The archers along the city walls must be negated first. Our infantry cannot begin breaching the gates while they have arrows raining upon them. How many Ashvaks in the camp that joined us?"

"About 1,800 for now, but more can join us at short notice," Haryashva replied. The Ashvaks had never accepted Pramshu as their King, and their combined strength was at Ikshvaku's command.

"And we have 900 archers with us," Ikshvaku calculated. "I have a way to reach Avisari's bowmen, but we will need all your men."

"It will be done."

"The siege weapons will be ready by nightfall tomorrow," said Revata, leader of the Aikshvakus and de-facto general of the army. "And our craftsmen are confident that they can break down the city gates."

"We cannot rely on siege weapons alone," Ikshvaku said. "I need our men to infiltrate the city as soon as possible. We must secure quarter after quarter till we have the Nripalaya surrounded. Our priority must be to establish multiple points of entry into the city while we have the rebels distracted with the siege at the gates."

The King kept his sons away from this campaign. Vikukshi and Nimi were seventeen and sixteen respectively, but Ikshvaku would not have them wage war on their uncles. "Get the men to build sturdy ladders," Ikshvaku commanded. "We will ramp them against the walls and climb once the archers are dealt with." He thought of his wives, Sarmi and Nivritti. With Sarmi, their first night together was the only real passionate moment they had shared. War, Rakshasas, nation-building and finally Dasavarsha had kept Ikshvaku too occupied to even spend time at home, let alone foster a romance with his first wife. And with Nivritti, though there had been sexual tension in the early years, their marriage was only a facade that was never consummated. No matter what he did from here on, he knew that he would not be able to undo the disservice he had done to both his wives.

"We need at least 1,000 ladders for enough warriors to be able to climb together," Haryashva suggested, breaking into Ikshvaku's guilt-ridden musings.

"Then we must begin immediately," Ikshvaku said, his steely gaze returning. "Our attack on Avisari must be relentless."

The Siege of Avisari

"The siege of Avisari taught Ikshvaku many things, and effectively made him a better ruler. He shifted his capital, learnt to make more defendable cities and generally became more militaristic. He also began to obsess with the matter of his succession."

King Bhagiratha to Sudasa

Year 53, Seventh era

"Ikshvaku does not hide his forces," commented Sharyati. "More than 4,000 men amass brazenly outside our walls, just outside the range of our archers. If those warriors find a way in, our 3,000 men may not be enough to defend the city." News of Ikshvaku's return had been confirmed a few nights before, when he sent a messenger into Avisari. The brothers had accepted it with an air of fortitude. Ikshvaku's return was their worst fear come true. But that did not mean that they could evade facing it.

"Our archers will greater the odds soon enough," Pramshu said confidently. "He will rush his soldiers against the city walls in a sacrificial frenzy."

"It would be unwise to rely on your premonitions, brother," said Nabhaga wearily. Pramshu wore the title of King publicly, but in private the brothers were a council of equals including Karusaka and Narisyanta."A second line of swordsmen should be ready behind the archers in case Ikshvaku's men try and scale the walls."

Pramshu scoffed, and even Sharyati said, "That is unlikely. They have no means with which to climb the walls."

"No *visible* means," Nabhaga corrected. "Perhaps that is why Ikshvaku does not hide his forces. His appearance of boldness is meant to distract us from what lies hidden."

Sharyati considered the speculation, aware that Nabhaga possessed the keener mind amongst them. "It is possible," he accepted. "We will allot men to form lines behind the archers."

"And arm both the archers and the swordsmen with boulders," added Karusaka. "If Ikshvaku's men reach our walls' feet, let us rain them upon their skulls."

"Will you reveal your big plan to me now?" Haryashva asked. "How do we take the Avisarin archers out?"

"Would you rather not see it instead?" Ikshvaku offered. "Send for the Ashvak commanders. It is time."

Avisari's walls were ancient clay and wood-baked superstructures, built by the three regents who ruled it between Marici and Ikshvaku, Ardra the Bear being the last of them. Ikshvaku thought of him now, remembering the beast of a man who was an early mentor to him. *I wonder what you would feel today, Bear. We try to penetrate the very walls you and your predecessors committed themselves to protecting.*

Ikshvaku knew that his plan could work only once. The attack had to be on all three of Avisari's walls together, so the Ashvak riders were split into contingents of 600 each. He allotted 300 archers to each set, taking time to explain the idea to them in detail, answering their queries and finessing the strategy together. Maharshi Vasishtha's final instructions were to begin battle at the break of dawn, just as Surya emerged to take its place in the sky. No warrior slept that final night, and the King walked amongst the ranks to offer encouragement.

The first steed galloped ahead just as a sliver of the Sun became visible on the horizon, hundreds more charging ahead on either side. An eager archer sat on each horse, his arrow loaded and the string tense. He would get only one real shot for the entire battle, and he was determined to make it count for his King. As the Ashvak charged his horse towards the wall they came closer and closer to the Avisarin archers' range, but the reverse was true as well. He allowed himself a moment's glance back, reassured by the second rider keeping up with them. Closer and closer to within the range, until at last the horse veered away just before that imaginary perimeter. At the very edge of its curve, the archer sprung up on the horse's torso and launched himself into the air. Momentum carried him high and deep into Avisari's range, but it gave him all the time he needed. Taking careful aim, he locked his eyes on some targets and released his volley of arrows. Many hit their mark just as he fell to the ground in a sickening crunch. The second rider was beside him, urging him to get on. He tried to ignore the pain and obeyed, allowing the Ashvak to carry him to safety as the Avisarin arrows rained around them.

On each of the three walls Ashvak riders charged head-on before veering off-course and giving air to leaping archers. Hundreds of them were successful, their arrows piercing clean through Avisari's archers taking aim from the walls. Secondary lines of riders pulled these archers back out from the fields just as their jobs were done. Ikshvaku saw the archers manning Avisari turn into a severely depleted force. It gave him grim satisfaction. These were *his* men. They were meant to give their lives for *him*. Solar blood coursed through all their veins, and how lightly it was being spilled here. Yet those men up there had made their choices, and there was still time for others to repent before they too paid the ultimate price. The seal of Surya would have to await its revelation to the Suryavansha at large.

Pramshu observed Ikshvaku's tactic unfold from the southern wall, taking cover as the arrows shot towards them and pierced his archers. He grunted in frustration—the first move belonged to Ikshvaku. But there was little he could do from within Avisari except wait for Ikshvaku to make his next move. "Send for Nabhaga!" he commanded, raising his voice over his men's screams and groans. Nabhaga would think of a way to counter this.

But Ikshvaku was already on his second tactic by the time Nabhaga climbed his way up the wall. Dozens of rider pairs charged at Avisari's walls head-on once again, this time balancing ladders between themselves. And behind them ran waves and waves of swordsmen, eagerly awaiting their successful placement. Ikshvaku was coming at Avisari with his full might, and Pramshu did not know what to do.

"Steady!" Nabhaga shouted to the men lined at the wall. Only a pitiful number of archers remained, the rest were swordsmen who uncertainly held boulders in their hands. "Do not let their ladders find a hold on our walls. Crush their skulls with those rocks if you have to."

He spotted Pramshu trying to make his way towards the stairs-ready to leave the wall. He grabbed his elder brother's robes and pulled him back, forcing his gaze towards the battlefield. "Ikshvaku rides among those men, putting his life on the line just like any warrior. If you wish for these men to fight for you against their original King, you need to fight with them."

Pramshu pulled himself free of Nabhaga's grasp. "There is no need for me to do so directly, brother. I am needed at the other walls too, men need to feel my assuring command. You take care of this wall." And with that he was gone, leaving Nabhaga to observe Ikshvaku's army run towards them with no fear of death in their blazing eyes.

"Steady!" Nabhaga repeated to the men, hoping it instilled as much courage in his heart as in theirs. He directed the archers to fire at the charging riders. If he could crush the ladders he would dent Ikshvaku's plans considerably. The archers' aim was good, two steeds went down, ladders and riders disappearing in an exploding cloud of dust. But not all arrows found their mark, and soon the riders were at the walls, mounting their ladders up against them. Nabhaga joined his men in throwing boulders down, grimacing as some of his throws found their mark in crunching sounds of confirmation. Yet, the sheer onslaught of warriors climbing was too much, and soon Ikshvaku's vengeful swordsmen were on the wall with blood in their eyes. They slashed and hacked with relentless fury, more men climbing up constantly. As the first spray of blood washed on Nabhaga, he decided that it was time he made himself scarce from the wall.

Ikshvaku worked in clinical precision, disabling the enemy rather than killing him as far as possible. His sword stabbed into knees, ankles and wrists, leaving only the danger of bleeding out. He moved resolutely, jabbing and pushing at men to throw them off the wall if need be. His eyes scoured for his brothers constantly, disappointed not to find them fighting among the men. Yet, as he made his way down the wall into his city and tried to take as little lives as he could, Ikshvaku noticed that the soldiers did not hesitate when they attacked him. They clearly recognised him as King Ikshvaku, yet they came at him with deadly intent. Each defender of Avisari wished to have his blood on his blade. How could Pramshu and the others have converted these men so easily? How could they wean loyalty away from Ikshvaku in a matter of years? He had thought himself to be a well-loved King, yet every new soldier that charged at him only reiterated the opposite.

He finally knocked the sword off one and grabbed him by the neck. "Why do you fight for them?" he snarled. "Why do you fight for Pramshu?"

"You are no King to me!" the man replied defiantly.

Ikshvaku loosened his grip instantly, his heart beating fast and loud. "I am no King to you," he repeated. "Why do you say that, brother? I put my life on the line for you, when I cleansed the Kamyakvana of the Rakshasas. I have brought you peace, security and prosperity. What more do you wish from your King?"

The man sighed, feeling helpless without a weapon in his hands. He was only a warrior after all. What real discourse could he have with a son of Surya and Marici? "I am a warrior of Vitabhya, oh Manava," the soldier said. "My grandfather was soldier in Marici's army, tasked by him to take dozens of clans to the confluence and settle them there. They named their town Vitabhaya—*without fear*. It is called Vitabhya now, and we have grown up to stories that we are a city of warriors. What glory we once held when Marici was alive, this was the lament of my father and grandfather. That glory was never renewed, for when you declared a kingdom you made Avisari your capital. Archers and swordsmen were found only in the north, you made it seem. None in your elite contingents were from the south, not a single from Vitabhya. When you went into Kamyakvana, did you call upon us to join you? When you marched west of Sindhu from our own city, did you invite us to follow you? How can I call you King, when you never looked upon us as loyal subjects?"

King Ikshvaku let his sword dangle by his side, so disarming was the soldier's candid statement. The man was right—Ikshvaku had developed his kingdom with undue neglect to the south. It seemed so obvious to him now, yet he was but blind to it moments ago. His elite contingents were populated by hardened Ashvak riders, Avisarin swordsmen and Sringaran archers; there were no warriors from Vitabhya or Harayupa. Their disdain for King Ikshvaku was justified, but did it also justify Pramshu's rebellion then?

"What is your name, Vitabhyan?" Ikshvaku asked.

"My parents named me Govanda, but in battle my friends have always called me Half-sword."

"Half-sword?"

"I once faced the misfortune of having my sword break during battle," Govanda explained. "The name has stuck ever since."

"And what will you do now, Half-sword?" Ikshvaku asked. "I cannot kill you, even though I surely must. Yet I cannot let you go, knowing that a fierce Vitabhyan walks the walls seeking death for my men."

"Will you trust me if I promise not to take the sword again?"

"Why will you take such an oath?"

"Because you will take an oath yourself, King Ikshvaku," Govanda replied. "You promise to better yourself. You promise to turn your attention to the kingdom's south."

"I do," Ikshvaku said truthfully.

"Then let me go," Govanda said. "There are enough men in need of medical aid. I will tend to them regardless of what side they fight for."

"Be safe," the King said. "And find me again after the battle. We have much more to talk about, Half-sword. And I will have need of your counsel."

The corridors of this palace were unfamiliar to him. In Vitabhya he knew every hallway, every nook and cranny that a young boy could hide in. But in Avisari he was a stranger, and young Narisyanta now felt very afraid. Shouts of men fighting echoed to him from every direction, and he knew not whether he ran towards the source of danger or away from it. He heard Sharyati call out to him once, but the voice echoed back and forth before he could determine its origin. Sweating in anxiety, he walked onward into a dark corridor, a faint light shining through at its other end.

The tip of a sword cut at his neck in that darkness. "You are Narisyanta, the youngest," a voice growled malevolently.

"Yes," he confessed immediately. But would that save him?

"Where are your brothers?"

"I do not know," he said, though he knew that the interrogator would not believe him.

"How many men guard them?"

"Fifty," Narisyanta said, praying that his honesty would pay off.

"Kneel!" the voice commanded.

Narisyanta obeyed, managing to protest meekly. "I am a son of Vaivasvat Manu, brother to Ikshvaku the King!"

A sword rested on his shoulder and then retreated to take aim. Narisyanta prayed to Surya, demanding courage now that death was upon him. Then, just as the sword was about to begin its deadly swing down, a voice shouted into the darkness. "Haryashva, no!"

Haryashva desisted and turned to find Ikshvaku face him from the distance. "He is a traitor!" he protested.

"He is my brother," Ikshvaku shouted back. "And he is only a boy. Let him go."

Narisyanta could have sworn that Ikshvaku's gaze now turned to him. "He is the youngest of my brothers," the King's voice echoed. "At his age I was only learning to hold a sword."

Haryashva's sword withdrew, and Narisyanta used that moment to scamper down the corridor and disappear into the darkness of another. The King walked up to his friend, his face awash in blood and grime. "You must leave my brothers to me, Haryashva," he said gently. "Find and capture them, but do not put them to death, yet. I wish to converse with them when this is over."

"The city is over-run," Sharyati said dejectedly. "Ikshvaku's men overpower ours at every corner. And they say Ikshvaku himself patrols the corridors looking for us."

"Ikshvaku will take time to reach us," Nabhaga said. "The Nripalaya's many corridors are vast and not entirely well-linked. He will have to navigate through dozens of passages manned by soldiers loyal to us before he can reach the central hall." Yet there was no doubt that he would, it was only a matter of time. "We are vulnerable here. We must find a way to escape the city."

"There is no escape," Pramshu said, his attention on the screams echoing in the hall. "The city walls belong to Ikshvaku, and by now his men would have broken through the gates. Wherever we run, we will find ourselves surrounded by his men."

"But we cannot sit here either," said Sharyati. "We still have fifty loyal men standing. We can use their protection and try to make way for the southern gates. Once outside the walls with stallions between our legs, there is no way Ikshvaku can capture us. And we only need make it as far as Sringara. From there we can disappear into the Himalaya."

"And into ignominy," added Nabhaga with distaste. "The valiant sons of Manu, brothers to Ikshvaku the First King, who captured kingship in his absence and fled when he returned to take it back. I do not wish that legacy upon us, dear brother."

"Nor I," said Pramshu. "We will make our final stand here. If you wish to run, I will not stop you."

Sharyati sighed. "Do not make me seem the coward, brothers," he said. "If you stay here then I will as well. Let us prime our swords, Ikshvaku and his men will be upon us any moment now."

"Where are Karusaka and Narisyanta?" Pramshu asked, noticing their absence only now. They were but youngsters swayed by his ambition. He would bear the brunt of Ikshvaku's vengeance upon himself, but none of it was due on the young boys.

"Karusaka is safe," Nabhaga assured him. "But Narisyanta is lost in the Nripalaya. I can only hope that Ikshvaku's blade will spare a life so young."

"I will find him," said Pramshu, making way towards one of the hall's large, wooden doors.

Both Nabhaga and Sharyati rushed to stop him. "It is too risky to venture out now, brother," Nabhaga said. "We do not know where Ikshvaku is, nor do you have any hints to Narisyanta's last known presence. He is an intelligent boy. He knows we are here. If he is safe, he will make his way here himself." Pramshu nodded and agreed, silently cursing Ikshvaku for placing such young boys at so much risk.

Ikshvaku and his men broke into the hall just as Narisyanta entered it from another end. The rebel brothers were surrounded by fifty men—like young Narisyanta had promised. Ikshvaku's eyes met his, and he tried to send a reassuring signal to his brother. But just then a rebel charged at him and the look was replaced by his characteristic, blazing fury. The siege of Avisari was more than two days long now, and King Ikshvaku was past the point where he tried to spare Suryavanshi lives. His sword cut swift, with lethal expertise. Haryashva moved behind him, tackling the rebels that managed to swing out of Ikshvaku's deadly path. He glanced at his King and remembered the Ikshvaku he had first met. That young boy was an exceptional warrior. This fearsome King was a dangerous, marauding killer.

It was over within minutes; Ikshvaku, Haryashva and Revata dispatching the soldiers with practised ease. And soon only the rebel brothers remained, four sons of Vaivasvat Manu facing their eldest. Sixteen years separated Ikshvaku from Pramshu, and not once had they engaged in the sort of companionship that brothers invariably do. As Ikshvaku's gaze locked with Pramshu's, the King found himself staring with regret. They looked upon each other as strangers, the blood tie seeming vacant when there were no common memories to reinforce it with.

"You only had to ask me," he said. "I would have made Kings of each one of you."

Pramshu and Sharyati stared back, hostility still present in their eyes. Nabhaga spoke. "You did not give us the chance. You chose to keep a nephew closer to you than your own brothers. You ignored us at every turn."

Ikshvaku nodded in grim agreement. "Errors that now seem far too grave. But it does not take away from your crime, my young brothers."

"Then kill us and be done with it," said Pramshu defiantly. "I care not for your sermons."

"But before you do that, I will have you know that there is a traitor in your midst, dear brother," added Sharyati maliciously. "We do not know who he is, but he extended much support to us when we originally captured your city."

Ikshvaku frowned at the acrimony in his voice. He knew that the boys' uncles had egged them on well, but who was this unseen partner? For one wild moment he allowed himself to imagine a traitorous Pururava, but that could not be possible. "He has let you down in the final test, then," Ikshvaku said. "For here I stand, my city and kingdom returned to me. And I possess the final symbol of authority, the seal of Aurvan Surya. The only question remains is what am I to do with you. I cannot kill you. It will break our father entirely, and I cannot bring him so much pain. But I cannot have you around us anymore either, for no longer will I ever be able to trust you."

"Exile then," Haryashva suggested aloud, long knowing that his friend would be unable to slay his brothers.

Ikshvaku nodded. "Exile indeed. As rightful victor at Avisari today and as King of the Suryavansha, I hereby banish you from Aryavarta. You shall not be found east of the Sindhu, south of the Himalaya or north of the Vindhyachala. Where you go from here is of no concern to me. But any man who spots you or your descendants in Aryavarta again is duty bound to the Solar King to wage war on you and wipe you out."

Pratishthana

"Your own home lies across the ruins of a much older city, probably the greatest of ancient Aryavarta. While Prayaga stands at the southern bank of the Yamuna-Ganga confluence, Pratishthana was established at the northern. Ila was its proud founder, and Pururava the first King."

King Bhagiratha to Sudasa

Year 55, Seventh era

Young Ayu exerted as much strength as he could, his puny hands digging deep into his father's gut. Pururava laughed aloud in paternal delight, observing his son exhaust himself in futility. He looked equally the son of both his mother and father—hair the black of dark Himalayan caves, and grey eyes shining through milky white skin.

"You are too strong," Ayu declared in frustration, stating it as if it was the most unfair fact in the world. His three years should not get in the way of his combat-ability as far as he was concerned.

"As are you," Pururava said to his son. "I am just a little stronger. But certainly you will bridge that gap soon?"

"Yes!" Ayu said confidently, not daunted in the least. "I only have to grow as tall as you." He was oblivious to the many years it would take him to scale his father's height.

"Only, yes," Pururava said in good humour.

"Is Ikshvaku *dada* stronger than you?" Ayu asked. *Dada* was the dialectical word for grandfather, and Pururava could imagine

Ikshvaku's expression at being called grandfather at the young age of thirty-seven.

He allowed himself a reminiscent chuckle before responding. "Ikshvaku dada is stronger than everyone. The day you beat him you will be the strongest warrior on Earth!"

"When will he reach here?" Ayu asked, almost as if he would challenge his grandfather to a duel the moment he arrived. His pronunciation was clear for a three-year old, his vocabulary expanding on a daily basis. Pururava knew that Ayu inherited this acuity from his mother. In the years since Pururava met Urvashi, he had come to see Apsaras as the fierce, matriarchal tribe they were. Their origins lay beyond the Himalaya, in lands that the Suryavanshi referred to as Ti Bhota or simply Bhota—best translated as *stark raving mad*. The Apsaras taught Pururava to understand them like no man ever had. They were, without a doubt, Aryas, in ancestry and fact. Their only mistake was to have fought on the Asura side in the Great Wars, and so their land became Bhota while his became Aryavarta.

"When will he reach here, father?" Ayu asked insistently, jabbing at his father's stomach.

Right on cue, the curtains of Pururava's grand halls parted and King Ikshvaku and his royal party entered. Pururava recognised all the familiar faces he was fond of—Ikshvaku, Haryashva, Vikukshi, Nimi, Varman, Maharshi Vasishtha and his beloved aunts, Sarmi and Nivritti. Pururava descended from his couch and greeted each, touching his aunts' feet with deep reverence. He met Varman as a simple pupil and Haryashva as an old friend. Then the two Kings embraced each other in strong kindred spirit.

The journey from Prasthala to Pratishthana took Ikshvaku's convoy of twenty people less than a week to complete, a feat previously unheard of. Part of it was due to swift sail downstream from Vrukasthali, but a significant portion was owed to a new message and transport system Ikshvaku devised. Haryashva had explained it to Pururava the last time, when he made it from Harayupa to Pratishthana in less than three days. "Way points have been established across the kingdom, often in villages and settlements that previously had no direct routes to larger cities. Thousands of horses have been distributed among them so that there is a well-maintained stable at each. A messenger that needs to take word from Avisari to Vitabhya can change steeds at every waypoint, no longer limited by anything but his own endurance. When we first set it up,

Ikshvaku and I had a race from Harayupa to Navapari, except we had to go through Vitabhya and Vinasana first."

"How long did it take you?" Pururava had asked.

"A little over four days," came the proud reply.

"And who won?"

"It's complicated," was the only reply Haryashva had offered to that.

"You can join us again whenever you desire, dear nephew," said Ikshvaku, breaking into Pururava's thoughts. The Lunar King shook out of his reverie to find all eyes on him. The gathering broke into a shared round of laughter at the blank look on his face, Pururava Aila was rarely spotted out of step with the world around him.

"Apologies, uncle," Pururava said graciously, accepting the mirth with a sheepish smile.

Elder Prince Vikukshi walked up to his aunt, Ila, eager to ask something troubling him for a while. "What lies downstream once the Yamuna and Ganga merge? Did you not explore ahead, aunt?"

Ila was the Somavansha's grand matriarch, its eldest member now that Maharshi Atri had ceased any active involvement in tribal affairs. She was also Pratishthana's founder and first citizen, proud leader of the great Lunar expedition that discovered these lands. That seminal journey was made ten years ago but the spark of exploration and innovation in Ila's eyes had not dimmed one bit. She smiled and ruffled Vikukshi's hair, remarking to herself how much he resembled his father at that age. Nimi was different though, taking nothing from Ikshvaku while bearing a certain ruggedness that did not seem his mother's either. "The forest takes over entirely a few yojanas downstream of Pratishthana," she informed him. "We call it Naimisharanya, and it extends just north of Krivi to as far-east as we have explored."

"The third and most dangerous forest of Aryavarta," Pururava remarked grimly, gesturing for his guests to take their seats. "We have enough reports of Gandharva and Rakshasa presence in it. If our estimates of Naimisharanya's size and density are anywhere near accurate, then their population is gravely large."

"Have there been any raids?" Haryashva asked.

"None yet," Pururava replied. "But scouting parties have been spotted observing Pratishthana from afar. For now, the Apsara strength aligned to us manages to keep them at bay."

"Where is dear Urvashi?" asked Sarmi. "We have heard enough songs of her beauty, and I am so eager to meet her."

"Urvashi will be joining us tomorrow," Pururava said. "There is a guild of Apsara traders in Yamaprastha, and she's gone to negotiate a treaty between us." Lunar society allowed far more equality between man and woman than Solar. Ikshvaku could never have Sarmi or Nivritti as his political regents—ancient Suryavanshi families would not accept it. But Pururava could position his wife as a representative, and the Somavanshi would see it as nothing extraordinary. It might not have been possible had Ila not shown the way for Lunar women, which was an irony as far as Ikshvaku was concerned. Ila was a Solar, first child of Vaivasvat Manu. What heights could she have achieved as Queen Ila of the Suryavansha?

Attendants brought in fresh drinks and snacks for the gathering, placing wooden trays full of dumplings and mashes that were new to Vikukshi and Nimi, it was their first experience of stepping beyond the Suryavanshi lands. They dug in like the rest, enjoying the Lunar tribe's spicier preparations. "I hope the food is to your liking, Nimi?" Ila asked fondly.

His mouth full of piping hot rice mash, Nimi settled for simply nodding earnestly. "Ayu, will you not come here and sit next to me?" asked Nivritti.

Young Ayu was awe-struck, not used to meeting so many new people together. He had pictured Ikshvaku as an old, towering man. To find him young and manly was surprise enough, but he had certainly not imagined him to be carrying such a large family in tow. Unfortunately for him, even in this diverse group there was no one of his age. Vikukshi and Nimi were so grim and old, sharing private jokes and looks with each other, all the while ignoring him.

King Pururava sensed his son's wonder and replied for him. "Ayu is just deciding who to make friends with first. And I do not think you are top on that list, sister Nivritti."

Ikshvaku's wives laughed in gentle mirth, remarking amongst themselves and Ila on Ayu's fair complexion. Local brew was brought in after the food was done, Varman commenting immediately that Soma was absent.

"Soma does not grow in these humid lands, General," Ila informed him. "But perhaps Maharshi Vasishtha can develop some batches for us?"

"I will certainly give it my best, Ila devi," replied the seer. "But I do not think Soma will grow along the Yamuna and Ganga. It needs the dry, almost arid airs of the north. I have been to Ahikshetra however, and Soma will flourish in the vales that surround it."

Pururava said to his son, "Ayu, why don't you take your uncles for a tour of Pratishthana? I'm sure you know the city better than I do by now!"

Neither Ayu nor Vikukshi and Nimi seemed too keen on the idea, but at a nod from Ikshvaku his sons rose to leave. When the boys were gone the Solar King turned to his nephew. "When you invited me to Pratishthana, you did not tell me it was for a serious discussion," he said. Pururava's subtle attempt at sending the young ones away had revealed his intent.

"But you anticipated it nevertheless, or you would not have brought Haryashva and Varman along," Pururava defended. "So no harm done?"

"None at all," Ikshvaku said. A different gathering of Aryas might have asked the women to leave at this point, but the Kings were not such men. Their discussion commenced, Pururava detailing Ikshvaku on the extent of the Gandharva and Rakshasa threat in Naimisharanya. When Pururava finally asked for some of Ikshvaku's finest warriors, the briefest of frowns appeared on the latter's face before being replaced by his usual poise.

"I must be honest with you, Pururava," Ikshvaku said. "I cannot spare too many men at this point. Narantaka is still free and alive in Dasavarsha, and his name comes up in more scout reports than I am comfortable with. I must maintain a state of constant vigilance."

"Shift in," Ila said matter-of-factly. "I have been saying this to you for years now. Come to Sarasvati. Vinasana could be perfect for that."

"I plan to do just that," Ikshvaku replied. "But not to Vinasana. The city is our father's vision. Let it remain the spiritual-beacon-on-the-Sarasvati he intends it to be. I will build a new capital for myself and my descendants, and there is another reason for not having a capital on that river. The Sarasvati forms a natural border between our kingdoms, and you must always remember that we are separate political entities. We are kinsmen and allies today, but it will not necessarily remain so forever. Any future King who has a capital along the Sarasvati will inevitably look beyond it and wonder why his armies have not marched there yet. Let the river be undisturbed, even mythic. Aryavarta is blessed with an abundance of rivers, and we have claimed most of them. Let one remain with rshis and the tribes of Asura-descendants."

"If I did not know my husband better, I would think he is becoming sympathetic towards Rakshasas," said Sarmi.

"Rakshasas do not inhabit the Sarasvati, actually," Ikshvaku said. "But you are right in spirit. I talk about their kindred tribes—Gandharva, Yaksha and Vanara. Sarasvati is their home more than ours, it sustained them for many centuries before the Solar tribes returned. But we are dishonouring our host, my dear wife, by digressing too much. He requested a favour of me, and I was trying to explain why I cannot deliver it fully."

"Rather you were telling me how our old enemy might yet return," Pururava said, not offended by Ikshvaku's candid refusal to share his warriors with him. He knew Ikshvaku well enough to know that his forthrightness was intrinsic. "If I were but in a better position, I would send my men to you instead. Narantaka is a threat to Aryavarta itself, not just to Suryavansha."

"Every Anarya is a threat to Aryavarta," said Varman. "The Rakshasa in Naimisharanya is as dangerous as the Dasa creeping closer from west." It was Varman's attempt to acknowledge that Pururava's concerns were no less graver than Ikshvaku's.

"Then unite," Ila said, as if it was the most obvious thing to do. "Narantaka knows that you are not the sole master of Aryavarta, Ikshvaku. And he knows that he will find kinsmen in every forest of this land. Similarly, the Gandharvas and Rakshasas of Naimisharanya know that Pururava does not have the Suryavansha's formidable army. Our enemies know our weaknesses, but how easily they vanish if we are one dynasty in place of two. Why does Pururava need to ask you to help him? Why is the presence of Solar warriors in Naimisharanya not taken for granted?" It was the best summation of Ila's eternal ambition—a complete blurring of the lines between the Solar and Lunar tribes. *There are two parts in a day*, her mother had once told her. *The Sun rules in one and Moon in the other*. Young Ila had innocently asked even then-*Why do they not rule together, mother?* If only she were a man, a marriage to one of Maharshi Atri's daughters would have sealed the fate of Aryavarta forever. It was a tragedy, the immense potential of an individual lost only because of their gender. But Ila was long past the age when she cursed the world for what it was. Now she accepted the truth without letting it affect her own actions—that the world belonged to her father, uncles, sons, brothers and nephews. Not her mother, aunts or sisters. And never her.

Her thoughts kept her oblivious to the long look that passed between Ikshvaku and Pururava. Friends for more than a decade, they thought they had a consummate understanding of each other. And yet all this while they were oblivious to the reality that stood obvious now—both of them were products of Ila's vision. Ikshvaku remembered his seven-year old self, listening to Ila's narrations of Marici and his grand ambition. She was the one who taught him the meaning of *Raja*. Pururava pictured his mother as she sent him off to Avisari, placing a stone on her heart as she sent her son away to give him the best preparation for kingship she could provide.

"There are two parts in a day," Ikshvaku finally said, remembering the same words said by their mother. "The Sun rules in one and Moon in the other. Together they make the basic unit of time that governs human lives. And yet there is no part in a day when they rule together, dear sister. The Sun needs to set before the Moon's glow lights up the night sky. And when the Sun rises again the Moon must go into inevitable slumber. A boundary always exists, as it must between our dynasties as well."

Ila opened her mouth to counter, but Ikshvaku raised his hand and stopped her. "Before you argue with me on how far we can extend this metaphysical analogy, let me add that there are several practical concerns as well. Who will be King in your scenario? Would you rather I give up Solar reign, or would you have Pururava relinquish all that he has achieved these past years? When the King goes to war or when he returns, will a Vasishtha preside over the proceedings or an Atri?"

Ila fell silent, unable to answer these questions. Ikshvaku used the opportunity to veer discussion back to his nephew's original request. "I will spare you 500 Ashvaks, no more. It is all I can do for now, Pururava. I must build a new capital first, erect it to become a fortress the Rakshasas never dare look upon. I owe it to my successor, and I must do so in the ever-reported shadow of Narantaka to the west."

On his third night in Pratishthana, King Ikshvaku decided to broach the matter that brought him to Pururava's capital. But he would have to wait for the evening to unwind, for there was a hearty social gathering with all members of either royal family in attendance. Varman, Haryashva, Devapi and Vasishtha were the honoured guests, and Sura was in ample availability. Ikshvaku was inclined to share the brew with his sons as well, but at a stern look from Ila he desisted in the attempt. "They're men now," he suggested quietly. "Not in my house they're not," was Ila's determined reply. Later in the evening the gathering turned to Maharshi Vasishtha, requesting him to share the history of Soma and Sura, and any other brews that he knew of.

"Soma, Sura, Seedhu, Madhu and Arishta," Vasishtha listed. "These are the inebriants known to the people of Aryavarta since the beginning of their time, and I have stated them in descending order of divine significance. Soma is the Indra of all brews, its distillation a true art that cannot be mastered by all."

"And who was the first master then?" Ila asked.

"How could anyone know? Soma's origins are deep in our past, when the First and Original Devas walked the earth. But true Soma's distillation follows an exact procedure, anything else produced is just an Arishta, a spirituous liquor. And the technique was passed down only in select family lines. Even among the Devas there were some who did not know how to produce it."

"Like Surya," guessed Ikshvaku.

The Maharshi nodded. "Which is why Solar tribes did not know of it before they returned to Aryavarta. Then there are the common brews, Sura and Madhu, one by rice and the other by honey. These too, are primitive drinks, though not accorded as much significance as Soma. Perhaps that is because they are easier to make, often even by accident. Rarity does attract its own exaltation after all, especially in matters of wine and brew. But both Sura and Madhu can be found wherever men are familiar with rice or honey."

"And what of Seedhu, guruji?" asked Sarmi, sparing a mischievous glance towards her husband.

"Seedhu, rum made from sugarcane molasses. I daresay that King Ikshvaku could expound on its history better."

Ikshvaku's fondness for all things sugarcane was legendary, and even princes Vikukshi and Nimi snickered at Vasishtha's comment. The King smiled indulgently, taking a sip of Sura and silently comparing it with Seedhu. The sugarcane's obvious sweetness was missing, but the gentle bitterness of rice was equally palatable. He felt sure that the Sura produced in ordinary Lunar households was more raw and significantly more bitter than this royal version.

"Seedhu is a brew unique to Aryavarta," he said, enjoying the audience's attention on him. "For where else have men learnt to grow sugarcane? It is said that Tvastra Deva was the first to take its sweet gulp, but I agree with the Maharshi-how could anyone know?"

The night grew heady soon after that, with Urvashi inviting Ikshvaku's wives for a special tour of Pratishthana's private forest. Ila retired to take care of the children, insisting that young princes should follow a strict routine lest they form a bad habit. Ikshvaku found his opportunity when he was finally left alone with Pururava and Haryashva. The Sura had settled in well, compelling even Varman, Devapi and Vasishtha to make their apologies and retire for the night. Both Varman and the Maharshi were men who favoured Soma, and only in temperate amounts. The Sura's rougher, more direct approach to inebriation did not suit their palate as much, nor their constituency.

"There is something I mean to ask of you, Pururava," Ikshvaku said, sharing a look with Haryashva before he began. The Ashvak knew what the King meant to ask.

Pururava looked across from the shadowed lights of his hall, sensing both Ikshvaku and Haryashva staring at him intently. "Ask anything, uncle," he said earnestly.

"Give me your son," Ikshvaku said simply. He had never been one to dally with his words. "Ayu is at the ripe age of three. He is like molten metal that can be forged into whatever weapon the smith desires. Let me sculpt him, like we once did you."

And yet, for the first time in his life, Pururava felt that his uncle hid something from him. "For how many years would you take him away?" he asked.

"Ten," answered Haryashva, making it clear that he knew what Ikshvaku hid. "And there can be no contact between you in that time."

Pururava looked from Ashvak to King, momentarily feeling envious of their relationship. How could an outsider become so close to Ikshvaku? How could their bond blend so deep that they shared secrets he knew naught of? "Something is amiss, uncle," he said. "I have not known you to be a withholding sort of man. Will you not tell me what you really intend?"

Ikshvaku nodded, refilling his cup with Sura and passing the pouch to Haryashva. "I am building an elite group of warriors, nephew," he replied. "A hundred men that can take on thousands, such would be their ability. There exists such a group in my army. I call them the Aikshvakus, my most loyal and fierce fighting force. But they are ageing, endless years of war beginning to take its toll on their bones. To replace them, I cannot take men who are already grown to adulthood. A sword once forged can be melted and created anew, but not men. I need young bodies and minds, ones that can be sculpted into whatever intended form."

"You wish to rob children of their childhood?" Pururava asked, not believing his ears. This sounded more like Rakshasa dispassion than Solar innovation. Then it hit him—had Ikshvaku heard of such practises from Narantaka?

Ikshvaku did not seem offended. Indeed, his look told Pururava that he had battled such thoughts himself.

"Ten years of nothing but strict martial training, preparing a young boy for the very extremes of life, where death lurks like an ever-present shadow," said Haryashva, speaking for his King. "Imagine a force of 100 warriors forged through such harsh measures. They would be invincible."

"And children still," Pururava said, unable to accept the proposal. "I cannot encourage such a program. And I certainly cannot enlist my son in it."

Ikshvaku sighed, draining his cup in one gulp and going for another refill. Pururava frowned-he had not known his uncle to indulge in drink with such abandon. "Complacence is our greatest enemy, Pururava," Solar King said wearily. "We see ourselves as mighty kings, riding horses amidst a populace only too happy to kneel at our passing. But outside our borders, wild tribes await for the perfect moment of weakness. To the west, Narantaka raises an army for a purpose we can easily fathom. Closer to your borders, Gandharvas observe your city daily and memorise its routine. And you know what? This land is *theirs*, not ours. They have lived here longer, and are thus more prepared to die defending it. We cannot win against this resolve if we are unwilling to take radical measures ourselves. And we must think of our descendants. Our achievements will mean nothing if we cannot secure a safer, more prosperous future for them. This is our final duty as Kings."

"And this is what you propose, uncle? To pick up young boys and put them through a rigour even many grown men would fail at?"

"Not grown men who have *already* passed through such rigour!" Ikshvaku countered, inverting Pururava's logic. "Do you not see it? These boys will emerge the highest quality of tempered metal, unbreakable in the face of insurmountable odds. An invincible army of 100 men, and your son an immortal among them."

"Five years with the Suryavanshi have made you a man fit to be Lunar King," Haryashva added, pressing Ikshvaku's point further. "Imagine what ten can do to young Ayu."

Rajavasa

"Irrigation, transport, trade, farming, pottery—there is no human endeavour that did not benefit from the efficiencies of Ikshvaku's reign, and Rajavasa was its living embodiment. Within a few years it became the nexus of his kingdom, weaning trade away from Prasthala and Harayupa."

King Bhagiratha to Sudasa

Year 56, Seventh era

"Are you afraid?" Nimi asked, smiling encouragingly.

"No!" Ayu lied. Truth be told, he was petrified. What four-year old could face a leopard and not instinctively want to run to his mother? But he was an *Aikshvaku* now, or at least training to be one. He had to display a level of courage commensurate to his title, not his age.

Nimi seemed to understand, and placed a reassuring hand on his nephew's shoulders. "Stay with me, little one. I will ensure no harm comes to you."

But Haryashva detected the display of filial sympathy between his wards and roared loudly. "Spread out! I want a distance of two swords between everyone. Let the leopard choose his meal well."

Nimi gave Ayu a helpless shrug and walked afar sideways, winking at him as if this was any normal situation. Ayu gulped involuntarily, studying the leopard as it paced ever closer, its gaze going to each potential victim. This was a wild beast brought from the Himalaya's upper reaches, still hesitant around humans. But these were mere boys, Nimi being the eldest at twenty. It strolled closer to them with increasing confidence before one of the boys charged at it. The animal retreated a few steps but did not flee.

"Hold!" Haryashva commanded. "Let it choose its opponent."

The eager Aikshvaku backed off, though not without giving his mates a smug grin. Ayu gripped his tiny sword tentatively and prayed to Soma to spare his life on this day. But as he looked upwards he found the royal balcony, where King Ikshvaku observed with cold eyes. His face was impassive, unsympathetic even.

"Turn around, you dolt!" Nimi shouted from somewhere out of his vision.

Ayu complied to find the leopard staring right at him, its teeth bared aggressively. The young Lunar tottered backwards. The leopard leaped into the air and Ayu fell to the ground with a loud wail. He continued to cry for a while before realising that the end had not come. No mass of claws and teeth ripped into his flesh, and his body had not erupted in blood and pain. Plucking courage, he opened his eyes. Blood was spattered on the ground around him, but it was not his. At some distance away lay the leopard's lifeless body, only its head was missing. Ayu whirled around reflexively to find it discarded some distance behind him. Then he finally looked to his left and saw Nimi, a bloodied sword dangling from his right hand. Comprehension hit him in an instant, as did a lifelong gratitude to his uncle.

Nimi let the sword fall from his hand, unable to take it any longer. He stared defiantly into Haryashva's narrowed eyes. "Enough," he said. "These are boys, and we are their guardians. If they die within the King's very walls, how can he claim to protect his vast citizenry?"

Haryashva stood silent. Nimi's defiance was for the King to deal with, not a trainer Ashvak. He marched the Aikshvakus back into the barracks, letting Ayu pick himself up and join the group without aid. Soon only Prince Nimi stood on the training grounds, unable to leave because his father's eyes were locked directly on him from the royal balcony. King Ikshvaku stood wordlessly and assessed his younger son-in truth the son of Narantaka. The King wondered whether he was alone in spotting a resemblance in Nimi's smile, or in his arrogant smirk. Did Haryashva not notice? How long would the likeliness escape Varman or the Maharshi? Father and secretly-adopted-son looked at each other for a long time while the sun disappeared into the horizon. From the shadows of the royal barracks, Haryashva observed the encounter in equal silence-knowing his friend's secret without needing to be told.

Ikshvaku's muscles strained at the pressure, fibre and tendon threatening to rip apart any moment. But the King held on as resolutely as the rest of his men, pulling hard as they yanked the lumber out of water and placed it on the mud. Countless more pieces of wood floated gently on the water; it was clear to all that their labour would continue into well after sunset. Maharshi Vasishtha had chosen the spot for the city well. Kamyakvana's northern borders were not too far south, close enough for timber to be in ready supply. And Iravati was a benign tributary here, still afar from Harayupa where it picked up momentum as it rushed into the Vitasta. The settlement was on the river's west, giving King Ikshvaku a wide view of Aryavarta as he looked across. It was meant to remind him of where his attention must lie, though that could never happen as long as Narantaka was alive to the west. It was titled Rajavasa, or Abode of the King.

The city was carved partly onto the face of a sheer cliff which at its eastern end tapered flat onto the Iravatati. On the north, outside the city's formidable walls, stood vast farmlands of maize and rice. In its design, Ikshvaku had taken inspiration from Vitabhya-which too was constructed partly on physical contours banking a major river. Rajavasa was protected on the north and south ends by manned walls, on the east by the Iravati and on the west by the ragged cliff. Its Nripalaya, King's Quarters, was Aryavarta's largest man-made construction ever. And now only the docks remained, space already allocated at the city's south-most clearings. But to build them would be no easy task. Layer upon layer of wood had to be placed to bring them at a sufficient height, with provisioning for a deck at a lower level as well. Iravati was a river that waxed and waned, its water levels increasing with the rains and falling in winter when the Himalayan glaciers froze up. The lower deck had been easy, placed at less than a man's height above the muddy bank. But the upper floor stood at a staggering eight *ikshvakus* high, for that was the measurement Vaivasvat Manu used. All of Rajavasa's river traffic could be accommodated once the docks were ready, and a separate team prepared boardwalks for what would undoubtedly be a dense gathering of traders, fishermen and travellers.

"It would be well if you rest, my King," said Half-sword, otherwise known as Govanda. After the siege of Avisari he found Ikshvaku again as commanded. And proved himself to be a master architect, soon becoming one of Vaivasvat Manu's finest pupils.

Ikshvaku accepted the dig with good grace, smiling wryly as he wiped sweat off his brows and beard. "No time for rest now, Half-sword," he said. "The docks are our last task. With them Rajavasa will be complete. Then we can rest."

Half-sword nodded, knowing that the King would not rest if his men were not afforded the same luxury. But to allow the entire team of 800 men to take a break at this point would bring their construction to a halt for the day—and time was running out. Rajavasa's population had swollen since its establishment, but without a well-functioning dock the city could not keep up with its citizens' burgeoning demand for wood, metal, clay, grain, gems, figurines and jewellery. Maharshi Vasishtha had generously allowed a portion of his ashrama to be used as a temporary dock, but he prohibited the passage of fish and meat through its premises. Yet since he alternated his time between Vinasana and Rajavasa, Govanda knew that some fish trade did ply under Ikshvaku's silent consent.

Govanda saw Ikshvaku gesturing the men towards another piece of floating lumber and rejoined the group, the fatigue in his bones could not diminish his motivation. He knew that the men around him shared this sentiment, such was the rejuvenating effect of watching one's King sweat it out with the common folk. Half-sword had heard that Ikshvaku led from the front, but he imagined it only applied on the battlefield. That the King would build Rajavasa with his bare hands, pouring as much sweat into its bricks as any other labourer, was something most had not expected. The collective zeal that it generated made it possible for a city so vast to be established within a few years. As night fell their work continued, and now they were aided by the light of not just the moon, but also the Suryavedi.

Inspired by Vinasana's ritual altars that were alit all day and night, the Suryavedi was a fire-altar that was Ikshvaku's spiritual assertion of his divine claim. Designed by Maharshi Vasishtha, it was an intricate conglomeration of bricks and wood, with five different brick-types being put to use. They symbolised, as Vasishtha explained, the five kinds of meters that rshis used to encode their prayers-usnih, pankti, viraja, tristubha and jagati. The design is adaptive. *If further meters are composed, we can alter the Suryavedi accordingly without needing to kill its flames,* Vasishtha had patiently detailed to King Ikshvaku. And this was important, for the Suryavedi was to be burning glorious at all times. There were even arrangements to cover it during rain with the flames only slightly reduced, and massive planks of wood could be erected within moments to protect it from strong winds. As long as the Suryavedi's fires were alit, Maharshi Vasishtha had declared, the Suryavansha would prosper. Three hundred rshis were assigned to man it constantly, replenishing its wood and fuel at regular intervals. The King began every morning with a prayer under its flames, taking blessings from the day's first union of sunlight and fire before having the lead rshi garland the seal of Surya around his neck.

The Suryavedi's flames formed a halo around the Nripalaya now, which was located between it and the docks. Under its warm glow, men pulled the other pieces of timber out of the water and hauled them up for the upper deck on pulleys imported from Madra. Ikshvaku called it a day just a few hours before sunrise. This had been their routine for weeks, a few hours of sleep punctuating days of hard and lasting labour. But when the King could bear it with fortitude, his men had no other choice but to follow suit.

The Nripalaya was open to all those who volunteered to help build Rajavasa, its various chambers and floors their accommodation while the city was being constructed. It was not unusual for Ikshvaku to find fresh faces roaming his halls, youngsters who had volunteered perhaps only to visit the King's grand palace. They would leave in a few days, supposedly exhausting their reserves of Solar patriotism. He did not mind this; Rajavasa was the *King's Residence* in name but in reality, it had to be a people's city. If some of them wanted to devote a few days of hard labour to reside in the Nripalaya for a few nights, then they would not be turned away. The only problem, as both Haryashva and Varman liked to remind him, was that any of these people could be a Rakshasa spy or worse—an assassin. They were right, but the solution was not to close the doors on Rajavasa's citizens. It could be countered only with spies of their own, blending with the masses to detect if there were any Rakshasa sympathisers.

The irony was that one Rakshasa sympathiser lived within the Nripalaya with Ikshvaku's will and consent. Nivritti was his wife for seventeen years now, and they had come to share a love that was true, even though it was not consummated. But Nivritti was a Rakshasi at heart, a woman who was distinctly Anarya in thought and ideology. She possessed an instinctive disgust for Arya rituals, unable to understand the significance of bowing and praying around a few pieces of flaming wood. And she religiously disapproved of every anti-Rakshasa campaign. Indeed, if not for Nivritti's counsel, Ikshvaku might have given in to Solar elders' desire to 'rehabilitate' captured Rakshasas as slaves. She added her opinion to any decision on Rakshasa matters, and avoided doing so only when the matter pertained to Narantaka. There was enough sincerity between Ikshvaku and her for him to know that she still held love for her ex-husband, as much as she did for Ikshvaku himself. But she was mindful enough not give any indication of it, and in public expressed the requisite amount of disgust and fear of Narantaka that suited a Solar Queen.

Rajavasa's docks took seven long months to complete, and when they were done Maharshi Vasishtha suggested a grand prayer to officially inaugurate the city. The ritual was long and elaborate, meant to symbolise the completion of a mission. But King Ikshvaku was not moved by the symbolism. His enemy still survived in Dasavarsha, and Ikshvaku would have to deal with that threat before he could bequeath his kingdom to his son. He still did not allow himself to debate which son that would be.

Father and Son

"Nimi has been a fascination to me. Mysterious, inscrutable and remotely chronicled, he was still a loyal son of Ikshvaku. When this tale is done, I will tell you of the grand kingdom Nimi founded—and the role it played in my own life."

King Bhagiratha to Sudasa

Year 57, Seventh era

The Rakshasa resisted the urge to join his companions on the battlefield, remaining hidden in the tree while he watched Suryavanshi valour on display. He felt a grudging respect for their prowess, the perfect co-ordination in their movements and the precise swing of every sword. Their leader was a man called Revata, and he was the epitome of their strength. The Rakshasa felt sure that only Raja Narantaka could face this fiery Solar and come out victorious. Revata was death incarnate, hacking through Rakshasa flesh and bone with a fluid ease that was hypnotic to watch. He looked almost bored, insolent even, acting as though he had done this a hundred times before. And he had—Kamyakvana was early hunting grounds for the Suryavanshi and their King. Revata was not only General of Ikshvaku's army, but also leader of the Aikshvakus—the crazed, battle-hungry force of elite warriors that had served Ikshvaku since the beginning of his reign.

Slowly but surely, Revata and his men finished off the Rakshasa party. Not a single soldier in their group lost his life, such was their invulnerability. Raja Narantaka was right, the Rakshasas were not ready to face the Suryavanshi yet. But would they ever be? Could they ever better or even match such war capabilities? They could, with the right planning and execution—Raja Narantaka was sure of that. The Rakshasa's mission was near its end. He had completed his report of Ikshvaku's capital, making it as comprehensive as ordered. And now his party was discovered and slain. General Revata did not leave it at that though. He set guards around a perimeter for two more nights, and his horsemen patrolled the forest's boundaries for a full week. It made it difficult for the Rakshasa to make his way back home, but not impossibly so.

Aryavarta was home to his ancestors once, and its rivers and terrain seemed intuitively familiar to him. He knew roughly how far west the Sindhu would be, once he crossed the Vitasta and finally escaped Kamyakvana's clutches. Suryavanshi presence was sparse here, represented by a handful of villages and local militias organised with the King's consent. Beyond the Sindhu he was a free man, back in Harivarsha—Dasavarsha to the Suryavanshi. A month's journey brought him to Harautii, Narantaka's nascent capital. The Rakshasa leader was unrelenting in his questions, seeking to squeeze every last bit of information out of his spy.

"Rajavasa's two walls are impenetrable," the spy reported frankly. "Thick and high walls of magical brick brought from Trigarta, manned by unerring Suryavanshi archers. And they have turrets at regular intervals, where they have planted stronger, deadlier longbows. On the western front, its settlements are carved into the cliff, which is too sharp for us to climb."

"How many soldiers protect it?"

"At any given time, 4,000 men protect Rajavasa, and Ikshvaku can summon a further 2,000 from surrounding villages at short notice. They once staged a week-long drill where horsemen rode in from Prasthala, Harayupa and Navapari as if the city was under attack. Ikshvaku expects your attack, my King."

"As he well should. Our own army is close to 3,000 strong. A few more contingents from the west and we will be ready to march. How long does it take for riders to reach Rajavasa from Prasthala?"

"Just under six days, my King. Ikshvaku's stallion express system is comprehensive."

"And from Harayupa and Vitabhya?"

"Harayupa can send men by river as well, but on land the horses take close to ten days. They have to cross east of the Iravati and then cross back again when they near Rajavasa, for all along the western bank lie the Kamyakvana's marshes. And Vitabhya would take longer still, more than twenty days."

Narantaka chuckled dryly. Even after wiping the Rakshasas out of it, Ikshvaku could not venture through Kamyakvana. It would seem that the forest was putting up a stronger resistance than they had. "Then Prasthala is the only city that could help Rajavasa in time," he said. "We must take the city within a week. Any longer and the Suryavanshi will be able to repel us."

But in his heart Narantaka knew that it would take more than just numbers and timing to overpower Suryavanshi warriors. His men were a courageous bunch, but nowhere near as organised or well-armed as Ikshvaku's polished forces. And unlike the Solar King, Narantaka had no men he could place his trust in. Only brute force wielded his contingents together, that and the promise of loot once they marched into Rajavasa. His horses were as inexperienced as his men—wild beasts that were not entirely amenable to be tamed for warfare. The mere sight of blood drove most of them into a frenzy, their instinctive motivation to flee getting the better of them. His archers were, if he was to be honest with himself, woeful. Not all of it was their fault though. Part of the blame rested on their primitive bows, not as precise or strong as the ones Solar archers carried. And the arrows were of wood, more susceptible to the wind and prone to breaking.

The best of his spies could not broker a treaty with Trigarta or Madra for metal and weapons. The cities may choose non-alliance when it came to Aryavarta's tribes, but they could not betray Aryavarta itself. Narantaka respected them for it, he expected no less from a people that claimed indigenous inhabitation as ancient as Rakshasas. Aid was equally scarce from the far west, where King Enmerkar and his city of Uruk looked upon Narantaka's people as savages much like the Suryavanshi did. But his propaganda served him well, attracting many second-generation descendants of the Rakshasas who once occupied Kamyakvana. Solar tribes were cast in an invader light in his narrative, no mention of first Marici and then Ikshvaku's attempts at brokering a peaceful coexistence. The numerous Rakshasa raids into Solar cities were conveniently omitted as well. Solar tribes were vile Daeva descendants, laying false claim on a land their forefathers were evicted from centuries ago. The momentum of this propaganda was strong enough to attract many local Rakshasas as well, though they referred to themselves as Parshuas.

Morale would be the least of his problems when the march to Aryavarta finally began. But keeping the disparate tribes that populated his army in check would be a tougher task. There was no way Parshuas could be persuaded to fight alongside Arians, or Asagartiyas with Yavanas. Among other quirks, Aspasois would fight only after a heavy night of drinking and other revelry, but Kambojas took up the sword after an intense morning ritual. And he would not be able to control them if not for their strong tribal commanders. But therein lay what Narantaka thought to be his finest move. His title of King was an illusion, a mirage cast in the desert so that his soldiers could summon the courage to go up against King Ikshvaku and his Suryavanshi warriors. All real power resided with the tribal commanders, and they accepted him as King only because it secured a tentative peace with other tribes. They would rally their men together in his name, and follow the ambitious journey that ended with his sword at Ikshvaku's throat. But the final key in this campaign would be the one secret Narantaka had over Ikshvaku, and he would relish its deadly revelation when the time came.

"Easy now. Do not let passion control your movements. Let your training and instinct come to the fore," Ikshvaku instructed, sparring with his second son.

Nimi took a deep breath and nodded, transferring his sword momentarily from right hand to left to wipe the sweat in his palm. "I will not rejoin, father," he said as he swiped, following the sequence of movements that formed today's lesson.

"You would dare disobey your father's orders?" Ikshvaku asked, lazily deflecting Nimi's swings. There was no anger in his voice. Like his father had done with him, Ikshvaku encouraged his sons to speak their mind, even if what they said bordered on dissent.

"No, not if you order it. But you haven't, yet."

"Nor will I, son. But I must try to convince you nevertheless. I admit to you now that I have been excessive with the Aikshvakus. The day you quit, Prince Ayu would have surely lost his life had you not intervened. I think now to the moment, and am ashamed to see myself standing motionless on the balcony. My wisdom and judgement were clouded in the days following the rebellion, but the haze has lifted now."

Nimi's moves did not falter at his father's confession. Ikshvaku was an exacting master and candid discourse would not be valid excuse for his pupil to make a mistake. He continued, "The Aikshvakus are only children, I see that now. And while I stand by my original intent, I accept that my methods were wrong."

"In that you will continue to raise an army of boys named after you, even if their training is softened," Nimi said, completing the sequence and beginning it anew.

"You need not put it that way. Their rigour will only be made consistent with their age. But you cannot argue against the merit of a training program that captures boys young and sculpts them into warriors."

"I love Haryashva as much as you do, father, and I respect him too. But I can easily imagine the radical side of him taking over once again. And you have always been unable to say no to him."

"Which is why I have decided that Haryashva will no longer train the Aikshvakus. You will."

This time Nimi did stop, frowning at his father. "Me? A teacher? I am still a student myself. And not a good one at that."

"Quite the opposite. You have learnt enough, with diligence and discipline; and I have nothing more to give. But you can give much to those boys. They look up to you, idolise you even, for you once saved the youngest among them. Be their guru, Nimi. Train and command these Aikshvakus into the fiercest force ever assembled, one that will serve under your brother when he is King."

Nimi sighed. Whether he was truly convinced or not did not matter. He could not bring himself to refuse his father's persuasion. So he nodded in acquiescence. "But the command will be mine alone," he set as a condition. "I cannot do my job if Haryashva, General Revata, Varman or even you interfere."

"Haryashva, Revata and Varman will stay away, I promise you. But I cannot withdraw from this myself. The Aikshvakus are *my* children, and my vision for them is clearer than ever before. My interference will be limited to timely confirmations from you that your direction remains true."

"Fair conditions," Nimi conceded. He was silent in thought for a while before he spoke. "So Vikukshi will be King after you. You are decided in this, father?"

Ikshvaku opened his mouth to reply, but his son cut him off. "I know what our traditions are. Primogeniture has always been our people's way, but you've never made it law."

"Do you wish to be King?"

"Not really, but it pains me to think that you are partial to one son."

His raw honesty tore at Ikshvaku's heart, and the Solar King realised that he could no longer keep Nimi in the dark. After a long moment of uncomfortable silence he said, "There is a secret I have withheld from you, my son. A terrible secret that could change everything you feel about me."

Nimi waited, a peculiar sense of dread spiralling in his gut.

"Before I confess it to you, I wish to tell you one thing. I cannot make you a Suryavanshi King, for reasons that will soon be clear. But I earnestly desire to see you as King nevertheless, for what a fine leader you will make. So no matter what happens between us now, I declare you free to form your own dynasty. Free to carve a kingdom anywhere you desire. And your line will never be enemy to mine."

Nimi guessed the truth moments before Ikshvaku uttered the words, but the full confession hit him like a boulder, crushing him. "I am not your father by blood, my son. You were born to a Rakshasa, one who was also husband to your mother."

The question came out of Nimi involuntarily. "Did you kill him?"

"No, but I should have and will."

"Who?" Nimi said faintly, strength seeming to drain out of him as the answer dawned on its own.

"Narantaka," Ikshvaku whispered.

The silence that followed was the longest of Ikshvaku's life, and for a while he wondered whether Nimi would tighten his grip on the sword and attack. But at the most important revelation of his life, Nimi's expression had turned inscrutable again. He looked at Ikshvaku with hollow eyes, his voice betraying no emotion when he said, "Twenty-one years I have been kept in the dark. And you made my mother hide it as well."

"I did."

"Who else knows?"

"Only my father by my confession. But Haryashva has surely guessed by now."

"I could kill you right now, father."

"No, you could not. But you have fair reason to try, and I would not begrudge it. I have loved you as my own son, Nimi. When we captured Narantaka, you and your mother were left abandoned. You were about to be slain by Rakshasas, and I could not leave you to that fate. Yet, had I brought Nivritti to Avisari as anything but my wife, I could not have given you protection and anonymity. It did not take me too many years to fall in love with her, or with you."

"What does sentiment matter when blood holds you back so strongly?" Nimi countered. "No one knows my Rakshasa lineage, they think me to be a true son of Ikshvaku the great." It was still not an expression of the desire to be King. Nimi never held that aspiration for himself, learning long ago that happiness could be achieved even in anonymity. But he spotted a vital flaw in Ikshvaku's reasoning, and he could not leave it unexposed.

"It is not about what people may know or think," Ikshvaku explained. "I have a duty to my forefathers, especially to Marici. To call you Suryavanshi King is desirable to me, but dishonest and unfair to him. I became King under the grand ambition of fulfilling his dream, of establishing a Solar homeland in Aryavarta. To bequeath that ambition to someone not of Solar blood, even if he is my son, would be supremely selfish of me."

In spite of himself, Nimi understood Ikshvaku's point. He knew his *step*father, Ikshvaku operated under a strong personal principle and considered Marici his chief deity. His ancient ancestor was everything to him, and preserving Marici's legacy was the undeclared duty of his life. But Nimi argued nevertheless. "Then how can I train the Aikshvakus? Is that not selfish of you?"

Ikshvaku's response was disarming in its honesty. "It is, beyond doubt. But it is also safe. The Aikshvakus are a creation of my vision, they owe no debt to Marici or Surya."

Nimi chuckled quietly. "You have made this mistake before, father. With Narantaka and your brothers. Your brothers betrayed you, and Narantaka stands as your greatest threat. Why trust his son?"

"I do not trust his son, I trust mine."

Nimi frowned again, conflict apparent on his face. "When were you going to tell me this? Had I not argued today, had I not pushed you-when would I have learnt the truth?"

"I don't know," Ikshvaku replied honestly. "Perhaps I needed you to push me, to summon the courage. I cannot imagine your pain and conflict, but I will do whatever I can to ease it. How would you have me penalised?"

"I want to meet him," Nimi said determinedly. "Once, as son and father."

"He will not let you return," Ikshvaku warned. "If need be, he will kill you."

"No, he will not. But he could try, and I will not begrudge it," Nimi said, echoing his father's words in a sincere display of loyalty.

Emotion took over Ikshvaku, and he pulled his stepson in an embrace, partly to hide his tears. "You are *my* son," he whispered earnestly.

"I am," Nimi replied. As they pulled away, he added, "But my mother comes along as well. She has a right to meet him. And a right to stay, if she so desires."

"I will stop neither of you," Ikshvaku said. "But talk to her. She might not want to accompany you."

Suspecting that there were still things he did not know, Nimi made way for his mother's chambers. The Nripalaya was planned as a central main complex, flanked by wings on the north and south ends. Queen Nivritti occupied the south wing overlooking the docks, where lines of boats shored up along the Iravati's banks. One look on his face as Nimi walked in, and Nivritti knew that Ikshvaku had finally confessed.

"How could you not tell me?" Nimi asked, pain and accusation echoing in his voice.

"I wanted to put it behind us forever," Nivritti replied. Her tone was unapologetic. She held no regrets in her life, and still considered it a wise decision to keep Nimi ignorant of his true origin.

"You are a Rakshasi," Nimi said. "A free woman who probably enjoyed equal status with Narantaka when he led Kamyakvana. How can you live among the Suryavanshi so easily? Do you not feel crushed by their patriarchy?"

"What Suryavanshi do you speak of? Manu? Ikshvaku? Maharshi Vasishtha?"

"They are different, I know," Nimi said dismissively. "But Suryavanshi traditions are distinctly patriarchal." He chuckled wryly before adding, "By their custom, I am Narantaka's son, no matter how earnest Ikshvaku's upbringing has been."

Nivritti knew what he referred to, feeling disgusted at the memory of how nonchalantly a Solar priest had once put it: *Grain produced from a piece of land belongs to the landowner, even if the farmer is another. Similarly, the child born to a woman belongs to her husband, no matter who planted the seed.* In Nimi's case, Narantaka was both *owner* and *farmer*. King Ikshvaku's innate discomfort with such misguided aphorisms ensured that the priest was adequately penalised and debarred.

"Ikshvaku is different," she replied. "In many ways, I am more free with him than I was as a Rakshasi. I loved Narantaka, yes, and he loved me too. But Rakshasa custom allowed him to 'love' as many partners as he liked. And those partners paired with others as often as they desired. That was simply the Rakshasa way, and I was expected to be like everyone else. I resisted, and so men had their way with me. For many years, Narantaka's love was not enough for him to find anything wrong in that. But one day an allied commander's son went too far. When Narantaka saw the abuse writ on my body, he slew him and gave his head what he called the Bear treatment. The vengeful commander betrayed him at the last moment, leading to his defeat and capture by Ikshvaku."

Nivritti paused, old memories surfacing and taking her back to a time she thought she had forgotten. But it was important she answered Nimi's questions. "The commander's men were looking for us after that, and you were but an infant, less than a year old. Ikshvaku gave me the dignified life I always wanted, and raised the son of his enemy as his own. No Rakshasa I ever knew was capable of such nobility. My own father maintained several wives, and routinely put them through various imaginative modes of abuse. The only thing *egalitarian* about Rakshasa society is that a woman may become commander too, and then inflict the same torture on lower men and women, if she so wishes."

Nimi realised then that Ikshvaku was right. "So you will not come with me to Dasavarsha? To Narantaka?"

"And neither will you!" Nivritti snapped. "Ikshvaku is your father and your place is here!"

"I will return, mother," Nimi assured her. "But I must meet him once, I must set my sight on the man who brought me to this world. Especially since he happens to be my father's greatest enemy."

The world seemed different to Nimi now, a perennial awareness cast on him that he was a Rakshasa. Years ago, Vaivasvat Manu had explained the meaning to him: *Rakshasas were the youngest sons of Asuras, brave warriors in their final wars. They were charged with the protection of Asura dwellings in the forests and around water bodies. Thus their named is derived from the word Raksha—protection. In the old world, a Raksha-sa was a fierce and brutal guardian.*

But in the new world he was a defeated and exiled tribal, thrown out of his homeland by mighty King Ikshvaku and his Suryavanshi armies. Till a few weeks ago, Nimi was oblivious to this righteous sentiment. But now it was a living, breathing part of him. It did not waver his loyalty to Ikshvaku, but it gave him better perspective on the great Suryavanshi-Rakshasa divide. Yes, the Rakshasas started it. Yes, they rejected Marici and Ikshvaku's overtures. Yes, they were raiders, looters and more. But every war had its chunk of collateral, and countless innocent Rakshasas had been sacrificed in the name of that cause. Was this a new war brewing in Aryavarta, or was this but another episode of a battle that had raged centuries? Once he would have gone to Manu with his questions, letting them pour out of him in a rush. But Vaivasvat could offer him little solace now.

His journey was slow as he took his time among the scattered villages and settlements. He conversed with the locals, picking up news of their contact with Rakshasas to get word on Narantaka's possible whereabouts. But he got his first hint only when he crossed the Sindhu, learning at a settlement on its western bank about a city called Harautii. It was Raja Narantaka's capital, the locals told him. They referred to themselves as Arians, and had a well-rounded knowledge of Aryavarta and its Solar King.

It took him another two months to finally make it to Harautii. There was no map he could use to guide him, and often he went in false directions till he turned around to retrace his steps. Dasavarsha was the geographical opposite of Aryavarta—its rivers running through arid lands and basins while Aryavarta's waters flowed through lush forests and fertile plains. Situated on the Setumanta's western bank, Harautii's entire stretch was visible from the mountains across. It was not large for a city, closer to the size of Sakala than of Prasthala or Vitabhya. No organised structures could be discerned, and the roads seemed to run in random patterns that were probably hastily constructed as and when the need arose. Nimi felt a sudden rush of pity for these people. Had their leaders made peace with Marici, had they accepted Ikshvaku's offers of conciliation, their fate could have been so different. The prosperity of Aryavarta would have inherited to them as much as it did to Solar or Lunar tribes.

Finding Narantaka inside Harautii was not too difficult. The Rakshasa Raja had nothing to fear in his capital, and one could call on him without facing any significant barriers. This was more a commentary on Ikshvaku's moral principle than on Narantaka's courage. Assassination and espionage were not to Ikshvaku's tastes, he would rather meet his enemies in open battle. Nimi stood in a line as people went up to Narantaka one by one, presenting their problems and asking for his resolution. His decisions were swift, incisive and rational. After a while it was Nimi's turn, and he stepped up to face his biological father.

Narantaka's eyes were curious and perceiving. "You are from Aryavarta, are you not, stranger?"

"I am, Raja Narantaka."

Narantaka frowned with interest, assessing the young man in front of him. There was something familiar about him, as if he had seen him before. "Yet you are not Suryavanshi. You do not possess their bearing. Who are you? And what brings you here?"

"My name is Nimi, and I am King Ikshvaku's second son."

The Rakshasas around Narantaka started to speak, but he raised his hand sharply and they fell silent. "A Suryavanshi prince in Harautii. That is a dangerous move, young Solar. I will not ask a third time. What brings you here?"

"I recently learnt a truth that compelled me to come," Nimi replied calmly. Fear was not an emotion he was familiar with, and he wondered now whether it stemmed from his Rakshasa blood. "I learnt that my mother was once your wife, and that I am your son."

Narantaka shot up as Nimi completed the sentence, a look of utter shock on his face. He walked closer, hands spreading wide to signal his men to stay back. "Swear that this is true," he whispered.

"It is true, whether I swear or not," Nimi said simply. "We were saved by Ikshvaku after your capture, and in Avisari he made Nivritti his wife."

A look of pure venom came upon Narantaka. "My wife's name was Akaya, not Nivritti."

"She changed her name, which was a smart thing. You lived in the Nripalaya just a few chambers away."

"We named you Udavasu."

"I know, she told me."

"You are truly my son?" Narantaka asked, willing himself to believe the young man.

"I am. Nothing else could have given me the courage to face you."

Raja Narantaka embraced his son, aware that all eyes were now on him. The second son of Ikshvaku was in fact his offspring, and his lover still lay within his clutches. "Why did you not bring her?" Narantaka asked, his fury towards Ikshvaku stronger than ever before. The man had stolen his home, his people, his treasures, and his family. But Narantaka would avenge it all yet.

"She did not wish to come," Nimi replied matter-of-factly. "She has found happiness with him."

Narantaka clenched his teeth, his eyes screaming murder. "She probably said that to avoid worrying you unduly. Rakshasi Akaya would find nothing happy in living as the wife of a Suryavanshi."

Nimi did not debate the point, and Narantaka continued. "We will bring her back, together. You are a blessing from the Ahura deities. A signal that my intent is right, my actions justified."

"I cannot do that, father," Nimi replied. It was strange calling this man his father. Narantaka was the only *enemy* he had ever known, the only thing standing between Solar tribes and complete prosperity. "My life belongs to the Suryavansha. Ikshvaku saved me and raised me as his own son. That is a debt I must repay with sincerity."

Narantaka frowned, not accustomed to being denied so casually. "You owe him no debt. He has held you and your mother captive for twenty-one years, and hid this knowledge from me even when I was his ally. He betrayed me. What would you do back with him? If word of your origin is out, the Suryavanshi will never accept you as one of their own. They will keep you away from any real power. But with me, your father, you can be King."

"I came here to meet you, to learn of your past and your motives. Perhaps in knowing you I can know myself better. But then I must return, for I have no desire to be King."

Narantaka stared, taking deep and heavy breaths as he tried to keep his anger in check. His own son had returned to him, only to stand defiant, in the presence of all his subordinates and commanders. He gave Nimi a mock grin. "Have you ever seen a lion, my son? I think not, the Suryavanshi have not ventured into their lands yet." It was true, though Nimi had seen images carved on clay and heard ample descriptions. But he imagined the lion to be no more ferocious than the leopard, and if he could take on one he could take on the other.

"Worry not," Narantaka said, sensing his thoughts. "We do not hold any lions here with us. But I have observed them at close range, and the male lion is a fantastic beast. It is the only animal I know that kills its own progeny, if it so desires. But do you think it is that uncommon among Rakshasas? Ikshvaku shall not have you back, and I recommend you accept this in peace."

The other Rakshasas stepped closer, ready to kill him at Narantaka's command. Nimi smiled, keeping his eyes on Narantaka. "I am your blood, combined with Suryavanshi military upbringing. You may send these men at me, if only to see what a fine blend that makes."

Maharshi Vasishtha recited aloud, his booming voice carrying across the Suryavedi to the many present denizens.

"This is the Godhead, the might of Surya.
The soul of all that moves not or moves.
Auspicious are the Sun's bay-coloured horses,
with bright and effulgent hooves.
Meet our shouts of triumph, bear our prayers,
the brilliant presence of Devas has risen.

Like a man follows a maiden, so does the Sun the Dawn,
refulgent Goddess with changing hues."

Ikshvaku did not possess the natural command over raw Sanskrit that his ancestors did, and it took him time to memorise Vasishtha's words and get his pronunciation right. He was chanting along by the fourth recitation, just in time for the sun to emerge fully out of the horizon and begin its daily journey across the visible sky. He pretended not to notice Nivritti's accusatory gaze. Nimi had gone to Dasavarsha with his permission. Anything that happened to him would be Ikshvaku's fault, and last night they had argued over this.

"He is only a boy, not even of the famed Solar blood that gives you your valour," Nivritti had complained.

"He will be alright," Ikshvaku had replied, believing it only as much as Nivritti did.

"You have never given me the chance to bear you a child. I hope you do not lose the only one we have," Nivritti had said.

Maharshi Vasishtha's incantation was recited a hundred times, Soma passed around freely during the latter recitations. Ikshvaku appreciated it for how conducive it was to spiritual endeavours, but Seedhu remained his favourite brew. It was well past noon when the ritual was finally over, Vasishtha satisfied that Surya Deva had been adequately appeased. In the evening, Ikshvaku called Haryashva and Varman to council.

"Nimi is in Dasavarsha," he said to them without preamble. "Soon he will return, but Narantaka and his forces will be close on his heels. We must be prepared to defend Rajavasa."

Varman asked what Haryashva already knew the answer to. "What is he doing in Dasavarsha? How could you let him go alone? I would have sent a thousand men with him at least!"

"Nimi is not my son by blood. Nivritti was once wife to Narantaka, and Nimi was born to them before I brought her to Avisari." Now that the confession to Nimi was made, Ikshvaku felt no shame in admitting the truth to anyone else. His eyes went to Haryashva, looking to apologise for the years of secrecy. But Haryashva blinked in assurance, as though to say, *You need not explain yourself to me, my friend.*

Varman was silent for a long time, unable to believe that his student had kept him in the dark for so many years. Ikshvaku had approached him as a boy once, seeking aid and guidance from him with sincere humility. In the years since, that respect had diminished a little, replaced by a sense of authority and leadership. Varman did not mind it in the least, his loyalty was to the Solar banner and its prime line. But a secret so sinister was not something he had foreseen, and he did not know how to accept it now. "Is that why you spared Narantaka's life?" he asked. "Did the Rakshasi beg you to?"

"The Rakshasi in her was dead when Nivritti stepped into Avisari. And sparing Narantaka's life was crucial in finding the seal of Surya."

"You brought Narantaka to Avisari, letting him sleep just a few rooms away from his wife and son. Any man who takes such risks is irresponsible, and I'm not sure I can trust your leadership anymore."

"I have paid for that mistake, Varman," Ikshvaku reminded him, speaking of Drishta's death. "Our failures in Dasavarsha were a direct result of my trust in Narantaka."

"And now you trust his son and make the same mistake again?"

"Nimi is *my* son, not his," Ikshvaku said with force, his tone brooking no further argument on the matter. Then he added, softer this time."You know him. So often have you commented that he reminds you of me even more than Vikukshi does."

"I talk of his mannerisms, not of a physical resemblance," Varman defended, turning to Haryashva and adding, "Why do you stay silent? Do you have nothing to say?"

"Trust has always been your greatest weakness," Haryashva said to Ikshvaku. "Me, Narantaka, Pururava, your brothers and now Nimi. How many of these investments of faith have turned on you? And might any turn still? Remember your brothers' final warning. There is still a traitor among us."

"What will you have me do then? Banish Nimi for no fault of his?"

"Nimi is innocent, I agree with that," said Haryashva. "And banishing him is not the solution. But to give him responsibility, to keep him close to any sort of power would be unwise. Who knows how changed he will return, what thoughts he may have been fed by Narantaka?"

"Exactly," agreed Varman. "And Nimi could have told him all about Rajavasa, giving him the knowledge he needs to mount an attack."

"Can you so easily forget the Rakshasas we recently slew?" asked Ikshvaku, referring to General Revata's recent battle in Kamyakvana.

"Do you really think that Narantaka does not have a dozen more spies active in our city? His report of Rajavasa will be complete even without Nimi's contribution."

"Nimi can tell him much that his spies are unable to discern," argued Haryashva. "But it seems to me that your mind is made, Ikshvaku. I fear Varman and I are wasting our breath."

Ikshvaku sighed, reminding himself that both Varman and Haryashva spoke out of loyalty and concern. "Vikukshi will be Solar King after me," he said to them, his tone reassuring. "Nimi will be kept away from any Suryavanshi power, but he is the only one who can train the Aikshvakus. Permit me that last indulgence, my friends."

Narantaka surveyed his seed anew, grudgingly admitting to himself that in battle Nimi was the mirror reflection of Ikshvaku. His movements and pivots, his calm slicing and slashing, and the overbearing fatality of his blade—all were a tribute to Ikshvaku. It was a strange sight, and Narantaka could almost imagine that it was his own younger self moving like a Solar King. Nimi dispatched twenty-six men with a disconcerting ease, not seeming to mind the coat of Rakshasa blood painting his body. When it was over, he turned to the rest, who now tread behind their leader and let Narantaka take charge.

"A fine blend indeed," Narantaka said agreeably. "But how long can you sustain yourself, my son? A hundred more men stand behind me, and thousands can gather within moments. Has Ikshvaku trained you to take on an entire army alone?"

"One or two at a time, taking soldiers as they come. There is never an army, father. Only a finite line of men waiting to meet their deaths."

Nimi's bravado was starkly reminiscent of his younger self, and Narantaka found himself smiling fondly in spite of the situation. "Well said. I expect nothing less from a boy who claims to be my son. And yet, you wish to fight alongside your stepfather. A warrior such as yourself deserves the right to this decision, as much as it may discomfort me."

Nimi's tense frame seemed to relax, though Narantaka noticed that his breathing had not escalated after the fight, a technique commonly taught to Suryavanshi warriors. If only Nimi could stay—he could bring discipline and training to his disorganised mass of soldiers far better than Narantaka's other partners. "But I ask you to reconsider one last time," Narantaka continued. "Stay with me, Udavasu. These are your people, your true kinsmen. You owe them, just like I do."

"What is it that we owe, father?"

"To reclaim our homeland," Narantaka said simply, surprised that Nimi had to ask. "Aryavarta belongs to us. And we will take it, city by city."

"What then? Parshuas, Arians, Yavanas and the others will settle down in Aryavarta, leaving their own homelands behind? How many Rakshasas does your vast army really contain? And how many of them actually descend from those that once lived in Kamyakvana?"

"Careful," warned Raja Narantaka. "Do not raise your voice to the King."

Nimi nodded and bowed his head, acknowledging Narantaka's authority. "If you permit, Raja Narantaka," he said. "I would like to return now." There was nothing he could learn from a man so blinded by vengeance.

Later that evening, when Nimi's horse disappeared into the far horizon, Narantaka visited a priest's hut. His own forefathers were priests once, before the coming of Solar tribes turned them into raiders and warriors. Narantaka consulted this one often, and she noticed his heavy mood the moment he walked in.

"Seed should be cast multiple times, often systematically," she said, her reference plain for him to perceive. "To sow a single seed, and spend the rest of your life worrying over its existence is a fool's errand." Her hut was a shabby, smelly dwelling that was constantly engulfed in smoke from the ganjika plant, a Rakshasa priest's favourite much like Soma was to the Arya Rshis.

"And what would you know of farming or children?" Narantaka taunted, not wishing to engage with her deliberate banter today.

"What do I know of fate and destiny, of future or dreams?" she retorted. "But you turn to me for guidance there. And is seed-concern not what brings you here today?"

"Udavasu's fate is for him to bear," Narantaka said. "I cannot change it, even if I know it."

"Then what would you have me divine for you?"

"My fate," Narantaka said. "My final fate. Will I return from Rajavasa? Or will my blood soak the earth of my forefathers?"

She closed her eyes and clasped his hands in hers, murmuring esoteric chants in a language even he did not understand. "Ikshvaku is the Day, and you are Night," she chanted, still in trance. "He is the Sun and you are the Shadow. And I see only Darkness in Aryavarta's future, no Light for a long time to come. Darkness will triumph in Rajavasa. You will return to Harautii alive, Raja Narantaka."

The curtains to Nimi's chambers parted and Elder Prince Vikukshi walked in. A year elder to Nimi and the mirror image of their father, he looked every bit the heir apparent he was. And like his father, knowledge of Nimi's true origin did not diminish the immense love he held for his younger brother.

"I am happy to see you back, Nimi," he said as they embraced, his affection genuine. Inheriting strong Solar blood from both his mother and father, his face bore archetypal Suryavanshi features—distinct jawline and nose, framed by sharp and rounded ears.

"I am happy to be home, brother," Nimi replied. There was no awkwardness between them, they were blood-brothers even if born to different parents. "And now there is work to do."

Vikukshi nodded. "The Aikshvakus await your command. But will you not tell me of your journey? Of your encounter with our greatest enemy?"

Nimi smiled, not the reluctant curve of Ikshvaku or Vikukshi but the easy, infectious grin that was so rare in him. "Dasavarsha is a ragged land, not capable of the sort of prosperity Aryavarta lends us. And Narantaka is a formidable man, his aura almost as powerful as our father's. I stood my ground against him, brother, but only I know the fear that raged inside me."

Vikukshi knew Nimi well enough to recognise his modesty when he saw it. Nimi's utter fearlessness was a cause for much envy in their younger days. "How many men did you slay?" he asked, imagining a high count.

"Twenty six," Nimi replied honestly. "Not much, if you ask me."

Vikukshi shrugged, returning Nimi's brotherly grin. "Come then, brother. We must prepare. And I have even thought of a battle nickname for you."

"What is it?" Nimi asked warily, expecting a lewd joke somewhere in the name.

"Janaka," Vikukshi replied. "A *patron* in colloquial dialect. I like to think of Janaka as a benevolent guardian—a perfect title for my Rakshasa brother."

"Nimi Janaka," Nimi said aloud, sounding out the name. "It does have a nice ring to it. I think I like it. But the full title should be Nimi Udavasu Janaka."

Vikukshi nodded. "Mother Nivritti told me of your original name. Nimi Udavasu Janaka—fierce Solar warrior taking on Raja Narantaka's Dasa forces."

"Nimi Udavasu Janaka and Vikukshi Kshuva Aikshvaku—taking on Raja Narantaka's Dasa forces together," Nimi amended.

Dasa

"Later commentators have faulted Ikshvaku for letting himself be surrounded in Rajavasa. Indeed, it certainly was a risky judgement, but Ikshvaku was counting on numbers being on his side. He should have known better though, for war is rarely a predictable matter."

King Bhagiratha to Sudasa

More than 5,000 warriors amassed around Rajavasa in just a few weeks, creating a vast military complex and populating inns with grim soldiers from all parts of the kingdom. On the eve of battle Ikshvaku visited the royal barracks, meeting with the veteran soldiers that formed the older Aikshvakus. These men had dedicated their lives to the Solar cause as much as him, and each one of them could have been King were he born to the right father.

Revata was among them, a few years younger to Ikshvaku and his second-cousin by blood. He was this elite contingent's leader, and General to the entire Suryavanshi army. "Is it true, my King?" Revata asked, voicing what all veterans wanted to know. "Prince Nimi is actually the seed of Narantaka?"

Ikshvaku nodded, seeing no reason to hide it from these men any longer. "But he is *my* son, and I trust him completely." Many of them had contributed their sons to the Aikshvaku program, and he felt the need to assure them that their sons were in reliable hands.

"Then so do we, King Ikshvaku," said Revata solemnly. "We are ready for battle."

"I am happy to hear it," Ikshvaku said. "But there is one more thing we must do to prepare." He gestured to the large leather pouches brought in and placed by attendants. "Maharshi Vasishtha has concocted something special for us, a Soma fit for warriors as they wade into battle. It will heighten our senses, lighting within us a fire akin to that which powered our Deva forefathers. This is Samarsoma—*battle Soma*. And I wish to partake it with you on the eve of battle, my friends."

They poured the Samarsoma into bowls and passed it among themselves, drinking with the King as equals. Fond stories were shared, battle anecdotes from the many times they raised swords together. Kamyakvana, Dasavarsha and Avisari—three great campaigns had brought together this elite force, and the inebriant gently made its way through their veins like adrenaline charging up for the big release. There were a few good-spirited japes at the King as well, for even great Ikshvaku had slipped in battle once or twice. But soon the discussions turned serious, and one warrior was brave enough to voice what many others wondered. "We have known of Narantaka's whereabouts for many months now, my King," he said. "We know how sparse his security is in Harautii. We even suspect that he has spies in our city. Why have we never tried to kill him? A single man could walk up to him and slay him, archers can shoot an arrow from hidden corners, and we could have invaded Harautii before he had the chance to bring the Dasa force to our walls. Why have we not done any of this?"

King Ikshvaku was not a man to be offended, and he knew that the warrior spoke out of loyalty, not dissent. "It has been suggested to me often enough," he confessed. "And I marvel at Haryashva's respect for my authority, for left to him, an assassin would have killed Narantaka long ago. But we must ask ourselves a vital question: are we Arya because of who *we* are, or because of who our forefathers were? To me, the answer has always been the former. I dread a society where an individual's standing is determined solely by that of his or her parents. To call ourselves Suryavanshi is our birth-right, and that is all it denotes, a blood tie. But the title of Arya aspires to nobility, to a superior morality, and it has to be earned by deed and toil. I could not assassinate Narantaka for the same reason that I could not my kill my brothers—murder and connivery are Anarya traits, and they leave me no different than my enemy. As for marching an army into Dasavarsha, I have made that mistake before and paid severely. I have put countless men in harm's way far away from their homes, I will not do so again. Let the decision to go to war be the enemy's, not mine."

It was a compelling response, and no man found reason to counter with it. King Ikshvaku was famously candid, but notoriously laconic with his soldiers. But the Samarsoma was affecting him as much as it was them all, its heavy undertones threatening to turn the gathering grim and introspective. Ikshvaku sensed it and called forward the comedian among them, commanding him to put on a show. The comedian was welcomed raucously, and his wide grin reflected his delight at being called to performance by the King.

"Let us begin with a riddle," he said, making it clear that this was no extempore. "Divide yourselves into the separate units. This will be a contest. Let us see which unit knows our Devas the best." The veteran force was divided into ten units of fifty soldiers each, and by stoking that healthy inter-unit rivalry, the comedian had his audience well engrossed. He turned to Ikshvaku and bowed. "I request you to refrain from participating, my King. For certainly you are well versed with the Riddle of the Vishvadevas."

"I am," Ikshvaku replied, gesturing to a few men to refill their bowls. "Let me be the arbiter in case of dispute then." Manu had taught him the Riddle of the Vishvadevas long ago. It was a simple prayer uttered at community gatherings, where particular Devas were called upon one by one. The trick was that no Deva was called by his name, only by a few attributes.

"A fine proposition," the comedian-warrior replied. Then he called out a few friends from his own unit and barred them from participation as well, confessing, "This lot has previously heard the riddle from me, and it will be unfair of them to play."

"The first query," he said when the units were finally settled down and their enthusiasm adequately curbed. "He is a youth, brown-skinned, active, manifold he decks the golden one with ornament. Who is he?"

Quite a few men volunteered the answer. "Vayu Deva!" Some argument followed on who replied first, but Ikshvaku finally decided in favour of the Iladevi unit, named after his sister.

The comedian continued. "Luminous, he occupies the place of sacrifice. Sage among the Gods. Who is he?"

An even larger number shouted the answer this time. "Agni!" Ikshvaku was able to choose a single victor with much difficulty.

The comedian put a sour loser in his place by snapping, "Funny to see you vying for this one, Kulvan. I have seen you run into the water like a monkey at the mere notion of fire set upon you!"

It was welcomed with uproarious laughter that took some time to quell, for poor Kulvan's fear of fire was everyone's favourite source for jests. The comedian's third and fourth queries were put together-"One brandishes in his hand a metal knife, firm in his seat amid the Deities. Another holds the thunderbolt, wherewith he slays Vritra."

Varuna and Indra-the latter was answered in a collective roar, but only one man could guess the former.

"The fifth Deva bears a pointed weapon. Bright he is, and strong, with healing medicines. Who will guess this one?"

This one too was easy, for Savitra Deva was considered a brother of Surya and his name was taught to every Solar child. But none could guess the next one. "Thief-like, he watches well the ways. And knows the places where treasures lie." The comedian had to supply the answer himself—Tvastra Deva. He followed it up by a few well-directed jibes at some of the known kleptomaniacs and hoarders in their group. Even the King let out a suppressed chuckle at one of them, "And this chap here, laughing away to glory. The first thing he did, as soon as he was born, was steal his own father's hair! The poor old man has been walking around bald ever since, while he is easily the most hirsute beast I have ever seen!"

The comedian was practised at his art, and he allowed his audience to have a round of laughter before continuing the show. "The seventh with his mighty stride made three steps to where the Gods reside. Who is he?" It was a reference to Vishnu, imagined as a dwarfish-being by the Lunar rshis of Atri. The Iladevi unit got this one too, and now it had a lead over the others.

"Two with one dame ride on with winged steeds, and journey forth like travellers on their way." The Ashvins, and it was another easy one. Before he began the last query, the comedian added a caveat. "None shall shout out the answer now! Those who know it can raise their swords, but only that man may answer who I point to."

It was a command delivered in vain, for the eager calls of Surya and Soma broke out even before he could finish the query, "The last two are highest in the heavens. Worshipped with oil and ghee, Imperial Kings."

They were forced to turn to Ikshvaku for the final arbitration, and the King declared the Iladevi unit as victors. Samarsoma continued to course through them as they climbed the city walls come morning and faced Narantaka's gathered Dasa force. Each among them ready to die in defence of Rajavasa. A lone man stepped out of the Dasa line and walked towards Ikshvaku's infantry contingents lined outside Rajavasa's walls. When he was within their archers' range, he dropped his weapons and walked on ahead with his arms in the air. No archer fired, and none would till the King gave his command. He walked through Solar infantry ranks all the way to the gate, and arrogantly stared at King Ikshvaku.

"King Narantaka has a message for King Ikshvaku of the Suryavansha," he declared.

"And what is Narantaka's message?" Ikshvaku asked.

"He offers to leave your city and its people alone and return to Harautii, on one condition."

"What condition is this, Dasa?" growled Revata.

"That King Ikshvaku hand over *both* his wives and sons. Present them to King Narantaka as slaves and we will retreat." The Dasa bared his teeth in a wolfish grin, easily aware that Ikshvaku would never accept the condition. The Dasas, it seemed, were here for war. And by Surya and Samarsoma, they would have it.

"Thrust it like this," Vikukshi grunted as he plunged his sword up the ribs of a Dasa, and said while pulling it out. "It cuts through the heart and bleeds the man out in seconds."

Nimi watched unimpressed. "I prefer a simple beheading." He turned right and sliced his sword in a calculated arc, cutting through the throat of a charging Dasa. War had erupted outside Rajavasa in a manner they had never experienced before. Dasa lines collided hard against Solar formations at Narantaka's war cry, pitting more than 10,000 men in a frenzy of blood and dust. Nimi spotted Haryashva's Ashvaks in the distance, making sweeping runs through enemy ranks and throwing their formations in disarray. Varman led another contingent of horsemen that sought to flank Narantaka's forces, pushing their numbers into a tighter space that the archers could aim at. And further in the distance, obscured in a cloud of sand was King Ikshvaku, taking on Dasa soldiers like a common Solar warrior. Nimi frowned and shook his head. Both his fathers were rash, predictable men—Narantaka pitted his vast force against Rajavasa in a brutal, tactless fashion, attrition and collateral his only stratagem; Ikshvaku waded into the carnage unmindful of his vulnerability, always seeking to set an example by being the first to put his life on the line.

The brothers picked up their shields and turned back-to-back, systematically moving through the charging Dasa line and reducing its numbers. They looked to each other with both envy and respect, for each considered himself the sole inheritor of Ikshvaku's perfected swordplay. And yet both now moved like their father, their sequences mirroring each other in a fashion what was symmetrical. "That's thirty nine for me already," Vikukshi boasting his kill-count.

"Do not forget the tale of rabbit and turtle, my brother," Nimi warned. "I am only getting warmed up." He did not add that Vikukshi moved headlong into the Rakshasa line while he cleaned up the back.

He worked up a heavy sweat by the time they ventured recklessly deep into Dasa formations. As he was beginning to spare a thought for how they would retreat, a loud Dasa horn blared into the air, momentarily causing both sides to stop and turn. A large section of Narantaka's army still stood away from battle, and now they moved aside to reveal a fearsome sight unfold behind them. Nimi counted hundreds of aurochs mounted by masked Dasas, wearing helmets with horns as large as those of their mounts. He heard Ikshvaku's distinct voice break out in the distance, ordering his men to fall back in line and prepare for the second wave. Haryashva and Varman moved their cavalry closer to the city walls; horses would be no match for the sheer brutality of aurochs.

"How can we take on vrishabhas?" Vikukshi asked aloud, using the Sanskrit term for the sight they beheld. Aurochs were dangerous, lethal creatures and these looked twice the size of a normal bull. A single beast could rampage through their lines with ease, crushing bone and flesh.

"Fear not, brother," Nimi said, suddenly remembering young Ayu and the leopard. "As long as we maintain the city walls, Narantaka's vrishabhas are useless." He pulled Vikukshi back towards Rajavasa, guiding the rows of men Ikshvaku commanded to retreat into the city. The King himself remained outside, guarded by his Samarsoma warriors. The Dasas' main attack was on Rajavasa's northern front, but now Narantaka spread his armies, snaking them towards the south gates. At the north entrance, Nimi found Haryashva. "Where is Ikshvaku?" the Ashvak asked, raising his voice above the clamour.

"Still outside," Nimi shouted back, breaking through the rows of men storming in and moving closer. Haryashva ushered his cavalry in and made to exit the walls and join Ikshvaku. But before he could, the King's loud command carried through and the north gate was shut. Ikshvaku and his 500 Aikshvakus were the only Solar representation defending the city's north.

The Final Secret

"History has an uncanny way of repeating itself. Centuries ago the armies of Aurvan and Tapin, Surya and Soma, united to bring final victory to the Devas. In a way, so it was with Ikshvaku and Pururava as well."

King Bhagiratha to Sudasa

"Do you remember the first time we raised swords together?" Ikshvaku asked Revata. The veteran contingent was formed like an arrow's head, and the King was at its absolute tip with Revata by his side. Behind them were two men, then three, four and so on till they formed thirty rows of Samarsoma-charged fighters. These were the Aikshvakus, 500 of the most capable Suryavanshi warriors alive.

"At Navapari," Revata replied. "I was part of your convoy, and only fourteen years old. There was a Rakshasa raid, and every man, woman or child capable of holding a weapon waded into battle behind you."

"I was not much older myself. And your valour compelled me to take you in my main force," Ikshvaku added. "I have never regretted that decision, Revata. Will you make me regret it today?"

Revata smiled, confidence glinting in his eyes. "Give the command, my King. Let loose the arrow. We will speak of regrets when we roast the heads of Dasa aurochs. That should be a particularly good meat!"

Ikshvaku returned the smile before giving the command, and from the walls Nimi watched horrified as the veterans galloped head-on against Narantaka's line of rearing vrishabhas. Ikshvaku was the first to crash against the aurochs, and within moments he disappeared in a storm of man and beast. Revata stayed close to his King, his stallion managing to manoeuvre through the auroch ranks. Both were sons born in the house of Aurvan Surya, and they moved more like one deadly force rather than two disparate warriors. Their swords hacked into vrishabha hides and through Dasa heads as they penetrated deeper into Narantaka's formations through momentum alone.. Ikshvaku knew from war-ridden instinct that dozens of his men would have perished. But he allowed himself some comfort—his life was on the line as much as theirs. None could say that King Ikshvaku sent men to die for him. King Ikshvaku would die with his men, if need be. But not today. The seal of Surya hung proudly around his neck, protecting him with Aurvan's legacy.

The rest of their run through Dasa formations was a blur to their addled minds. Samarsoma was a brew that brought headiness in progressive waves, and their motions were guided more by its effects than by their training and expertise. The force of 500 was reduced to half, and then a quarter. But the auroch cavalry suffered severe damages as well, and Ikshvaku was satisfied to find dozens of beasts turning around and fleeing at the sight of their fallen kin. Rajavasa's north and west borders were now completely surrounded by Dasas, and Ikshvaku's men had to force their way through enemy lines as they barged towards north gate, the only place where Suryavanshi still made a stand outside the walls.

Then another horn blared out, further in the distance. Two horns followed in its wake, all seeming to come from different ends of the battlefield. Ikshvaku frowned as Narantaka's forces began to withdraw, forming back into lines and ranks away from the city walls. The horns continued to blare, getting louder and louder till the armies they heralded came into view. Unmistakably Suryavanshi banners fluttered among them, their horses and armour appearing distinctly Solar even from a distance. Comprehension dawned upon King Ikshvaku, and he let out an involuntary laugh. "It's my brothers," he said to the men, still laughing. "They warned me of this when I exiled them. They told me there was a traitor in our midst. But even they did not know then who it was. Now it all makes sense. It was Narantaka who allied with them, all those years ago. He fostered their rebellion, perhaps planning to end me in Dasavarsha."

The King continued to laugh wryly, his men joining. Death did not scare them, and they agreed with Ikshvaku when he said, "Could you ever have imagined Suryavanshi banners marching alongside Dasa and Rakshasa? Call out the rest of the forces. Throw at these traitors everything we have, and defend the walls."

Raja Narantaka had come to Rajavasa with a plan for breaking its walls, and Ikshvaku's brothers were crucial to that. Pramshu, Sharyati and Nabhaga each brought with them hundreds of infantrymen and aurochs. Their forces could have been larger, but the years since their defeat to Ikshvaku had been harsh on them. Pramshu scoured the breadth of Dasavarsha and travelled further west to the great city of Uruk. King Enmerkar, its ruler, too derived vague descent from the Surya of a previous era. He graced Pramshu with 500 cavalry units, moved by Pramshu's appeal towards kinship and a shared forefather. Sharyati's natural leadership skills gave him command over several horse-tribes north of Dasavarsha, and they now assembled as the Shakas, the tribe of Sharyati. Nabhaga's relatively petty force comprised of defeated Suryavanshi warriors, those who had chosen the rebels' side in the siege of Avisari. Spending four years on the run and in hiding had done them little good, and they resembled more a rag-tag bunch of mercenaries than the disciplined warriors they once were. Narantaka relished the thought of what might be going on in Ikshvaku's mind right now. Had he suspected that his brothers were secretly aligned with Narantaka, or was this the shock that Narantaka wanted it to be?

The leaders met in council outside the walls of Avisari, allowing Ikshvaku time to regroup as they formulated their plan of attack. "When this is over, Rakshasa," said Pramshu, somehow appearing even more arrogant than his elder brother. "Then Aryavarta is ours. Your group of Rakshasas will retreat to Harivarsha."

"That is our agreement," Narantaka confirmed. That was not always his plan, but Nimi's tirade had brought home a vital point—Asagartiyans, Yavanas, Kambojas, Parshuas and the other tribes of Harivarsha could scarcely be expected to settle down in Aryavarta. This was a place of loot for them, not one to make homes in. Thus, after he had destroyed Ikshvaku, Narantaka would leave Aryavarta to its fate. And he would install a friendlier King in Ikshvaku's place, even if that was Ikshvaku's own brother. But he was not too sure about the other two, Sharyati and Nabhaga. They eyed him with a constant wariness not unlike the suspicion Ikshvaku and Haryashva had reserved for him. And they made no effort to hide that they were loath to align with Rakshasas. They were doing this only out of necessity, but then so was he.

"How the fates have reversed on our brother," Pramshu commented. "Four years ago he had us surrounded, his men converging on our city from all directions. Today, Ikshvaku will face his first and final defeat, and it matters not that he has the seal of Surya."

"Which will be returned to me," Narantaka reminded them. Nothing would come in the way of his intent to melt Solar metal and cast it in Rakshasa mould.

"As agreed," said Nabhaga. "Ageing artefacts hold no meaning for us."

The extra contingents of aurochs these brothers brought with them was crucial to breaching Rajavasa's walls. Long, hulking pieces of timber had been sharpened at the end, tipped with rare metal that could break through reinforced clay bricks and wood alike. Two aurochs were needed to lift a single log, and a minimum of four were required to carry the elaborate machinery that went with it and converted it into a potent ramming device. Four men had to follow every such ram, their job to pull the ropes that lifted the log in one direction before sending it hurling forward in the other. But before he could put these machines to use, Narantaka needed to push the Suryavanshi into their city. So he threw at Ikshvaku everything he could muster—wild Yavana axe warriors, lethal Parshua hammer wielders, nimble Arian archers and more. Untamed vrishabhas tore through Solar ranks, throwing their resolute formations out of order and sending terror down the lines. Archers thwarted them constantly, raining arrows that were tipped with poison at suggestion from the wily Asagartiyans. Ikshvaku had originally positioned 5,000 men outside his city walls, but Narantaka's unrestrained rampage dwindled that number to less than 3,000. He took no small losses on his side as well, but a large chunk of his force was yet to join the havoc. And once the walls were breached, Pramshu and his brothers could send their infantry into the fray.

After two days of endless battle Ikshvaku finally ordered his forces completely within the city, and Narantaka quickly manoeuvred the siege aurochs into position. He was wary of Rajavasa's longbows, mounted on the turrets that dotted its walls at regular intervals and jutted out of the western cliff. Their thick, strong arrows could easily pierce auroch flesh; and a single auroch down in his set of four would render the entire ram immobile. But the longbows were clumsy, taking time to recalibrate their aim after a shot was fired. The aurochs made slow progress, the rest of his infantry staying behind while they crept up to the city walls. Their attack commenced at nightfall, taking advantage of the natural Suryavanshi disinclination towards fighting in the dark. Sharpened logs rammed hard into Rajavasa's bricks, even as Ikshvaku's archers wasted their nimbly arrows on the aurochs' thick hides. But the attack was relentless, and by the third night they breached the walls. Narantaka let his untamed vrishabhas loose, allowing them to maraud through Rajavasa's streets and cause chaos among its citizens. They were aided by his soldiers' ravenous loot-lust, and only the restraint imposed by Pramshu and his forces ensured that Rajavasa's women were spared the plunder.

"It's them," Haryashva confirmed. "The men have spotted them at the helm, taking Rajavasa lane by lane."

King Ikshvaku was quiet for a long time, contemplating the actions of his brothers. Did power and rule mean that much to them, that they would side with Dasas? But then, did that not make their drive stronger than his? When he entertained Narantaka for all those years, only for the hope of finding the seal, did he not do the same? "Spare them no mercy," Ikshvaku finally said. "Four years ago I prevented you from killing my brothers, and was unable to do so myself. We will not make the same mistake twice."

Varman was to continue putting up a resistance on the south wall; the Dasa ranks were still climbing it and charging through Rajavasa. Vikukshi and Nimi were assigned to Haryashva, and theirs was the task of securing Rajavasa's north gate. King Ikshvaku and Revata would clear a path inside the city, cleansing the city quadrant by quadrant once it was secure. Other leaders were set to the job of evacuating the city's civilians, caught under the heavy crossfire of Dasa and Suryavansha. But even as he marshalled his forces with the ease of a consummate commander, Ikshvaku was aware that the numbers were no longer on his side. Narantaka's aurochs had taken a heavy toll on his army, and his brothers' forces had tilted the balance heavily in their favour. What meaning would a simple law have held to them, had Ikshvaku instituted primogeniture years ago? Would they have abided by it only because it was law? He doubted it. The desire for power, once ignited, could never be sated. And in this analysis he was no different from his brothers.

By the time the Sun set on the fourth day, Narantaka controlled most of Rajavasa's southern territory and Varman was forced to suffer the only loss of his career. At the north gate, Haryashva and Ikshvaku's sons managed to subdue the Dasa rampage and close the gate shut once again, repairing its damaged holes with temporary wooden arrangements. Soon they were joined by King Ikshvaku and his men, a severely depleted force. Climbing onto a turret mounted next to the north gate, Ikshvaku scanned the city and turned his eyes to the Suryavedi-feeling oddly relieved to find it still burning. Dasa units raided unchecked in various pockets of the city, but even in the chaos of battle the Suryavedi was left untouched. But with the rshis manning it whisked away to safety, it was fast running out of wood and ghee. Soon its flames would be reduced to embers, even without Dasa intervention. Ikshvaku was not a superstitious man, and his spirituality extended to a sceptical inquiry that had no place for portents and premonitions. But he allowed himself to speculate what would happen if its flames died out. Would that mean his end, would it mean a lethal fate for his sons as well?

The north gate secure, they reconvened a line of archers on the wall and turned them on the Dasas inside Rajavasa. They heard a roar in the distance, and a loud Dasa horn sounded from the Nripalaya. Revata voiced what it suggested, "They have taken the Nripalaya."

"They cannot hold it if we block the south gate as well," Ikshvaku said. "And we must rely on Varman to provide that advantage." The battle was slipping away from Ikshvaku's grip, and for the first time, he felt anxiety.

"Numbers are not on Varman's side. Will he be able to clear the south gate?"

"He must," Ikshvaku said grimly, trying to push doubts away. "And we must cut-off the Nripalaya. If we can surround Narantaka's forces within it, we may win this battle yet."

But by the fifth morning, it was King Ikshvaku and his dwindled forces who were surrounded near Rajavasa's northern riverbank, making their camp in the ample greens of Maharshi Vasishtha's ashrama. None dared voice what all were thinking—this battle was close to being lost. King Ikshvaku's reign was drawing to an end, ironically in the very capital he had built as his legacy.

"One more day," said Haryashva. "We need to hold out only one more day. Contingents will arrive from Prasthala and Harayupa by then."

"As will Dasa reinforcements, surely," said Nimi. "Narantaka will not rely on only one army. A backup is surely on the way, especially now when they can press their way to victory."

"It never ends," said King Ikshvaku. "The war, the death. It is a part of life as much as anything else. I am the First King of Aryavarta. I forged this kingdom, this army. I will not go down this way." Ikshvaku turned around and faced his men, looking into their tired eyes and bloodied faces. "Aikshvakus!" he shouted, his voice roaring. "This is the day we prove ourselves! Sword, blood and fury—these are the things we are known by. Let us show our enemy their meaning!"

The men roared back in his wake, loud calls of Surya and death ringing out and carrying over to their enemies. And then a horn rang, almost as if in response to their passion. They turned towards the source, floating up to them on the Iravati river. Large, black flags fluttered on dozens of ships. They carried the same image, a silver moon shining in the night-sky. It was the Somavanshi banner, signalling that the Lunar warriors had come to Ikshvaku's aid. Hundreds of men came ashore, marching in smart formations and with gleaming weapons. At their head was their King—Pururava Aila of the Somavansha. The balance of numbers had just been turned once again.

"The Nripalaya belongs to Narantaka," Ikshvaku said, apprising Pururava of the situation. "But soon we will have him surrounded from all sides." There was no time to spend on exchanging pleasantries. "My brothers are allied with him. Their forces were small, but together they outnumbered us. With your men we can tilt that in our favour."

Ikshvaku was smeared in a thick, crusty layer of grease and blood. So were his men and there was a distant, almost vacant look in their eyes. Pururava could not imagine what they had gone through in the past few days. "How many Dasas stand alive?" he asked.

"Less than a thousand, I estimate. Most of them are within the Nripalaya's outer compound. But a significant few are dying at the south gate as we speak." Corpses lined around them, both enemy and own. Pururava knew what Ikshvaku did not voice: the Suryavanshi had suffered more losses than could be imagined.

"How could this happen, uncle? You built Rajavasa's walls to be impenetrable, learning from your own siege of Avisari."

Ikshvaku's eyes darkened. "Rajavasa was built to withstand even the finest stratagem," he said. "But what could its walls do against a relentless onslaught that spared no thought for tactics and diversions? Narantaka brought more than 10,000 bloodthirsty Dasas to my gates. He had aurochs on his side, and my city is but built of clay and wood. And he had my brothers to aid him."

Pururava fell silent, knowing how it must pain Ikshvaku to accept that his grand city had failed in its ultimate test. He followed his lead through burnt farmlands and deserted dwellings till they were within sight of the Nripalaya's outer compound. A friendly scout peeked through from one of the huts and approached at Ikshvaku's signal.

"Varman has the south gate blocked," the scout reported. "And he converges on the Nripalaya. Haryashva and your sons await on the western side."

"Then everything is in place," Ikshvaku commented. "Let the Dasas sleep for one more night. Send message to Varman and Haryashva that we rain down upon the Nripalaya at dawn."

The Solar charge on their King's quarters reflected Narantaka's earlier attack on Rajavasa's outer walls. Ikshvaku committed all his men to the cause, letting them run at the Nripalaya unmindful of Narantaka's archers taking aim from its roof and upper balconies. They overran its outer pavilions within moments, breaking into the inner chambers and eliminating the resistance Dasa by Dasa. A frenzy came over Ikshvaku that he had never felt before. Was this the after-effect of Samarsoma, or was it the seal of Surya powering his limbs to an invincible degree? As he hacked through torso after torso, his teeth were bared in a wolfish smile. He was enjoying this, not losing count even after his kills crossed three digits. He did not know who his sword longed for more, Narantaka or one of his brothers. But neither were to be found, and in a few hours Ikshvaku was brought the not-so-surprising news—his brothers had fled. Cowards that they were, they were nevertheless smart enough to realise that the battle had gone away from them. It would not have been possible without Pururava and his Somavanshi warriors adding to Ikshvaku's strength. But Ikshvaku found himself respecting his greatest opponent, Narantaka. At least the Rakshasa chose to stand and fight, while his own brothers turned tail and fled. Their tales would not end on this day, but Narantaka had lived his last.

After countless hours of beheading and dismembering, Ikshvaku heard the unmistakable roar of his lifelong enemy. Narantaka had finally cleared a direct path to him, and the Dasas made way for their King to approach the centre. On the other side, Ikshvaku's sons gathered with Haryashva and Varman. Narantaka turned his eyes to Nimi, surveying the enemy blood on his armour with pride, even though it was of his own men.

"Before I end you, Dasa," Ikshvaku said, pronouncing the name as a curse. "Tell me why. Why do we stand here such, facing each other like enemies?" He twitched from side to side like an impatient bull, raring to go at Narantaka's throat.

Narantaka snarled with menace and venom. "How does it feel?" he taunted. "How does it feel, having your home invaded by people who have no business there?"

"Is that what this is about, a conflict more than twenty years old?"

"This is about justice and revenge," Narantaka replied. "Justice for the countless Rakshasas you killed in Kamyakvana, for the genocide you committed under the guise of Suryavanshi patriotism. And revenge for separating me from my family. Your gods are the

Devas. Agni, Surya and Soma are the objects of your worship. I pray to them today, so that your people may better understand my curse. I curse you, King Ikshvaku of the Suryavansha. I curse that forever will Suryavansha Kings ache for their loved ones like I have, and Rakshasas and Dasas will be the cause of it. May this continue through generations till the end of your line. Now come, meet me in battle. Let only one of us remain standing alive today."

With that declaration he charged, exactly the way a Suryavanshi would have, sword jutting out from the cleave in his shield, and the shield held firmly ahead of him to use as a battering ram. For he had trained and fought with the Suryavansha, years ago. And even if he could not impart that technique to his men, he certainly retained flashes of it in his own bearing. King Ikshvaku charged back, and the two met at the centre in a clash of wood and metal, splinters exploding out in crunches and grinds. Narantaka was no longer the undisciplined, error-prone warrior that Ikshvaku had last met. He moved with precision, leaving no spots open for Ikshvaku to manipulate. His sword was a blur, and Ikshvaku only heard its angry whooshes against the wind as he swung it fast and lethal. He was a worthy adversary even two decades ago, now he was almost an even match.

For the longest time they were at a stalemate, their swords never managing to touch each other. Then, cut by cut, Ikshvaku gained the upper hand. Narantaka's swings turned slow and heavy, the whoosh of his blade ceased to be sharp and quick. Ikshvaku wasted no time toying with his enemy this time. When he saw the opening, he leapt up with surprising agility and brought his sword down powerfully through Narantaka's left shoulder, pushing it all the way down by his force. "Three cuts I had once promised upon your body," he said to him. "Consider the promise finally fulfilled."

But just as Ikshvaku pulled away, the Rakshasa found a spurt of dying strength and yanked a curved dagger out of his leather sheath. The blade was still lodged in his shoulder, its tip slicing into his heart. But Narantaka powered through the pain and slashed his dagger arm at Ikshvaku's neck. Ikshvaku's eyes widened in alarm, but before he could react the curved dagger sliced cleanly across his throat, and the Solar King saw his own blood gush out angrily. He heard men shouting in dismay and saw Haryashva charge towards him. But the dagger had done its damage, and Ikshvaku fell to his knees with blood spurting out even as breath finally ebbed out of

Narantaka, leaving only a triumphant gleam in his eyes. Haryashva reached in time to push his hands beneath Ikshvaku's head as he slumped to the ground, the acceptance of mortality evident in his eyes.

"Vikukshi is King after me," Ikshvaku croaked, barely able to speak with his throat slit. "But let Nimi go. Let him do what he wishes. The Bear and Drishta await me."

With that King Ikshvaku Manava followed his nemesis into the afterlife, bleeding out in front of his friends and sons. The seal of Surya hung loose around his neck, coated in a thick film of his blood. It was not the first time the blood of a Surya had soiled the seal, nor would it be the last. No one noticed, but around the same time that Ikshvaku breathed his last, the Suryavedi's final flame wisped into nothingness.

Elder Prince Vikukshi stood in silence, surrounded by the corpses of countless Dasas. The others walked up to him, their vengeful blood lust satiated now that every single Dasa lay slain. But no extreme act could bring Ikshvaku back, and none among them could imagine a life without him. It was Haryashva who broke the stillness, his voice heavy with a pain never heard before. "His funeral. We must conduct his funeral immediately."

The First King of Aryavarta's funeral was attended by more than a thousand broken men, their grief no less than that of the tribesmen that once gathered at the pyre of Marici. In the absence of a rshi, Varman conducted the prayer:

> Honour the King with your oblations, Yama, who gathers men together. Who travels to the lofty heights above us, who searches out and shows the path to many.
>
> Go forth, go forth upon the ancient pathways where our fathers of old have gone before us. There you shall look upon the Devas enjoying their sacred food, both Aurvan and Tapin.

Varman walked up to Vikukshi when there was nothing left of Ikshvaku but his ashes. "You are King now, my son," he stated simply. "We have a long task ahead of us."

"Indeed," Vikukshi said, feeling far older than his twenty-two years. "But we cannot stay here any longer. I name Rajavasa a land of death, unfit for inhabitation and prosperity. My father was right to stay in Avisari, and it is there that the Suryavansha must return."

Varman did not argue. To stay in Rajavasa meant staying with the memory and presence of Ikshvaku all around them, the city was his product. "And what of the Dasas?" he asked. "How long before their next attack, even without Narantaka?"

"Did you not hear his curse, uttered moments before his death? The Suryavansha is forever an enemy to Rakshasas and Dasas. That is our fate. We are Aryavarta's eternal protectors, destined to be the only wall standing against foreign invaders. It is a noble duty, one that would make even Marici proud. And on my father's ashes, I dedicate myself to this cause."

King Pururava came to bid farewell, his sense of loss no less than Vikukshi's. "Anything you need, any help I can provide. You only need to say it," he assured.

Vikukshi bowed his head in gratitude and took Pururava's leave, walking up to Nimi, who still stood staring at Ikshvaku's dying embers of the pyre. They stood together in silence for a while, seeking solace from each other's company. "What will you do now," Vikukshi finally asked, knowing that Nimi's pain was two-fold, for both his fathers had died today.

"Travel," Nimi said. "To the Himalaya and beyond. To a place where I can find some peace."

"And then?"

"Father gave me permission to establish my own kingdom," Nimi said slowly, pausing to see Vikukshi's reaction. Ikshvaku's elder son maintained his impassive expression. "I think I might exercise it," Nimi continued. "One day at least. But nowhere near your borders, brother. I assure you."

"Even if it were, I would only welcome it," Vikukshi replied sincerely. "The grand kingdoms of Suryavansha and Janaka will be a fitting tribute to our father." Then he withdrew the seal of Surya from his robe and extended it to Nimi. "Here, let this remain with your line."

Nimi retreated. "No. It belongs to the Solar King."

Vikukshi smiled gently, taking Nimi's hand and pressing the medallion in it. "Who is Solar, and who is not? Does not the ownership of this medallion prove your inheritance? Let it remain with your line," he repeated. "And none will ever cast your lineage into question. I'm sure this is what father would have wanted as well."

They parted ways that day. One was the son of a Rakshasa, and one day he would establish a glorious legacy. The other was the son of a Surya, and a long but troublesome reign lay ahead of him.

Epilogue

Sudasa, Year 920, Seventh era

Sudasa stood at the confluence's banks, reaching out a thousand years in his past and trying to visualise what these waters looked like back then. Prayaga stood on the confluence's southern bank, while Pratishthana once stood on the northern. King Pururava's capital was a dead city in Sudasa's Bharatvarsha, and the only remnant of its existence was the life-sized statue of Prince Suhotra, Late King Bharata's elder son and then High King himself. For the first time in his life, Sudasa wondered about the statue's history. Why was it established? What deeds did Prince Suhotra commit in his young age that his father committed a statue in his honour? He knew vaguely that it had something to do with King Bharata's Ashvamedha, but any further details were entirely lacking. King Bhagiratha's narration had brought Aryavarta's grand history to life, and every fact held in itself a question. He thought of Bhagiratha's concluding remarks, before he returned to Prayaga laden with awe for Aryavarta's history.

"The First King of Aryavarta ruled for twenty-two years," King Bhagiratha had said when the tale was done. "Quite short when you consider some of the later Kings. But his brief yet unprecedented reign influences us to this day. Our rivalry with the Dasas is just one of such aftermaths, as is the enduring Suryavanshi hostility towards Rakshasas. The Solar dynasty has seen many great Kings, and will no doubt see more still. But Ikshvaku remains the true Surya among us, and we retain his name to this day! My full title is Bhagiratha Sagari Aikshvaku. Do you think your line will remember your name a thousand years after, when thirty generations separate you?"

Sudasa did not think so, for what great deeds could he achieve in his life that surpassed the legend of Ikshvaku? "Do you know the names of all the Kings that separate you from Ikshvaku?" Sudasa had asked.

"Certainly, young one. We have detailed records of our line, just like you have of the Kings between Bharata and your father. Every tribe maintains only its own history, and Ikshvaku's life is a telling reminder that even the Veda is not free from the signature of a single tribe."

"I do not understand," Sudasa had said blankly.

"Ikshvaku does not find mention in the Veda even once, young one," King Bhagiratha informed him. "Not once! Nor is there mention of our tribe-the Suryavansha. Why do you think that is? How could so great a King be omitted from so great a collection?"

Sudasa did not have the answer, and Bhagiratha continued. "The Veda is almost entirely a Bharata creation. It may contain prayers that were composed before your dynasty arrived, but it has been collated and organised by your ancestors. It reserves glory only for your tribe. And Surya, my patron deity, he has no more than ten prayers dedicated to him—ten among the hundreds!"

Sudasa had never thought of the Veda as a tribe-specific collection before, assuming it to be as important to Purus or Suryavanshi as it was to Bharatas. "What do the Suryavanshi pray from then?" he asked.

"Suryavanshi prayers are mostly to Surya alone. Of Soma and Indra we care little, but of prayers composed by the first Maharshis we are consummate devotees."

"And what of Nimi, my King? Did he establish the Janaka dynasty of Mithila?" Mithila was a remote city, it lay far north of Prayaga and Ayodhya. Its current King, if Sudasa remembered correctly, was King Svarnaromana Janaka.

"Indeed he did," King Bhagiratha confirmed, looking pleased at Sudasa's conclusions. "Nimi travelled beyond the Himalaya, venturing into Ti Bhota and standing on the banks of the Rakshastala lake. The Janaka Kings of Mithila are from his line, but there is a secret to that which I shall reveal much later!"

Sudasa ventured a guess. "Did they also form the Eastern Suryavanshi?"

King Bhagiratha had laughed in good nature, eyes twinkling. "Certainly not. Do not confuse yourself by drawing connections where none exist. Contemplate on Ikshvaku's story, and see what you can learn from it. Remember this: Ikshvaku's was the true Age of Surya, and soon after his time power shifted to the Lunar dynasty-ushering in the Age of Soma. When you return to us and formally begin your training, I shall tell you more about it. Ikshvaku's descendants were great kings themselves, but they were no match for the ambition of the Somavanshi kings that followed Pururava."

"But one last thing-"

"Yes?" Bhagiratha prompted.

"Marici's medallion, the seal of Aurvan Surya. How did it find its way back to you?"

King Bhagiratha smiled. Sudasa had a curious, open mind like his father. It was a good trait for a young prince to have. "Go back to your tribe now, young one," Bhagiratha had said. "Tell your father that I humbly accept his offer to place you under my training. And when you return, I shall tell you how I came to acquire the seal of Surya, once it had passed onto Nimi Janaka's dynasty. But perhaps you might be more curious about the pearl-ring that your father wears around his finger?"

Sudasa raised his eyebrows. He knew the ring, but was unaware of the history behind it. "It is the moon-ring of King Nahusha, Pururava's grandson. It is a Lunar relic much like the seal of Surya is to us. And over more than a dozen generations it passed from Nahusha to your father. When we next meet, I will tell you about the ring of Soma."

Bibliography

Have you ever, like me, wondered, if Allahabad (Prayag) and Benaras (Kashi) are some of the world's oldest cities, who founded them? And when? If Rama was a glorious King of the Suryavansha dynasty, who was its founder? When did he establish it, and under what circumstances? Who composed the enigmatic collection of prayers we call the Rig Veda, and who were the people we insist on calling Aryans? Did they invade or migrate? Did they arrive or depart? The plausible history behind Hindu myths has always fascinated me, and much of my study of scriptures was as a historian, not a devotee, though people often confuse one with the other.

As I read a diverse and often conflicting range of historical opinions, a narrative formed in my mind. I call it *The Scrolls of Aryavarta*, and behind the shield of fiction and creative license I plot my speculations on the pre-Buddhist history of India. Here follows a list of some of the texts I consulted, in no particular order of influence:

1. **The Wonder that was India, AL Basham, Pan Macmillan 2004** This and a host of other books were instrumental in forming a broad world-view of the ancient era. It gave me vital insights on the tools, metals, wares and fabrics that could plausibly inhabit my fictional world.

2. **History of Early India from the Origins to AD 1300, Romila Thapar, Penguin 2003.**

3. **India a History, John Keay, HarperCollins 2010** By far one of the most fascinating and well written books on Indian history I have read.

4. **The History of the World, Frank Welsh, Quercus 2011.**

5. **The Hindus: An Alternative History, Wendy Doniger, Oxford University Press 2010** This and Doniger's other book, *On Hinduism*, were instrumental in giving me a paradigm for the early 'Aryans' and their tribal, nomadic existence.

6. **The Rig Veda and the Avesta: The Final Evidence, Shrikant Talageri, Aditya 2008** This and Talageri's other work on the Rig Veda provide the basic framework for the world I've created, from the geography and rivers to the ownership of Vedic prayers and the Rig Veda as a whole. My first exposure to the possibility that the Rig Veda is exclusively a text of the Bharata tribe comes from Talageri's works.

7. **The Vedas, Roshen Dalal, Penguin 2014** The last book I read as 'research' to fine-tune my world-building before finalising the manuscript. I used this work to identify historical inaccuracies in my work.

8. **Ancient Indian Dynasties, VS Mishra, Bhartiya Vidya Bhavan 2007** An obscure, inconspicuous book I found on the shelves of a bookstore in Lucknow. But it was also the most critical and indispensable book to my work. Genealogies are an essential component of any Purana, and are also carried in the Ramayana and Mahabharata. As a result, we are faced with several genealogies of the ancient Indian tribes, where different texts often feature different names and chronologies. VS Mishra undertakes the laborious task of collating all the genealogies, cross-referencing them and producing one comprehensive list. That list forms the basis for the overall family tree in my novels.

9. **Finding Forgotten Cities, Nayanjyot Lahiri, Hachette 2012** Used primarily to understand the Indus Valley civilisation and glean hints on how it could be plausibly connected to the Vedic world, if at all.

I have thus tried to imagine a history which is technically plausible, and for the most part have avoided anachronisms, such as potatoes in a Vedic India, which is just not possible! That being said, *The Scrolls of Aryavarta* is an exercise in fiction. The keen historian may indeed find much that is dishonest to her discipline, but she must allow me my creative license. For the rest, please do not let this work be your source for any historical facts!

Selected Chronology

The Scrolls of Aryavarta identifies two broad epochs of ancient Indian history: The Age of Devas and the Age of Vedas. This vast time period was divided by the people of Aryavarta into eras, or ages of man. Ikshvaku's tale is set in the Seventh era, which also heralds the beginning of the Age of Vedas. The Age of Devas comprised of six eras, each of which had its own set of seers, Devas, Asuras and Manus. For a wider reading of the chronology visit www.scrollsofaryavarta.com, which gives a timeline for the past six eras, before the time of Ikshvaku and Pururava. The Seventh era is said to begin with the birth of Vaivasvat Manu, so declared by Maharshi Vasishtha at his naming ceremony. Some of the events prior to this are thus listed as occurring some years before Year Zero of the Seventh era, but technically they fall in the Sixth era.

51 Years before Year 0	Marici Havishmani leads the Solar tribes to Aryavarta
Year 0, 7th era	Birth of Vaivasvat Manu
Year 32	Ikshvaku becomes first King of Aryavarta
Year 33	Haryashva arrives at Avisari
Year 34	Ikshvaku's Yaksha campaigns commence
Year 35	Ikshvaku weds Sarmi; death of Ardra
Year 36	Pururava begins training under the Suryavansha; Narantaka is captured
Year 41	Pururava travels to Trigarta and Madra
Year 45	Ikshvaku's Harivarsha campaigns commence; beginning of his brothers' rebellion

Year 47	Pururava weds Urvashi and becomes King of Somavansha; death of Drishta; Ikshvaku finds seal of Surya; beginning of exile
Year 52	Ikshvaku returns from exile
Year 53	The siege of Avisari
Year 56	Rajavasa is founded
Year 57	The sack of Rajavasa

Acknowledgments

The list of people I must thank for helping me write this novel is long, and I shall endeavour here to acknowledge them all.

First—to Ma and Pa. My mother forced me to write essays, poems, speeches and stories long before I was keen to do so myself. Her perseverance ensured that when I finally wanted to write, I had the skills and experience to do it. My father actively encouraged a reading habit, and as a result I had no dearth of inspiring authors to learn from. I would not be so intimate with the English language were it not for him. A special mention must go to Late Prof. Hari Ram Verma, who first inculcated in me a love for ancient Indian history. I wish I could have written this book years ago, when I could still place it in his living hands. All my English teachers ever, especially Revati and Manjari ma'am, Conrad and Andrew. My classmates in English A1 Higher at MUWCI, their command over the language and its literature set a standard for me to aim at.

At work, my deep gratitude to Mr. Partha Sarathi Basu. Without his encouragement and support I could not have finished this novel. Prof. Rohit Prasad was a great support during my college years.

All the friends who helped keep faith and motivation alive—Ramon (Avneesh), Modang (Mohit), Janki (Srikanth), Badke and Baby Daddu (Satish and Himanshu), Boriya (Amit), Takla (Manish), Spic Macay (Sumeet), Faddy (Fahad), Addy (Adnan), Jaundice (Misbah), Asad, Roy, Rakesh, Bittu, Kanha and the Barbadians—Old Man (Gautam), Tiffin (Gaurav), Laalach (Nikhil), Black Cobra (Rahul), Sir John Perrera (Amrut), Dehaati aka the Penguin (Narender), Bebbo (Vivek) and Lord Pinkerton (Narayanan).

The folks at Pirates: Captain (Mukund) and Sport (Kunal) and the Editor yet Unknown as I write this! I approached them with a confused, complex manuscript that was all over the place. But what you read now is a complete book, in no small part due to their contributions. Ashish Boyne for the fantastic cover. The authors Ashok Banker, Bhagwan Gidwani and Alex Rutherford for showing me how Indian historical fiction could be done right. The science fiction greats: Frank Herbert, Isaac Asimov, Arthur C Clarke, Stephen Baxter, Peter Hamilton and so many others, for inspiring me to write and for being the guiding light when it comes to the art of world-building. Samit Basu, whose brief communication with me was the trigger that set me down to crafting and finishing a novel. His GameWorld Trilogy features a Raja Amrit, and I hope he remembers that I've got the part when the movies are made.

My sister, Deepika. I finished this book after suffering through years of sibling apathy towards my work, but I thank her for it! My grandparents on either side, for all the myths and stories of my childhood that later evolved into a deep curiosity for all things ancient India. And finally, my wife, Divya. For putting up with a husband who returns grumpy from work and withdraws into a laptop by night. And for being my greatest fan and loyalist, without whose love and support this novel would not have seen the light of day.

What Next?

I see this novel as only one story in a vast world that encompasses all of ancient India's history. This history, to me, ends where the Ramayana and Mahabharata begin. Indeed, Sudasa's time is some five hundred years before the reign of Rama of the Suryavansha. But there is only so much I will be able to capture through the novels, and I fear I cannot dedicate my life to this like Ashok Banker has to his Epic India series. The website, www.scrollsofaryavarta.com, is where I will build most of this world's environment, tribes, cities and writings.

It already contains several detailed genealogies, maps and time-lines. There are notes on various cities and tribes, as well as articles on the trade, travel and culture of that era. There are short stories as well, and I will continue to add to them as Mukund edits scenes out of my novels! For example, there are tales on Marici, Kashyapa and Vaivasvat Manu that could not make it into this novel. There are moments in the friendship between Kashyapa and Atri I'd like to create, and the website is where I will share them with you.

For now, the next task awaits us. I first approached Pirates with a 150,000 words strong manuscript that ranged the *entire* span between Ikshvaku and Sudasa-covering one thousand years! We decided to tell the same story spread over several books, and thus Mr. Ikshvaku got his own novel. The heroes we now move to are Nahusha and Mandhatra, of the Lunar and Solar tribes respectively. Nahusha took the Somavansha to the peak of its glory and expanse, and Mandhatra destroyed it and brought the era of Pratishthana to an end. Sometime during this the Suryavansha also witnessed its first Queen, and she will be my first attempt at writing from a female perspective. These are the tales we will turn to next, and I hope you are there to join me as we witness the ring of Soma being forged.

Pirates? Because we firmly believe in stealing - we pick from our parents, style ourselves on our idols, snatch moments from real life. For every Mandela, there is a Gandhi. Claiming originality is audacity, conceit. We are all thieves, and the better among us Pirates.

Ahoy Reader! A pirate's oath: Books, finely crafted and stories, carefully picked.
We value your feedback.

*Other books by **Pirates:***

Anything for you, Ma'am by **Tushar Raheja:** Special 7th Anniversary Edition of the bestseller which is a part of college campus folklore now.

Romi and Gang by **Tushar Raheja:** If *Anything for you, Ma'am* reminded you of college, *Romi and Gang* will take you back to school!

Great Indian Democracy by Manivannan K: A Satire on Indian Politics.

12 Years a Slave by Solomon Northup: This special edition of the book commemorates the revival and the deserving success of an astounding, evergreen story in the form of Steve Mcqueen 's Oscar winning movie ***12 Years a Slave***.

Think and Grow Rich by Nepoleon Hill: The *most popular & influential* self-help book of all time.

Do you have a story?

For submissions contact: captain@pirates.ind.in

Author Bio

Amritanshu Pandey was born in Varanasi, grew up in Ajmer, Saudi Arabia, Noida and Jammu and acquired an International Baccalaureate diploma from the United World College in Pune. He followed it up with a B.A. in Economics and a post graduate diploma in management.

A keen amateur in the world of single malt scotch, he runs a malt reviews and coverage website at www.maltworship.com. The Scrolls of Aryavarta is his imagination of the Vedic and pre-Vedic history of India, and is a natural product of his life-long interest in ancient Indian history.

He is deeply influenced by thinkers such as Samuel Harris, Dan Dennett and Michael Shermer to name a few. It is his desire to create a similar debate in India and raise his voice for skepticism, rationality, tolerance and simple common sense. You can find him on Twitter @Amritanshu_soa, mail him at scrollsofaryavarta@gmail.com or simply visit his site www.scrollsofaryavarta.com